THE WINDRUSH AFFAIRS

THE WINDRUSH AFFAIRS

Maxine Barry

CHIVERS

| British Library Cataloguing in Publication Data available |

This Large Print edition published by BBC Audiobooks Ltd, Bath, 2008.
Published by arrangement with the Author.

U.K. Hardcover ISBN 978 1 405 64440 2
U.K. Softcover   ISBN 978 1 405 64441 9

Maxine Barry has asserted her rights under the Copyright, Designs and Patents Act, 1988 to be identified as the author of this work.

Printed and bound in Great Britain by
Antony Rowe Ltd., Chippenham, Wiltshire

PROLOGUE

1995

A bitterly cold wind was blowing through the bare chestnut trees as a sedate black car swept up the narrow country lane towards Rowhant Village and its squat Norman church. Standing outside, shivering in his vestments, the Vicar watched the approaching hearse and sighed heavily. He glanced at the young woman standing beside the big set of wrought iron gates and felt a wave of pity wash over him.

From inside the depths of the cold church, he could hear the gentle, respectful murmur of the mourners.

Elizabeth Jensen had had many friends in the village.

By the wrought iron gates, Harriet Jensen lifted her fair head and watched as her mother's flower-bedecked coffin was carefully removed from the hearse. Then, fighting back tears, she walked slowly towards the open church doors.

The clergyman's breath caught in his throat. It was her youth that made it all so hard. She was only just turned eighteen after all. And the contrast between her Nordic blonde hair and the stark black clothes was almost painful. As was the ashen pallor of her extremely beautiful face. But she managed a wan smile before

1

passing him, and the Vicar knew then that it was really her eyes that had cut him to the quick. The dark purple-blue eyes that lifted her face from being merely beautiful into being spectacular.

Ranked by sympathetic mourners, she took her place in the front, left-hand pew.

The Vicar snapped out of his reverie as the pall-bearers approached, the inexpensive coffin smothered in flowers.

He sighed and followed the coffin inside, nodding gravely to people he'd known since becoming Vicar in this small parish. But one pew at the front was empty except for a single, elderly woman. Since Harriet was Elizabeth's only relative, he was surprised to see the pew occupied. Out of respect, the rest of the congregation had chosen pews behind the front two.

The Vicar noted the iron-grey hair swept back in an old fashioned chignon, discreet make-up and simple jet ring on her gnarled hand, and recognized her at once as a 'lady'.

The service was a simple one. They sang Elizabeth's favourite hymns—How Great Thou Art, and Abide With Me—and, with a simple eloquence that his parishioners so appreciated, the Vicar spoke kindly of the woman they would all miss.

Then it was time to go outside.

Harriet, feeling numb to her core, rose when everyone else around her rose. She was vaguely aware of Sam Blenkinsop, the farmer for whom her mother had worked for the last ten years, taking her elbow and leading her gently outside. She looked so white that most people were afraid she was going to faint. The old aristocratic woman looked on, her eyes worried.

Harriet turned her mind and her face away from the burial of her mother, half-listening to the words that were so universally known, whilst another part of her mind went far, far away. *Ashes to ashes . . .*

She'd have to find somewhere else to live, of course. Sam had been so kind, telling her she could stay on in the cottage for as long as she liked, but she knew he would need it soon, when he found another cowman. Her mother had been such a good cowman . . . *Dust to dust . . .*

Perhaps she could find a bedsit somewhere? The Oxford Colleges were always in need of Scouts to clean the buildings, and she'd always been good at housework. From a very early age, she'd learned to cook and clean, so that Elizabeth wouldn't have to do it when she came home, exhausted, from the fields. *In sure and certain hope . . .*

Of course, she had no money. None at all.

Someone touched her. Dimly, she realised it was over, and now they'd be going back to the cottage. It was Sam again, leading her to his car. Sam Blenkinsop's farm was the driving force in the small village. Any jobs to be had were either on his farm, or working in his big farmhouse. But Sam's wife had a daily who'd worked for her for years, so there'd be no work there. And she didn't have her mother's way with animals. No, Harriet thought sadly, she'd have to leave Rowhant, the only home she could really remember.

Her step-father, the man whose surname she had legally taken when she was only five, had died when she was just seven years old. That was when she and her mother had come to Rowhant.

And here was where her life had always been. Being taught in the friendly school. Helping to weed their traditional cottage garden. Skipping down the lane to the barns to watch her mother with the new-born calves. Cooking dinner and tidying the house, humming as she vacuumed and dusted.

'We're here, luv,' Sam said gruffly. 'Mavis and Jean have done a grand spread for you.'

Harriet nodded and climbed stiffly out of the car. Mavis, Sam's wife, had been a pillar of support since Elizabeth had died, last Saturday morning. Harriet's mother had simply driven away to do their main weekly grocery shop, and had never come back. A lorry driver, asleep at the wheel, had seen to that.

One moment she'd had everything—a mother, home, and future. Then, after one visit from the police, she'd had nothing.

4

She smiled and thanked Mavis and Jean, looked at the groaning table of food blankly and turned away to greet the mourners coming in dribs and drabs through the door.

Back in the kitchen, Mavis and Sam's eyes met, Mavis biting her lip and turning away. 'She's still in shock,' it was Jean, her daily, who spoke for them all.

Sam sighed gloomily. 'I've just offered Bill Neale's oldest lad the job of cowman,' he said, to no-one in particular. Mavis sighed deeply. 'He'll need the cottage I suppose?'

'Ar,' Sam said. 'He's married with a young 'un on the way.'

In the tiny hall of the 150-year-old cottage, Harriet began to sense a growing panic within herself, aware of a roiling, frightening loneliness creeping over her.

What would she do? Where would she go? Even as she handed out sherries and thanked people for their sympathy cards, and reassured her friends and neighbours that she'd be all right, she wondered. *Would* she be all right?

A sudden rising wind, howling around the guttering and roof, set off an eerie wailing.

She shook her head, telling herself not to be such a idiot. She was not helpless, after all. Her exam results were good enough to get her into a decent secretarial college. She could work evenings—a barmaid's job or something—and put herself through secretarial school. She'd find someone to share

5

a flat with. She'd just have to bite the bullet and sign on the dole . . .

She felt, suddenly, overwhelmingly depressed.

It was at this moment that she noticed the old woman sitting in a big armchair near the fire. And Harriet realised she didn't know who she was. The mystery took her mind away from her own predicament for a moment. Could she be a relative of Sam's? But, if so why would she come to the funeral of his cowman?

Harriet frowned slightly. There was something about the woman that looked familiar. Oh, they'd never met, of that she was sure, but there was something in the shape of the nose . . the strong line of her almost arrogant jaw . . .

Harriet shook her head. No, it wouldn't come to her.

After an hour, most people began to leave. Harriet saw that the old woman was deep in conversation with Mavis and Sam, but thought little of it. Instead she stood at the door, shaking hands with people and thanking them for coming.

It was nearly two o'clock in the afternoon before Sam and Mavis took their leave—the last to go. Mavis squeezed Harriet's cold hands and said that she was to call at the farm if she ever needed anything. Sam gave her an awkward but well-meant kiss on the cheek, and then they were gone.

Harriet once more shut the door on the cold, wet day and walked back into the tidy kitchen.

Life went on—Elizabeth would have been the first to tell her so. And she should know. Twice she'd had to bury a husband and move on. And Harriet was her daughter. She'd just have to follow her example and do the same. She stiffened her backbone and walked into the tiny living room—and stopped dead. For there, still sitting in the big armchair by the fire, was the old woman.

Harriet blinked. 'I'm sorry,' she mumbled, her voice faint and surprised. 'I thought everyone had left.'

'No, I'm sorry,' said the woman Mavis and Sam had identified as the Honourable Frances 'Frankie' Powell. 'I thought Mavis and Sam would have told you that I was still here.' The Vicar's sense that here was a 'lady' had been perfectly accurate. Frankie was, in fact, the daughter of Lady Grace Powell, of Powell House.

Harriet moved towards the flickering flames of the fire, too tired and heartsore to ask the stranger what she wanted. Instead she slowly sank down into the armchair opposite and leaned her head wearily back against it.

Frankie felt a pang. How like her grandfather Harriet was, with the same Nordic white-blonde hair. Funny that none of Lady Grace's children had inherited that hair but it

7

must always have lurked there in the genes, just waiting to come out in the next generation.

Mark's daughter. Mark. Frankie felt her face soften as she thought of her younger brother. Mark, so full of cheek and vim and spunky defiance. So different from Arthur, who was the eldest. Arthur, Frances and Mark, the Powell siblings. Frankie shook her head. And now, only she was left. Herself and Grace. And this child—Mark's daughter.

Frankie sighed deeply, making Harriet look across at her curiously.

'I should know you, shouldn't I?' Harriet said at last.

It had been a strange day. An unreal one, in many ways. But right here, right now, there was only the wind and rain at the windows, the fire, and this old woman.

Frankie smiled. 'Yes and no.'

Somehow, that answer seemed fitting. Harriet merely nodded and turned to look at the fire once more.

Frankie watched her, understanding everything. Life could be bitter sometimes. But her niece was so beautiful too. Really, quite easily, the most beautiful woman that Frankie had ever seen—and in her time, she'd seen some of the most striking 'society women' of their age. There was something about Harriet Jensen's bone structure that did it. It was in the bones that true beauty lay. With looks like that, Frankie nodded to herself, the girl could easily catch herself a millionaire. If she wanted to. If she had someone to introduce her to the right people . . .

'I'm Frankie Powell,' Frances said quietly. And watched as the beautiful blonde ice-maiden in front of her suddenly sat upright. She watched the angry colour flood the pale cheeks. Watched the blue-purple eyes flash in vivid animation. And nodded sadly. So. It was like that, was it?

'You're a Powell?' Harriet all but spat the last word out, as if it were something vile. Something rotten. And who could blame her, Frankie thought sadly. Yes, indeed, who could blame her?

Harriet saw the old woman flinch, and suddenly felt ashamed of herself. Elizabeth would have been appalled at her bad manners. 'What do you want?' she asked ungraciously.

Frankie Powell sighed. What did she want? Why had she really come? Was it just to say goodbye to an old friend and her one-time sister-in-law? Or more . . . She looked back at her brother's daughter, and knew it was more. Much more.

She shifted her slight weight in the chair, her arthritis pinching. Harriet wondered if she should offer her another sherry, and then thought, no. Damn it, why should she? This woman, after all, was a Powell.

'What do you know about your father's

9

family, Harriet?' Frankie asked softly, half expecting a bitter outburst of fireworks.

And, indeed, for a moment, Harriet's eyes flashed. Then, slowly, blanked again. She shrugged one thin, elegant shoulder. 'Only that my father was Mark Powell. Youngest son of Lord and Lady Powell. That he married my mother against their wishes, so they cut him off without a penny. That they refused to even meet my mother, because they thought the daughter of a bankrupt farmer wasn't good enough for their precious son.'

Frankie winced, but knew that the girl was speaking no more than the stark, unpalatable truth.

'So you also know,' Frankie said softly, 'that Mark, who was my brother by the way, loved your mother deeply? That he defied his family to be with her? That he gave up everything to marry her? That he loved you both so very, very, dearly?' she asked, her soft, chiding voice, making Harriet flush uncomfortably.

Harriet looked away from the level, brown-eyed gaze of the old woman who was now identified as her aunt, and looked back to the fire. She sighed. 'I don't remember him,' she admitted flatly. 'I was only eight months old when he was killed in the plane crash.' Frankie nodded. 'My mother wrote to your parents,' Harriet's face became tight, once more, with remembered pain and anger. 'She told me so. She wrote and told them he was dead, and that he had a daughter. But they didn't care. They didn't want to see me. They didn't even write back. Perhaps they thought it was just a begging letter. But she didn't ask them for money,' Harriet all but shouted. She couldn't bear it if *this* Powell was secretly looking down her nose at her. At Elizabeth.

'I always liked Elizabeth,' Frankie said. 'When Mark told me he was going to elope with her, I was glad. Mother . . .'

The Honourable Frances Powell's voice faltered slightly. 'Mother wanted him to marry the daughter of a friend of hers, the heiress to a vast estate . . .'

'Marriage between them would have founded a nice little dynasty for your family,' Harriet translated bitterly. 'Why couldn't her other son have married her, if Lady Grace was so all-fired set on owning half of Gloucestershire?'

Frankie burst out laughing. She couldn't help it. For her mother would truly love to own half of the county, if only she could. Harriet, surprised by the sudden laughter, reluctantly smiled. Really, her aunt wasn't at all what she'd have expected from the snobbish, unforgiving Powell clan.

Eventually Frankie got herself under control, and answered Harriet's question.

'Arthur had already married a Baronet's daughter.'

'Bravo for Arthur,' Harriet muttered. 'So

11

Dad let the family down well and truly by marrying my mother?' she asked, her voice heavy with sarcasm and rich in defence of her mother.

Frankie sighed. 'The family saw it that way, yes,' she agreed sadly. 'But I kept in touch with Mark and Elizabeth,' Frankie surprised her by saying. 'When Elizabeth wrote and told me Mark had died . . .' her voice broke for a moment, before she carried on quickly, 'I was devastated. I was so glad when your mother told me she'd remarried. She deserved some happiness. I can't tell you how sad I was to hear about your step-father. You've taken his surname, I understand?'

Harriet shrugged. 'Mum arranged it. I think she wanted to forget all about the Powells.'

Frankie nodded. 'Yes,' she said thoughtfully. 'Yes, I can understand that.'

Harriet glanced at her aunt, curiosity raising its head. 'I didn't know she kept in touch with any of the Powell family,' she said, a question in her voice.

Frankie smiled. 'It was only the odd letter or two. Every year or so. But when I heard she'd died . . . I had to come.'

Harriet nodded. So, the mystery was explained. A sad little explanation, perhaps, but . . . She felt herself brighten. At least she wasn't totally alone now. She had an aunt. An aunt she'd never met before, true, but, nevertheless, someone.

As if reading her thoughts, Frankie took a deep breath and took the bull by the horns. 'I was wondering . . . if you didn't have any other plans if . . . well . . . you might like to come and stay with me for a few days? Or even longer, if . . .'

'Go to Powell House?' Harriet squeaked. 'Not on your nelly! Is . . . are . . . my grandparents still alive?' she added, defiance and shame vying for supremacy on her expressive face.

Frankie shook her head. 'My father died some years ago. Mother is still going strong. Arthur and his wife are both dead, but their son, Giles, has taken over running the estates. He has his own computer company too. But I don't live at Powell House,' Frankie said hastily. 'At least, I do, but not the new Powell House,' she added, confusingly.

And seeing Harriet's not unnaturally puzzled face, hastened to explain. 'The Powell family split into two distinct groups a long time ago, when my father inherited a Peerage. He and Grace, my mother, came into an estate and moved to the big country mansion that came with it. The house where they had been living, is where I live now. Quite alone. It's a big house, but not half so grand as a stately home . . .' she trailed off, but Harriet suddenly saw it all.

'You never married?' she asked quietly.

Frankie laughed and shook her head. 'No.

13

No, I thought, once . . . but . . .' she shrugged.

Harriet bit her lip, imagining the old woman rattling around a big empty house, lonely and cut off from her family. Reading between the lines, she imagined that her aunt and her grandmother didn't get on too well.

Suddenly, Frankie looked her straight in the eye and lifted her chin, almost haughtily. 'My house is big, but very run down, Harriet. I don't have much money, I'm afraid, and I'm damned if I'm going to ask mother for any. Or Giles. The house is in a small village, very much like this one, called Rissington Basset. There isn't much going on there. You might be bored. If you did want to come and live there with me, you'd have to get yourself some kind of a job. I can't afford to keep you. I only just get by myself.'

Her chin lifted yet another inch. Pride, humility, strength, were all there in her face. 'But if you want a home, Harriet Jensen,' Frankie Powell said simply, 'you have one.'

*   *   *

Across the Atlantic, as yet unaware of Harriet Jensen's existence, Vania McAllen walked to her large, walk-in wardrobe and extracted a long brown skirt. She barely glanced at the racks of gowns and high-fashion outfits culled from fashion shows in Paris. Milan, London and Rome.

14

It had been fun, at fifteen, to buy such gorgeously grown up, expensive, and feminine clothes. Now, at nearly eighteen, she didn't so much as stop to caress their silks and satins as she packed a suitcase full of dark, sober, business-like clothes.

There would be no use for fine Italian silk where she was going.

She paused and picked up the last photograph her father had commissioned of her. She looked younger than seventeen. She looked like a frightened child, in fact. Vania shook her head. It was no good being frightened. No damned good at all.

She went back to the wardrobe, selecting her plainest blouses, her neatest trouser suits and a few good accessories—a leather belt by Gucci, a Dior scarf, a pair of finest kid gloves in a gorgeous caramel colour. She added them to her case, checking it carefully. It would pay for her to look smart. When you had to job-hunt with no qualifications to show, outward appearances mattered more than anything. Dressed well, and impeccably groomed, she at least had a chance of getting a job somewhere.

Nothing about the case gave away the fact that it belonged to Vania McAllen, the fabulously wealthy heiress and only daughter of Chuck McAllen, the auto-king of the East Coast.

Vania couldn't help but smile at the title her father, a fifth-generation Scotsman, hated so

15

much. Not that it wasn't accurate. McAllen's Auto Dealership was a giant. It sold millions of used and new cars to the middle-American motoring public. As well as expensive, imported sports cars to playboys and millionaires. No matter what walk of life you came from, you didn't have to go further than McAllen's to get the car of your dreams.

For the son of a baker in one of Boston's poorer suburbs, the rise to multi-millionaire businessman had been quite a step up. But then, her father was quite a man. A man who'd married for love and worked like a demon, became a multi-millionaire and raised his only child almost single-handedly when his beloved wife had died four years ago.

It had been the gruff, acutely embarrassed Chuck McAllen who had taken his blossoming fifteen-year-old daughter to all those fashion shows, determined that she should not miss out on all the things her mother would have done for her.

Vania sighed heavily. Oh Dad!

She picked up the photograph, meeting her own green-eyed gaze with determination. Vania, like teenagers everywhere, was intrigued by her looks. But not obsessed. She knew her eyes were good, and her long, dark, brunette locks were striking and silky, but she'd have preferred to have been a blonde. She was sadly aware that she'd now stopped growing, and that her current height of five-

16

foot-seven was as tall as she was going to get. Nowhere near tall enough to be a super-model, which, at one time, had been her burning ambition.

Her wide, generous mouth twisted into a smile.

Being honest with herself—and Vania always was honest with herself, sometimes brutally so—she knew that if she chose to, she could still be a model. Her father could squeeze the arms of the newspapers and magazines, who relied on his big advertising revenue, to feature her face selling lipstick, car wax, or any other thing they chose. She knew the world was hers. Or at least, as much of the world as a rich, spoiled heiress of an indulgent daddy could wish for.

A cold sense of loss settled over her as she added a couple of pairs of fine Italian shoes to the sturdy side-pockets of the suitcase and snapped it shut decisively.

From here on in, the good life ended.

When she'd travelled before, taking a cruise around the Caribbean, or going on a skiing holiday to Aspen, she'd always travelled with big trunks of possessions. This single, carefully plain suitcase looked rather pathetic by comparison.

Vania put the case down by the side of the bed, her youthful strength making light work of its weight. Even though she'd always had chauffeurs to carry her luggage for her, she

17

wasn't incapable. Which was just as well.

She supposed she could thank her father's Scottish Highland ancestors for her surprisingly practical, down-to earth personality. Whilst her friends and contemporaries got themselves into trouble with too much drinking, or, even worse, too much experimenting with 'in' drugs, Vania McAllen had never given her father a moment's cause to worry about Rich-Kid Syndrome. She wasn't about to wrap her brand-new Porsche around a tree and get herself killed. She wasn't, in fact, ever going to get to drive the Porsche again, she realised. So much for her 17th birthday present.

Like everything else, she was leaving the car behind her.

She went back to the wardrobe, selecting a warm woollen coat and draping it across the bed, for when she was ready to go. It wouldn't be yet, of course, she realised, checking the Swiss watch on her wrist. It was still only eight-thirty.

She walked to the bedroom window and looked out of the McAllen Mansion across the city of Boston. It was cold, with an icy wind and lowering clouds threatening snow. Would London would be any warmer? Somehow, she doubted it.

Below, a fountain switched off for the winter was briefly lit up as a car pulled up outside the large, electronic gates. Vania felt herself tense.

Every sensor in her body tingled into life. Even if she hadn't known he was due for dinner, she'd have known it was him. Her body always let her know whenever he was near.

She watched as a uniformed guard walked to the side of the car, leaning in to check the driver's identity. Then the gates were opened and the car swept up the drive, the wheels crunching on the gravel.

Vania's heart began to pound as the car door opened.

One booted foot appeared. It was followed by a jeans' clad leg, and Vania felt herself, in spite of everything, laugh softly to herself. Only Brett Carver would ever come to dinner at the McAllen Mansion wearing jeans. Even cleverly-cut, designer jeans.

She watched him as he climbed out of the English Jaguar, unfolding his six-foot length with wiry ease. And why not? Having been raised on a farm in Kansas, Brett Carver had been lugging heavy machinery about, building his muscles, when she was still taking elocution lessons from Mrs DuBarry. As he shut the car door behind him, the lights from the house reflected off his head, turning his dark red hair into fiery auburn. As if aware of being watched, he suddenly turned, angling his head up.

Vania gasped and took a quick step back. But he'd know that she was there, just the same. Just as she always knew when he was around.

She caught a glimpse of his hard, tough, craggily attractive face, and thought she detected just a hint of a smile. Then he walked to the front door, which was already being opened for him by their butler. Vania bit her lip. She didn't like that slight smile. Didn't like the confidence, the cock-sure attitude it implied. But then, why shouldn't he smile?

She turned back to stare at her case and waiting coat, her mind torn between her upcoming 'escape' and the man she was escaping from. Brett Carver. The youngest son of a dirt-poor Kansas farmer, forced to leave home at fifteen when his family lost the farm, without even a High School certificate to his name.

His parents had managed to find jobs in the city, but they had five other mouths to feed besides Brett's. And the tiny apartment they had couldn't house them all. And so he'd left and worked his way east, until, one day, he'd washed up at one of the McAllen used car lots. The manager there had given him a job washing cars. Then fixing cars. As a farm-boy, he'd often turned his hand to repairing tractors and farm machinery, and was already a mean mechanic.

It had become something of a legend now, how Chuck McAllen had walked into one of his less salubrious car lots in Delaware one

20

day, and saw this pair of ragged-jeaned legs sticking out from under a Chevy that looked as if it would never live again. Of how he'd watched this kid, who talked with a laconic Kansas drawl, get the engine purring. Of how Chuck, who'd always wanted a son, had found himself strangely drawn to this youngster.

A job at the McAllen's prime showroom in Boston had followed. And Chuck, who'd been slightly worried that the country boy would flounder in the big city, slowly came to relax, as Brett took to big business as easily as he'd taken to selling cars.

Oh yes, Vania knew all about the legend of Brett Carver.

From mechanic to salesman. From mere salesman to winner of the coveted McAllen Salesman of the Year trophy, as the Bostonian buyers took to his easy Kansas charm and obvious knowledge and love of cars in their droves.

And then, inevitably, from salesman to executive.

For a kid who hadn't even finished high school, Brett had no trouble climbing the corporate ladder until he became Chuck's undisputed right-hand man. But not everyone was happy about that, of course. And Chuck's 'sleeping' partner, James Larner, liked it least of all.

But nobody listened to James, particularly Chuck McAllen.

21

When the young Chuck had bought his very first car lot, he'd needed capital. No bank was going to trust a poor risk like Chuck McAllen but he knew a man who would. Richard Larner, a small-time shop-owner, recognised a go-getter when he saw one, and had taken the only risk of his life when he'd backed Chuck, on the proviso that he be a sleeping partner, and that they'd share a straight 50/50 split.

Chuck knew it was a poor deal. He'd do all the work for only half the profit. But half of something was better than all of nothing. So he'd agreed, but had put in a proviso of his own—namely tying up voting rights and shares so that he would always have managerial control.

Of course, under his hard-headed leadership, that one lot had grown into an empire. During which time, Richard Larner had died and left his 50% to his son, James. Who'd had to do nothing but lean back and let Chuck make him rich.

The only thing James Larner lacked was power.

So when Brett Carver, a hick kid from Kansas appeared on the scene, there was little he could do but watch and fume as Chuck groomed him to one day take over control of McAllen's.

The 'city' had been fascinated by Brett's rise, just like everyone else, enjoying a rags-to-riches success as much as the next man.

Reporters coveted him, because he rarely gave interviews. Society ladies coveted him even more—not that he socialized all that much either.

He'd bought himself a very nice penthouse overlooking the harbour, and of course, had his pick of the very finest cars from the Boston showroom, but apart from that, he did little to live up to the new boy on the block image.

Oh yes, Vania thought, her heart twisting in her chest. He was some man, was Brett Carver.

And then, last year, her father had finally brought him home. No doubt he could see for himself how well those fine Parisian gowns fitted his fast-maturing daughter. And, by then, he had a dream of his own.

At first, she hadn't suspected a thing.

When he'd told her, last Easter, that he'd invited Brett over for the big annual dinner, she'd hardly been surprised. Or that excited. She'd been looking forward to spending some time with her best friend, whose parents had invited a film star over for the holidays. So the thought of missing out on a Hollywood hunk to play hostess to her father's golden boy hadn't particularly thrilled her.

But since her mother's death, she'd grown up fast, and knew that her father relied on her to fill her mother's shoes.

And so, at the age of sixteen, wearing an emerald green satin dress from London, with her hair piled high atop her head and her mother's emerald and diamond necklace clasped around her throat, she descended the stairs, aware of the two men talking in the hall, and met Brett Carver.

She could still remember that moment now as if it had only happened a second ago.

She'd spoken to the cook hours before, and knew the meal would be perfect. The flowers were dealt with, and the other guests were yet to arrive. She felt calm and in control. And then the man who'd been standing with his back towards her had seen Chuck look up, read the look of love and pride in his eyes, and quickly turned to look in her direction too. And her world had come to a crashing, shocking, pulse-shattering stop. He was nothing like she'd expected.

Reared on her father's stories about him, she'd expected a stereotypical farmer's son, complete with a stem of straw clenched between his teeth and freckles across his nose. The man who looked up at her was . . . amazing.

He was tall, about six foot, and had the hard, lean, but bulky appearance that some outdoors men had. Even though he was dressed in a perfectly tailored tux from Turnbulls, it couldn't hide the fact that the body underneath was solid, rock solid. He had the broad shoulders and well built physique of a world-class athlete.

His hair was red, but not the homely kind of

24

ginger she'd expected. Instead it was dark red, like mahogany with hints of fire in it. And there was not a freckle in sight on his face.

And his face . . .

Vania had never seen a face like it. Born and raised in Boston, attending the most genteel of schools, growing up amongst the tennis-playing, sailing, all-American WASP brothers of her friends, this face was like nothing she'd ever seen before. It was craggy. Hard. Solid, like the man himself. The nose was crooked, as if it had been broken at some point. (As indeed it had, during a bar fight he was trying to break up when he was eighteen.) His jaw and the planes of his cheek were razor-sharp and aggressive.

He shouldn't have been handsome, but somehow, he was.

Vania, halfway down the stairs, had stopped dead at the sight of him, unaware of her father's speculative and then downright pleased gaze as he watched the expressions cross his daughter's face. Chuck had been close enough to hear the short, hastily-drawn breath Brett had given, but he'd always known that his right-hand man couldn't fail but to be knocked out by her. Now, seeing his daughter's similarly awe-struck expression, he was well satisfied.

At the time, of course, Vania wasn't even looking at her father. Wasn't capable of looking anywhere but at the man who seemed

25

to dominate the room. Command the very air she was trying to breathe, if only she could get her lungs to work again. Now, in her bedroom nearly two years later, Vania could still remember the way she'd licked lips gone suddenly bone dry. Could remember the way she'd forced herself to move down those final stairs. To put out her hand in greeting.

She looked down now at her hand, remembering how it had felt to have it engulfed in his own. His fingers were long, tanned and held immense strength. She could imagine him crushing the bones in her hand without even raising a sweat.

Since then, of course, he'd come to dinner many times. Had taken her out on the harbour in his boat. Had escorted her to dances. And, since then, Vania had learned a great deal more.

Not least of which was that her father expected her to marry him. Had, in fact, re-written his will, whereby she inherited all his wealth, but only inherited his stock in the company on the proviso that she married Brett Carver before her twenty-fifth birthday.

Thinking about it now, she was disgusted at herself for not cottoning on to how her father was thinking, right from the start. Here he was with an only daughter—a beautiful enough child, mature, intelligent, but hardly a fitting heir to an auto dealership. An old-fashioned thinker. he'd always known that he'd have to hand on the company to a man.

And definitely not to James Larner, the leech.

Which meant he had to find someone else. And, like a gift from the gods, he'd discovered Brett Carver. Honest, hard-working, and with the toughness a businessman needed to survive and thrive. A good-looking, young, virile man. A man he'd trust with his company.

So why not a man he'd trust with his daughter?

Vania shot her reflection one last look in the mirror. She had to go down now, and sit and talk and eat and laugh and entertain them, and not let either of them guess what she was planning. She saw a woman dressed in a pale blue silk dress, a diamond and sapphire pendant nestled in the slight V of her breasts. She smiled grimly at herself. Vania McAllen. The girl with the mostest. Why, she'd even had her husband hand-picked for her!

Taking a deep, calming breath, she opened the door and stepped out onto the landing. From the open study door, she could hear voices.

Even now, she couldn't, in all fairness, find it in her heart to blame her father. After all, he was as good a judge of character as you'd ever find, and he'd passed that on to his daughter. Both of them had learned who Brett Carver was, inside and out. And it hadn't taken either of them long to sense a deep-rooted gentleness behind that hard exterior. And that the laid-back drawl was both a part of him, and a good disguise. That he was funny, and compassionate, and sometimes breathtakingly cunning. She also knew that he'd regularly sent money back home, and now, on his executive's salary, she knew that his parents and sisters were living in a big detached house in Wichita Falls. That they'd never have to worry about paying the bills again.

As a man to marry, she could hardly do better . . .

Vania moved slowly down the stairs, her mouth once more dry.

Soon she would be leaving this house for good. Tonight, at two o'clock in the morning, she'd put on that woollen coat, pick up that packed, anonymous case, and leave by the side door. She already knew the code that would turn off the burglar alarms and let her get through one of the side gates in the garden without any of the security guards knowing. She already had her journey planned. There would be no airport for her, where her movements could be so easily traced. No. There were always boat-owners willing to take passengers across the Atlantic, dodging customs on both sides for the right price, and she'd already paid a mini-fortune for her fare to Ireland. After that, it would be another anonymous boat-ride to mainland England.

In her handbag, she already had a big wad

of money to help her on her way. There could be no more liberal use of all those pretty green and gold credit cards of hers. From now on, everything she did, everything she bought must be untraceable. Chuck McAllen would have a private detective on her tail quicker than a flea jumping on to a dog. And she had no illusions that, once her father had found the note she'd written him, she'd be a hunted woman.

She walked across the hall towards the study, her heart leaping at the sound of their visitor's voice. The Kansas drawl was still there. It flowed over her like warm molasses, oozing into every pore. Oh how she was going to miss that voice . . .

Vania paused in the doorway, watching her father's face as he smoked his cigar. She didn't make a sound. For the first time since she'd purchased her phony passport and papers from a frightening, weasel-faced man in the Bronx, the realities of what she was doing were brought home to her. She might never see her father again. If only he wasn't so all-fired determined that she marry Brett. If only she didn't know him so well. But she did know him. And she knew that if she stayed, he would eventually wear her down. That he'd never give up. That, before she reached twenty, she'd be Mrs Brett Carver.

She knew it as well as she knew her own name.

Except, her lips twisted grimly, from now

on, she was no longer Vania McAllen. She was Vania Lane. Little Miss Nobody.

She saw her father notice her and get to his feet. She smiled at him, although her heart was breaking in her breast.

And then Brett turned, and those unexpectedly pale grey eyes were once more looking at her. Drinking her in. A welcome in their depths that invited her to fall into his arms.

All of this would be so much easier, Vania thought achingly, if only she didn't love him with every last atom of her being . . .

CHAPTER ONE

Today . . .

Harriet Jensen slowly opened her eyes, and for a few moments, she felt warm and safe and happy. Then, slowly, she remembered. Frankie was dead.

She listened absently to a blackbird singing in the orchard, its dulcet song filling the air, and then looked at her alarm clock. It was six-thirty in the morning. Time to get up.

When she sat up, a spate of coughing wracked her thin body. She could do nothing but wait until it passed, glad that the worst of the 'flu was over. Outside it was high summer, and a July sun threatened to bake them long before lunchtime. Summer colds were always the worst.

And when she'd caught the same 'flu that had ultimately led to her aunt's sad passing, she'd been too low to put up much of a fight.

Hearing the sounds of activity that were starting to come from the kitchens right below her window, she straightened up. Lingering 'flu or not, it was time to get moving. She walked to the small wash-basin against one wall and sighed at her pale reflection.

Vania had called in the doctor and he had given her a shot that had put her out for almost twenty-four hours. By the time she'd

31

awoken, Frankie's funeral was over. In a way, she was glad. In another way she was angry, and had said some harsh words to Vania. But that had been last week. And it hadn't taken that long for the two women to make up. It never would.

Harriet brushed back her long platinum blonde hair into a ponytail and then pinned it to the top of her head with a large silver clip. From her wardrobe she selected a long thin caramel-coloured skirt and creamy silk blouse. Sensible flat brown shoes completed the ensemble. She checked the mirror again, relieved to see the owner/manager of Windrush Shallows Hotel looking back at her, and not the ill-looking woman of just a few days ago. It had been a blow, losing Frankie, but not an unexpected one. And the doctor had been warning her for some days to expect the worst . . .

Harriet straightened her shoulders. Well, the worst was over. Time to get back to work. She'd let the full responsibility of running the Shallows rest on Vania's shoulders for far too long as it was.

When she and Frankie had first opened her aunt's country house as the newly-revamped Windrush Shallows Hotel, Harriet had taken this room on purpose, because it was right over the kitchens. She didn't want her first batch of guests disturbed by just the sort of sounds that had awoken her this morning.

Harriet walked quietly down the corridor to the neighbouring room and tapped discreetly on the door. It was opened almost immediately. The vivacious, good-looking girl who answered, grinned. 'You're up,' Vania Lane said, then frowned. 'Are you sure you feel up to it?'

Harriet smiled. 'I would still be in bed otherwise.'

It didn't surprise her to find that the American girl was already up and dressed, and looking gorgeously chic in a summer dress of dazzling white. With her long dark hair left loose, she looked more like a model than a tourist guide for Windrush Shallows.

'But you know, you don't need to get up so early,' Harriet said, watching as Vania dashed to her dresser to squirt a light floral scent on her wrists. 'You're not going out with the morning group until nine, are you?'

Vania walked with Harriet towards the hall landing. 'Nope. But Mr Amerheimer wanted to get in some early morning fishing. I'm just making sure he's got his hamper.'

Harriet smiled. it was typical of Vania to be so conscientious, and she knew, without doubt, that Vania's services were one of the many things that had made Windrush Shallows the success it had become.

When she'd first arrived at Frankie's house, the very day after her mother's funeral, it had felt like coming home. Nestled in a valley on

33

the Oxfordshire/Gloucestershire border, in the tiny and heartbreakingly picturesque village of Rissington Bassett, Frankie's house had come as something of a shock. From what she'd said, Harriet had half-suspected a rambling ruin of a place. Instead, she'd sat in the passenger seat of Frankie's old and temperamental Bentley, and gaped at the sight that met her eyes as her aunt had driven down the long gravel drive. The house was a gem.

Set in a huge but overgrown garden, it was made of beautiful, creamy Cotswold stone, with two huge bay windows dominating the front of the house, which was three storeys high. Ivy clambered good-naturedly all over the place, whilst the rear of the house stretched back haphazardly, revealing a dizzying number of rooms that, Harriet had soon learned, were all locked, unused, and covered in dust sheets.

It had been Harriet's idea to offer bed and breakfast that first summer. Unable to get a job, she'd been feeling guilty and desperate to put some money into Frankie's coffers. At first her aunt had been against the idea—not because she had a snobbish dislike of opening her home to strangers, but because she was convinced that the shabby, old-fashioned house wouldn't be good enough to attract visitors. But of course, visitors had come.

The village alone was a beauty spot that sold the tourists the moment they drove through it. The thatched cottages, the little stream that emptied into the River Windrush, the quaint, old-fashioned English pub, the gentle rolling Cotswold farm land. And of course, the house itself, then named Powell Manor. What American could resist living in a 'real' Englishwoman's home? For Frankie herself had been as big a draw as the house.

Worried and nervous at first, she'd soon begun to actually enjoy the influx of new faces. And Harriet hadn't minded rising with the larks and frying huge panfulls of sausages, bacon and eggs. By the time the summer was over, and they'd opened five more bedrooms to the public, she was able to whiz through them in a morning, changing sheets, hoovering, dusting, and changing the flowers; getting it down to a fine art.

And then the autumn and winter had come, and no more guests. The money they'd saved went. It was then, one night in December, just before Christmas, that Harriet had approached her aunt with an idea.

The Bed & Breakfast idea, Harriet had argued, had been a roaring success. Powell Manor had everything a paying guest could want—history, elegance, beautiful views, genteel atmosphere, and proprietresses who could cater to their every whim. So why not turn the whole of Powell Manor into a hotel? An 'English Country House Experience Hotel' was how she put it. And that was exactly what she had entitled the presentation she made to the bank, just two months later.

It hadn't been easy, either to persuade her aunt or their local bank manager. But she'd done it. And she'd done it by being very clever. If she'd tried to turn the house into a modern hotel, such as any tourist could expect to find in the capital, it would have cost literally millions, and Harriet had realised right away that no bank would lend them the horrendous sum they'd need if they went down that route.

So, instead, she'd calculated what would be needed to merely 'touch up' every bedroom in the house. She'd started by touring each room meticulously, and her heart had glowed with growing excitement as she did so. The house, centuries old, already had things a modern interior decorator would die for. Oak wainscoting, teak panelling, real Adam fireplaces, old, dirty, but original paintings. Flock velvet wallpaper that had faded over the years to a perfect shade that looked old because it was old. Carpets that had come from the Orient on sailing ships in the 1700s, little used and hardly worn. Powell Manor, Harriet had told the at first sceptical, but then genuinely interested bank manager, already was ideal for a newly antique-conscious public. All the house really needed was cleaning.

Of course, the bank manager had pointed out that modern tourists expected all the conveniences.

But Harriet had been ready for him. She'd had the long cold months of December and January to work out everything, and she had her argument well-rehearsed. Basically, what she proposed was to turn a disadvantage into an advantage.

Just think, Harriet had said. What do most wealthy tourists who come to England for their holidays really want? Buckingham Palace, English Country Gardens, Fish and Chips and a taste of 'Culture'. Well, Harriet had said confidently, just look around. What if we restored the garden to what it was in Victorian times? The original kitchen garden, with its mellowed brick walls, was still there. As were the apple, plum, and cherry trees. The chicken coops could be restored, so that the hotel could provide guests not only with its own organically-grown fresh vegetables (which, she'd pointed out cannily, were very popular nowadays) but with fresh eggs as well.

They could make good use too of the river Windrush, which formed part of the Manor's boundaries. Ideal for guests to get in a spot of old-fashioned angling right on their doorstep. Long ago one of Frankie's ancestors had purchased private fishing rights to it, so that would present no difficulties.

Slowly, bit by bit, by showing the bank manager her carefully worked-out financial plan proving how much thought she'd put into it, she convinced him.

37

Genuine four-poster beds would more than make up for having to go down the corridor to one of the main bathrooms. In fact, Harriet had prophesied, that touch of 'olde-world charm' would be one of the things their discerning guests would adore.

Can't you just imagine them, Harriet had cajoled the now thoroughly intrigued bank manager, writing home, telling their friends about this adorable country inn they'd found, where they'd had to take their towel and sponge bag and walk down a corridor to the bathroom? It would be high adventure to the pampered rich.

But the rich, Harriet had added, were no fools. They, above all else, knew the 'real McCoy' when they saw it. And Windrush Shallows was as real as it got, because it was real. And think, Harriet had added as the final cherry on the cake, what it would do for the unemployed in the nearby villages.

Most of the start-up money they needed was for labour: gardeners, and for the bluebell wood that fringed the house, a good woodsman. Then they'd have to hire maids and a cook. And the bank manager, well aware of mortgage repayments due to his bank from just such local people, was sold.

He'd given the go-ahead, and from March to May of that same year, Powell Manor was transformed.

Frankie had been bewildered, delighted and

fascinated, to see her home come to life again. Everything changed. The derelict fish-pond was emptied, cleaned, and stocked with ornamental goldfish, and the jungle of the garden melted into distinct areas—the flower-bedecked ornamental front garden, the walled kitchen garden, the newly-pruned orchard, and a newly-laid gravel walkway that meandered throughout the grounds, taking in the bluebell woods and the four-acre boundaries of the gardens. Harriet had even hired a local carpenter to build two small bridges across the river on their private stretch of it, so that guests could stand and look down into the water. Rooms that had not seen the light of day for years, received facelifts. Plumbers modernised and enlarged the house's six bathrooms, and the kitchens had the biggest refit of all. The library was very cleverly divided in half. One part became an office, where Harriet worked like a demon on administration, the other half remained very much a library, complete with its iron spiral staircase leading to a top floor of shelves, where guests could browse at their leisure.

Nobody but Harriet had thought they'd be ready to open their doors that same summer. But open they had.

Clever and well-placed advertising had ensured that they'd attracted just the right sort of clientele. Over ninety percent of their guests were tourists from overseas, whilst the other

39

ten percent consisted mainly of British guests who'd despaired of ever finding a truly 'English' hotel again.

Now, five years later, the hotel was always full in summer, and even in spring and autumn was never less than half-full.

Of course, Windrush Shallows was not huge. It had just twenty-five bedrooms in all, twenty of them for the guests, so there was never a feeling of being crowded together like sardines.

One of the first things Harriet had done was to hire a local cook with a reputation for English cuisine and every day at four o'clock, in the fern-bedecked, mirrored ballroom, tea was served, including scones warm from the oven, with local clotted cream.

Locals had quickly discovered this attraction, as well as dons from Oxford and businessmen from Gloucester. Now, 'Tea at Windrush Shallows' had become the event to experience.

And when, four years ago, Vania Lane had come knocking at the door, asking if they needed the services of a good tour guide and organiser, Harriet had made yet another golden decision, and hired her on the spot. And had never regretted it.

The young American girl had been an instant hit with guests and staff alike. She immediately made any home-sick American guests feel as if they were getting the attention they were used to, and at the same time, her organisational skills matched even those of Harriet. Within a month, both Frankie and Harriet wondered how they'd ever managed without her.

Vania had discovered a coach company that specialised in charabancs, the rounded, colourful, comfortable old coaches that had been around in the 1950s. And the novelty of having one of those pull up outside still bought gasps and sighs from new guests, who invariably reached for their cameras.

And those who elected to go on 'Vania's Tours' were able to choose from such delights as a horse-drawn buggy ride around a real working farm, a river cruise up the Thames complete with smoked salmon lunch, Saturday afternoons spent watching cricket on the village green, or lazy days spent wandering around Bourton-on-the-Water.

Vania, Harriet had soon realised, had the knack of knowing just what her fellow Americans wanted to see. In the four years that she'd worked for Windrush Shallows, the young woman had done everything from plotting the best route to Warwick Castle and Shakespeare's Stratford-Upon-Avon, to taking a wheelchair-bound guest around the Cotswold Wildlife Park to see the animals.

Now, as the two women walked down the deserted stairs to the enlarged kitchens, Vania cast her friend a quick glance. She was glad to see her looking better. Like everyone else who'd ever met her, Vania had quickly grown fond of Frankie Powell, and her death ten days ago had been a shock to them all.

Things were slowly getting back to normal, though, and as they walked into the kitchen, the smell of newly-baking bread made Vania's stomach rumble. Loudly.

Maisie Bryce, their English cook, looked up and smiled. 'Hello. You up and about then?' she asked cheerfully, her merry blue eyes running over Harriet's face. 'You're still pale, chuck. Want a cup of tea?'

Harriet smiled and sat at the table. 'When did I ever say no to a cup of tea?' she asked wryly.

During the last year, Harriet had run the hotel single-handedly, determined to take even the smallest burden from Frankie's shoulders, and now she could almost hear Frankie urging her to get on with her life and take the Shallows on to ever greater things.

Vania, reading the morning paper, suddenly looked across at her. 'Isn't it this afternoon that you have to go to Powell House?' she asked quietly. And Harriet felt her new-found sense of confidence drain away as she contemplated the will-reading.

Frankie's lawyer had been away when she'd died, and hadn't been able to get back to read the will until today. It was to be read at Powell House, only twenty miles away, although

Harriet had never been there. She wasn't looking forward to seeing her grandmother for the first time either. Not that Lady Grace Powell knew that Harriet was her granddaughter . . .

'Yes, it's today,' Harriet said, something in her voice making Vania's dark glossy head shoot up. Her green eyes narrowed.

'Are you worried about it, Harriet?' she asked softly, tossing the paper aside. 'Do you want me to come with you?'

Vania had always felt very protective towards Harriet. Her appointment at Windrush Shallows had been her first real, decent job, since coming to England. Now, the hotel felt like home. Was home. Harriet was like a sister to her. And she knew enough about the complicated Powell family history to know that this afternoon would be something of an ordeal for Harriet.

But Harriet smiled at her, and something about the way she stiffened her shoulders and lifted her chin defiantly reassured Vania.

'No, it's all right,' Harriet said. 'I'll be fine.'

Those words would prove to be somewhat premature however . . .

*　　　*　　　*

Whilst Vania was making sure that Mr Amerheimer had all he needed for a comfortable day on the river, across the

43

Atlantic, Brett Carver was waking up in the middle of the night to a phone call. He took it in the small study of his penthouse, padding naked to the large swivel chair and pulling towards him a notepad and pen. Whenever he got a call from Vincent White, he always made notes.

'Yeah? Go ahead Vince,' Brett drawled into the receiver, stifling a yawn. 'What's up?' Brett had outwardly aged little since Vania McAllen had disappeared. No grey hairs. No noticeable weight loss. Only those who knew him well had detected the way that the shadows in his eyes had deepened, becoming almost haunted.

'Just thought you'd want to know—Larner has petitioned the courts to have Vania McAllen declared legally dead.' Brett grunted. 'He can't get away with that. Not enough time has passed.' Brett's lawyers had already told him how many years had to pass before that could happen.

'Yeah, but he's trying it on anyway. You know James Larner.'

Brett did. 'Anything else?' he asked sharply. 'How did that witness in France work out?'

'It wasn't her,' Vincent White said regretfully. 'Sorry Brett. I know how much hope you were pinning on that. But one of my boys has come up with something else. Something in London.'

Vincent White, who ran one of the best private detective agencies on the East Coast,

44

had been hired by Brett and Chuck McAllen five years ago to find Vania McAllen.

And he was still trying to do just that.

'OK.' Brett said flatly. 'Keep on it. Let me know if you get word on anything, anything at all, won't you?'

'I will,' Vince said, and rang off. He stared at the receiver for several long seconds, shaking his head. That little girl sure had intended to disappear. He packed a case and headed to the airport. Next stop—Heathrow.

*   *   *

Back in his Boston penthouse Brett Carver also hung up. In front of him were papers about the takeover he was planning out on the West Coast. He had spent months working on it in utmost secrecy, sweating, manoeuvering, knowing that if he could only pull it off, he'd be set for life—he'd finally be up there in the big league.

But now he could hardly summon up the energy to even care.

Instead he went back to bed. There he lay, alone, in the darkness of the summer night, staring up at the ceiling for a long, long time.

'Vania,' he muttered softly. 'Where the hell are you? Why did you leave me?'

CHAPTER TWO

As Harriet drove the twenty miles towards Powell House, she forced herself to remember all that Frankie had ever told her about her family. Frankie's older brother Arthur had married late in life, a young widow with a son, Giles, who was only a few years old when Arthur had officially adopted him. Grace, Lady Powell, had not approved, blaming Arthur's wife for never conceiving a true Powell heir. But over the years, Grace's attitude had changed. Like his adoptive father, Giles Powell had quickly shown true entrepreneurial spirit.

Not only had he learned, by the time he was eighteen, all there was to know about running the huge multi-farm estate he would one day inherit, but he'd gone to Oxford, to St. Bede's College, to earn a First in Politics and Economics. After leaving, he'd set up a computer software company that had taken advantage of the new and growing games and toy market and by the time he was twenty-five, Giles Powell was already a multi-millionaire in his own right. After his father's death, he had taken over the running of the estates and was now Grace Powell's 'golden boy'. Whenever Frankie had talked about her nephew, she'd done so with fondness and admiration.

As Harriet turned the corner, a gasp of dismay left her, and she found her foot automatically pressing hard on the brake. Obediently, the car drew to a halt.

In front of her was a . . . a . . . palace! It was huge. Four storeys high, crenellated, it looked like a castle. No wonder Grace had such a high opinion of herself.

Grimly, Harriet reached into her handbag, straightened her shoulders, and put the car into gear. Lady Grace and the oh-so-popular Giles Powell might have Powell House, the land, wealth and title, but she had Windrush Shallows, and that was all she'd ever wanted or needed.

*　　*　　*

Standing in the blue salon overlooking the front of the grounds, Grace, Lady Powell watched the approaching car with narrowed eyes.

'I don't believe it,' she hissed. 'She's actually had the gall to come in your aunt's Bentley.'

Lady Grace was 89, but looked 70. Her hair was iron grey, and matched her elegant suit. She walked with the aid of a gold-topped cane, and her back was still ramrod straight.

Leaning negligently against the fireplace, her grandson looked at her fondly. She reminded him of an outraged cat, all offended dignity and hissing anger. At her words, however, he frowned and joined her, looking out of the big sash windows as Frankie's 1940 grey Bentley cruised sedately down the drive.

'The cheeky little . . .' He didn't bother completing the sentence, and instead shook his head. He didn't know whether to applaud her nerve, or laugh in disgust. He began to wonder if his grandmother's vitriolic views on Frankie's 'companion' might not be so far off the mark, after all.

He'd been immersed in his new company, when his grandmother had first told him that his Aunt Frankie had taken 'some young girl' under her wing. It was hardly earth-shattering news, and it had barely registered with him. And then the up-dates had starting coming in, causing his grandmother to come marching into his office, practically speechless with rage.

Frankie had turned Powell Manor into a Bed and Breakfast! Grace had squeaked the last three words, so shocked had she been. And Giles had, at last, been taken aback. For it had not sounded like something his shy, conservative aunt Frankie would do at all.

Grace had been beside herself. 'The ignominy of it. Mark my words', she'd fumed, stabbing the air in front of Giles's nose, 'it's that girl that's behind all this.' And Giles had been very much in agreement with her.

Although he'd never lived in the old house himself, its current use saddened him. He knew his own upbringing had given him old-fashioned views on things like heritage, but even so . . . he still felt uneasy.

Grace had promptly telephoned her daughter, demanding that she give up this foolish enterprise. But Frankie, rather to her mother's surprise had stood firm. It wasn't something Grace was used to.

And when it became official that Powell Manor was now called Windrush Shallows Hotel, Grace had been apoplectic.

It was then that Giles had begun to become seriously concerned. But Frankie herself had reassured him. She and Harriet knew what they were doing, his aunt had insisted. The venture had been well researched and she wasn't in danger of losing her home, or her savings, or anything else. It would work.

Eventually Frankie's confidence and matter-of-factness had convinced him. And she certainly seemed to be happy working with Harriet. But Grace had continued to fume and fret, predicting dire disaster. And yet no such calamity had happened. In fact, from what they'd heard from neighbours and friends in the area, Windrush Shallows was becoming quite popular.

Of course, Giles thought, all that would change now. He knew his grandmother well—and when the property returned to her, she'd be sure to shut the hotel down.

He heard the door bell ring and knew that Bates would be answering it.

49

Grace sniffed. 'She should be coming in through the side entrance,' she muttered, and Giles decided, wisely, to ignore the catty little comment.

Sometimes, he was sure, his grandmother forgot the times she was living in. And over the past few months Lady Grace had become ever more . . . eccentric. He didn't want to even think it, for she'd always been so sharp and had such a strong personality, but he was beginning to realise that perhaps senility was rearing its ugly head. Uneasily, he shook away the thought. She'd be mortified if anyone even suggested that perhaps . . . her age was beginning to tell, and in such a cruel manner too.

'Will Gordon be set up in the Library by now?' Grace asked, and Giles grinned.

'If I know Gordon, he is.'

'I don't see why he insisted that *she* be present,' Grace sniffed.

Giles took her gnarled hand in his in a comforting, calming gesture. 'Now come on, Grandmother,' he said softly. 'It's only natural that Frankie wanted to leave her a little something in her will. Whether you like it or not, Frankie was genuinely fond of her. She told us so, often enough.'

'Hah!' Grace snorted. 'Frankie never did have any sense. Letting a little gold-digger wangle her way into her home, turning everything upside down.'

Grace sighed. 'Yes. Well, best get it over with, I suppose,' she sniffed. 'Still, Frankie can't have left the little gold-digger much. She'd never leave anything valuable to an outsider.'

'No, she wouldn't,' Giles agreed, and together, with evident accord, they left the room.

Harriet was sitting on a powder-blue divan, nervously holding on to a glass of sherry that Frankie's solicitor, Gordon Keeler, had just poured for her. She was still feeling thoroughly rattled. She'd been shown into a library that made the library back at Windrush Shallows look like a second-hand bookstore. The antique globe in the corner alone must be worth tens of thousands of pounds. The rows of books were priceless. Everything screamed MONEY in letters so large she felt like laughing. And to think her father had left all this behind, willingly, for the love of her mother.

It was as she was thinking this that the door opened and two people walked in. Harriet knew that the impressive-looking woman with the cane and hauteur of a queen could only be her grandmother, but she barely noticed her.

Instead her eyes widened, filling with the image of the man beside the old woman. He was tall, she realised numbly, well over six feet in height, and seemed to dominate the room just by being in it. His hair was inky black, and fell over his forehead in a silken wave. The eyes above the strong cheekbones were dark brown, penetrating, and glowed like jet. He was wearing a suit so dark a blue it, too, was almost black, and so exquisitely cut it could only have come from a top London tailor. It somehow emphasised, rather than hid, his lean, powerful, masculine physique. A discreet gold watch circled his left wrist, but somehow, all these trappings of civilisation did nothing to reassure her. Without quite knowing how, she got the impression of a predator. Well-camouflaged, silent, and discreet perhaps, but a hunting animal nonetheless.

His chin had just the slightest hint of a dimple in it, she noticed, her bewildered and scattered thoughts doing their best to assimilate information and carry it back to her stunned brain. He was, she guessed, in his early thirties, and his mouth, which had a surprising full and sensuous lower lip, was curved into a slightly mocking smile. Only his eyes, which were carefully blank, gave her any hint that, perhaps, he wasn't quite as cool and confident as he might wish her to believe.

Giles, in fact, was feeling very far from cool. The moment he'd walked into the room and become aware of a blonde-haired vision rising to her feet like Aphrodite from the waves, he'd felt the earth lurch beneath his feet.

It was the same sensation he sometimes had when he was having a bad dream. A feeling of helplessness. The sickening sensation told him that he was no longer in control. That something way outside his influence—fate, had luck, destiny—had suddenly put an obstacle in his path.

He could hardly believe what he was seeing. The dark suit made her startling platinum hair seem even whiter. Her face—her impossibly lovely face—was as pale as milk. And those eyes . . . he couldn't believe it, they were almost violet. He blinked, unable to believe what his own senses were telling him. What his own brain was insisting was real.

'Ah, Giles. Glad to see you.' It was Gordon Keeler who spoke, shattering the tense atmosphere with all the finesse of a bull in a china shop.

Harriet took the opportunity to drag her eyes away from Giles's. She sank back on to the sofa, not because she'd been invited to, but because her knees had simply given out on her.

What was happening to her? Giles Powell was just another handsome man—a sophisticated man in his element. She shook her head, telling herself that her tingling reaction was just the aftermath of the 'flu. But, somehow, she couldn't make herself believe it. She glanced at the door as every instinct within her screamed at her to run.

Only a determined sense of self-control kept her from bolting, there and then. Giles, for his part, was relieved to be able to turn away from her to shake the solicitor's hand. 'Gordon,' he said simply. His voice was deep, and utterly English, Harriet noted. But then, raised by Grace, Lady Powell, what else could it be?

Stamped on his features, in his voice, in his clothes and his very background, were centuries of English aristocratic breeding. It mattered not a whit that he was adopted— Giles Powell, Harriet realised in dismay, was every inch the English aristocrat. She took several deep breaths, relieved to find she was getting back some sense of balance. Of perspective.

Gordon Keeler alone seemed unaware of the bad vibes in the room. As he moved back behind an impressive desk, Grace Powell glided stiffly to the biggest chair in front of the desk. Giles, clearly out of a long-established habit, drew it back for her. To Harriet the gesture was at once oddly touching, old-fashioned, and mildly irritating.

She reminded herself that she'd be out of this overwhelming house soon. She gave her watch a sneaky glance, unaware that as she did so, that Giles Powell caught the small movement of her head, and his lips twisted. In a hurry, was she? Couldn't wait to see how much all her scheming had netted her?

He smiled, a tight, angry, uncharacteristically vicious smile. The sooner the little baggage was sent packing, the better. Giles

54

didn't trust beautiful women. Not since he'd unwisely married and very swiftly divorced one in his foolish youth . . .

Gordon coughed. Giles, taking a slightly less throne-like chair turned it at an angle so that he could watch both his grandmother and Harriet Jensen, who seemed to be in no hurry to leave the sofa. Gordon, too, shot a glance at the pale young woman. Unlike Giles and Grace Powell he knew that Harriet Jensen was Frankie's niece. He only wished that he'd been able to persuade Frankie to inform her mother of that fact.

He glanced at Grace, noting the grim satisfaction on her face, and his heart fell. He next turned to Giles, but the other man was staring at Harriet as if . . . He felt his spine tingle. A man of some experience himself, Gordon knew what that look meant when he saw it in another man's eyes.

Giles Powell looked as if he hated Harriet and yet, against his will . . . *desired* her.

Oh hell! That was all they needed.

Harriet glanced up at the sound of the solicitor's cough, and for the first time Giles noticed how ill she looked. How pale. And those dark circles under her eyes . . . With a start, he found himself wondering about something he'd never even thought of before. Was it possible that Harriet Jensen had actually loved his aunt? That Frankie hadn't merely been a foolish, lonely, old woman,

55

when she'd assured him that Harriet was genuinely fond of her? Could it have actually been true?

Then he gave himself a mental shake. Hah! This vision of frail beauty hadn't even bothered to show up at Frankie's funeral. But she'd shown up for the reading of the will quickly enough. Oh yes. He knew her sort. Money. It was all women ever wanted. All his ex-wife had ever wanted . . .

'This is the Last Will and Testament of the Honourable Frances Davinia Powell,' Gordon began portentously, 'dated the twentieth of May, 1999.'

Harriet, very much aware of the dark gaze boring into her, fixed her eyes determinedly on Gordon.

Just look at her, Giles thought in disgust. She can't wait to hear what she's getting, staring at poor old Gordon like a dog at a bone. But he knew Frankie better than she did—his aunt had a sense of family every bit as well defined, in its way, as Grace Powell's own. His lips twisted. If she thought she was in for a big pay-out then was she in for a shock!

'Because he is fond of fishing, I leave my nephew Giles, my father's collection of antique fishing equipment and books, in the hope that this bequest will give him many hours of pleasure.'

Giles glanced briefly at Gordon and smiled. It was just like Frankie to think of something like that. Knowing how little he needed in monetary terms, she'd opted instead to give him something she knew he'd appreciate. He nodded, pleased to know that his aunt had been thinking of him.

Harriet watched Giles Powell's face as this was read out, slightly surprised to find that he looked happy with the small bequest, when she'd half expected sardonic amusement.

She felt herself relax. This wasn't going to be so bad after all. She'd made these people into monsters in her mind, when really . . .

'The rest of my estate, including my Bentley and all other properties and land, namely Powell Manor, or Windrush Shallows Hotel as it is now known . . .' Gordon's voice swept on, and Harriet, who knew the contents of the will, as Frankie had insisted she should, chose that moment to glance at her grandmother.

And saw her smiling in anticipation.

She doesn't know, Harriet thought, aghast. Frankie hadn't told her about the contents of the will. She felt suddenly sick. Grace thought that Frankie had left everything to *her!*

Giles saw Harriet look at Grace, and saw her beautiful face freeze. An expression, almost of horror, crossed her lovely features. He felt himself smile. So, the gold-digger had suddenly cottoned on to the fact that she was not going to have things all her own way, after all. His lips curved up into a smile. What a pity. After all the hard work she'd put into

57

worming her way into Frankie's affections too. Wasn't it a shame?

'I leave to Miss Harriet Jensen, currently residing at Windrush Shallows Hotel,' Gordon Keeler completed the sentence, keeping his voice as flat and emotionless as possible.

He needn't have bothered.

In that instant, complete pandemonium broke out.

CHAPTER THREE

'What?' Grace Powell screeched, for the first time in many years completely losing her dignity. She rose, trembling, to her feet, her eyes wild. Gordon, aghast, reared back in the chair, wishing himself a thousand miles away. At the same time, Giles too catapulted to his feet, all male energy springing into action. 'You've made a mistake,' his voice was a combination of firmness and cold, hard, fury.

Gordon, choosing to deal with Giles, rather than with Lady Grace, looked at him levelly. 'I assure you, there's no mistake,' he said quietly.

'Frankie would never leave the house to a stranger,' Giles stated, and so sure did he sound that both Gordon and Harriet exchanged a quick, knowing look. Since they both had exactly the same thought, at exactly the same moment, it was impossible not to

58

react with a mutual glance of understanding. For they both knew that Frankie would never have left her so much if she hadn't been family.

Giles caught the look that passed between lawyer and girl, and felt a cold fist of fury clench in his innards. What the hell was going on? Gordon had been Frankie's family lawyer for years. Why was he suddenly so close to Harriet Jensen? Had he, too, been taken in by her pretty face?

'Let me see that,' Giles snarled, whilst his grandmother slowly subsided on to her chair. Everything about her was quivering, like a dog straining at the leash. But she was willing, for the moment, to let her grandson do all the talking. It would give her time to think . . . Besides, she knew Giles well. He was a man very much like her own father had been—a man who got what he wanted. A tough-hearted, tough-minded man who took the world by the throat and told it what it was going to do. She watched him now with tight-lipped approval as he all but snatched the proffered will out of Gordon Keeler's hand. Before, she was sure, Giles had never really taken Harriet Jensen seriously.

Frankie had always been very evasive when they'd asked her why she'd taken the girl under her wing. At the time, Giles had been prepared to just shrug and let it go at that, not believing it was a sneaky campaign on the girl's part to wriggle her way into Frankie's affections—and purse.

Now, seeing his face so tightly controlled, but pale with rage, Grace let a satisfied smile cross her wrinkled face.

Now, Miss Harriet Jensen would realise what she had taken on.

Giles quickly read the will for himself, seeing in black and white Frankie's last wishes. When he'd finished, he lowered the papers back to the desk, and looked Gordon Keeler in the eye, pure steel in his gaze. 'So what's going on, Gordon?' he asked ominously.

But it was Harriet who answered. Harriet, who'd simply sat there, too stunned to move, as first Grace and then Giles had reacted like wolves at the first scent of blood. Harriet was appalled by the fact that neither of them had so much as given Frankie's last wishes in this whole matter a passing thought. After all, it had been Frankie's money.

Her face flushed in anger. Fire-hot anger.

Just who did they think they were?

'I'd have thought that was obvious,' she said, as surprised as everyone else at the cold, smooth, almost amused tone of voice that was coming out of her own mouth.

Giles wheeled around and took a half-step towards her, his eyes blazing at her impudence. Instinctively, Harriet was on her feet again, the age-old instinct of flight-or-fight washing over her. Only, this time, it was definitely not going to be flight. She was sick and tired of treading on eggshells around these people.

It was her against them. So be it. Of course, it was all very fine to make such a promise to herself, but coming face to face with Giles Powell's fury was something different altogether. For a start, she wasn't prepared for the way her body reacted to his. Just looking at him now made something hot and melting stir within her, sending a wave of heat washing over her face. Heat that had nothing to do with anger.

When his hands clenched and unclenched into fists by his side, her nipples tightened, tingling into hard budding life, and her breath caught. Again, it had nothing to do with fear.

As their eyes met, electricity sizzled between them. Harriet had never felt anything like it before. It confused her. She'd been too busy at Windrush Shallows to have much time for a social life. She'd been kissed and dated, of course, but never before had a man's mere presence affected her like this.

But she couldn't afford to be confused. Even as one stunned part of her brain was sending back astonished messages to her consciousness, telling her that she was attracted to this man, another, more logical part of her, was already telling her that fact was simply irrelevant. Her chin lifted slightly. Her amazing eyes flashed. 'Frankie wanted me to have Windrush Shallows,' she said flatly. 'What's so hard for you to understand about that?'

Giles stared at her, his dark eyes glowing like jet. What was wrong with it? The audacity of the wench! He wanted to . . . Taking a deep breath, Giles forced himself to relax.

'I don't think it's as simple as all that,' he said, forcing his voice back to normal, taking a determined pace or two away from her and towards the drinks cabinet. He simply didn't trust himself to be so close to her. He used the valuable seconds he'd gained to force his reactions back under control.

Damn her, he'd never expected her to be so beautiful . . .

Harriet watched him pour a glass of brandy and take it to his grandmother, once again feeling out-classed and out-manoeuvered. He was like a chameleon. One moment the roaring, raging lion, the next cool as a snake, all smoothness and charm.

'Giles,' Gordon said, his voice nervous but reasonable. 'I assure you, your aunt's will is perfectly valid.'

Giles glanced at him. 'Do you think so? How long have you been Frankie's solicitor, Gordon?' he asked smoothly.

'Nearly thirty years,' Gordon answered the question quietly, guessing what was to come.

'So you knew my aunt well.'

Gordon nodded. 'Yes. She always confided

in me. I'd like to think we were friends, as well as solicitor and client.'

'So do you think it was like Frankie to leave her estate outside the family?' Giles growled, not liking the way the lawyer's eyes darted away from his. 'Well do you? Don't look at her, dammit,' he snapped as, once again, Gordon shot a quick look at Harriet.

It wasn't hard for her to read his expression. Tell them, he was urging her silently. Just tell them, and then all this will be settled. But something previously alien to her was stirring now. She was angry, yes. But she was also elated. For the first time in so long she felt alive, glowingly, vibrantly, incredibly alive. She'd never had to fight for anything before. She had never had anything she wanted so much that she was prepared to do battle for it.

Now she was being challenged, and not just by the situation, but by the man himself Giles Powell. The oh-so-successful, handsome, Lord of the Manor. And she was utterly determined that Giles Powell was not going to have his way this time.

She quickly shook her head at Gordon. *Tell them nothing.* Giles caught the almost telepathic exchange between them and exploded.

'You're in collusion,' he said, his voice both shocked and furious. 'I don't believe it. Gordon, are you insane?' he queried, genuinely stunned, staring at the old,

63

previously trusted family solicitor as if he'd never seen him before.

Gordon sighed and shook his head. If Harriet wanted to keep her identity a secret, then it was not up to him to interfere.

'There are several other smaller bequests in Frankie's will—some jewellery to her mother, a small annuity to a charity . . .' He read the rest of the will, determined to do his job, then quietly packed away his things. All the time, he was aware of Lady Grace glowering at him from her chair.

As the solicitor left, Grace looked at the girl, hate burning like fire in her eyes.

Giles also turned to look at Harriet, who faced him with a level, determined stare. She looked so sure of herself that he wanted to take the few steps necessary to drag her into his arms and . . . and . . . kiss her into submission. Caress her into trembling acquiescence. He smiled. Spoke softly.

'Don't think you're going to get away with this, Miss Jensen,' he said. 'Please,' he held out a hand in a mocking gesture of appeal. 'I'd hate for you to go away from this house thinking you've won.' He sounded so utterly confident that it triggered some wild female defiance deep inside her. Harriet knew she shouldn't do it. Even as the impulse came over her, even as she felt her facial muscles rearranging themselves into a contemptuous, triumphant grin, she was telling herself it was

64

sheer folly.

Giles watched the impudent grin spread across her face.

And the urge to take her into his arms and crush the defiance out of her became so strong, he literally had to take a step backwards to restrain himself.

'Oh, but I *have* won, Giles,' Harriet said, her voice clear and lilting and full of life. 'I always knew I would.'

All her life, she'd wondered what had made this family believe that a woman like her mother—strong, beautiful, generous Elizabeth—could actually be beneath them. All her life, that thought had been there, like a rose thorn under her skin. Living with Frankie, though, she'd thought she'd finally managed to put the sour spectre of the Powell family behind her. But just a few moments of gazing into Giles Powell's dark, dangerous, seductive eyes, and she knew how wrong she'd been.

Now, all her disdain showed on her face.

And, for a moment, Giles was puzzled. The gloating he understood—he'd half expect it from a gold-digger who'd just learned all her planning had been successful. But this look of . . . distaste for them, seemed way too . . . personal.

A man of keen brain and good instincts, something told him that he hadn't yet got the whole picture here. That something more than greedy triumph was going on behind that outrageously beautiful face. That Harriet Jensen had some kind of hidden agenda that he didn't know about. But what? They'd never even met before. And so far, things were going her way, weren't they? So why this look of . . . antagonism?

Harriet noticed the narrowing of his eyes and sensed the man's brain working furiously. And suddenly, belatedly, she felt a frisson of fear work its way up her spine.

She had a tiger by the tail.

For an instant her fear showed, and Giles felt a primordial sense of sheer masculine dominance. It was heady, and wonderful. It made him smile confidently. But that was all drowned out a moment later by a wave of desire that rocked him, taking him on a current so strong he couldn't fight against it. In his imagination, he could see his own dark head coming closer to hers, the jet black of his own hair a stark contrast to her fairness. He could see her hair, splayed out on a pillow, her lovely eyes softening, welcoming, as she looked up at him, coming closer . . . His body hardened, every sense in him quivering into alertness. Skin tingled. Nerves leapt. An intoxicating, sensual, sexual, natural drug seemed to have been injected into his veins.

He'd had no meaningful relationship with a woman since his divorce eight years previously. Just an occasional one-night stand that had temporarily satisfied his body, but touched no other part of him. Suddenly, horrifically, he could feel himself being drawn to this woman. This mercenary, lovely, treacherous, greed-driven woman who was his enemy. Was he mad?

Harriet, fascinated by the flickering of emotions that were crossing his mobile, handsome face, suddenly realised that for better or worse, she was making one hell of an impression on Giles Powell. But then she began to feel heart-sore. Weary. As if she'd just come through a storm at sea, and was now tired and depressed.

And she was definitely not thinking straight.

What did she have to be afraid of? Why should she be afraid? If Giles did learn the truth about her, did manage to ferret out her secret, so what? It would only strengthen her hold on Windrush Shallows, not loosen it. She was in a no-lose situation. The thought made her laugh. She hadn't meant to laugh out loud, but the realisation that she was on tenterhooks for nothing, just seemed so damned hilarious all of a sudden that she couldn't help it.

Her laughter, dark, husky and warm as a summer breeze, made Giles tingle. It was so wonderful it rippled through his blood like quicksilver. To Lady Grace, it was the ultimate insult. How dared she laugh? How dared she laugh . . . at *them?*

Unaware of the effect of her laughter on the two Powells in the room, Harriet reached down for her bag, slung the long strap over her shoulder and glanced back at Giles. Her face was once more composed. 'Well,' she said. 'That would seem to be that.'

Giles smiled. 'Oh, I wouldn't say that,' he said softly, his eyes running over her, caressing as they went.

Harriet felt her pulse trip and bit her lip.

'No, I wouldn't say that at all,' he mused, seeing the flush of colour come to her face and resisting the urge to thrust his fist up into the air, and shout 'YES'.

'Let me walk you out,' he said, urbanity personified. Out in the hall, Giles walked beside Harriet to the main door.

She was tall and slim, and walked with the gentle swaying movement of a reed in the wind. At the entrance, he opened the door for her, the sunlight and breath of fresh air incredibly welcome. Harriet took a thankful step outside, then she felt a hand of steel hook around her elbow. Her body, moving forward, was suddenly abruptly halted, the impetus of her movement making her swing around, cannoning into him.

Her breath left her in a rush. She struggled wildly, a sense of panic rushing through her. He was so close. She could feel the muscle under the suit. Smell him. Touch the warmth of his skin . . .

Giles's eyes narrowed as he saw the expression on her face. And once again he was aware of the sudden surge of emotion between them. 'Hey, take it easy,' he snapped. not liking the look of fear and panic in her eyes one little bit. She was making him feel like Jack the Ripper.

'Let go of me then!' Harriet snapped, dragging her arm out of his grip. 'And don't ever touch me again!' She wasn't sure why she said that. It wasn't as if they were ever going to set eyes on each other again.

She only knew that something had happened to her the moment she'd met this man. Something she didn't trust. Something that she knew instinctively, could threaten her whole way of life. Her familiar way of thinking. And she'd been through too much already. She only wanted peace now.

And this man wasn't exactly peaceful.

Giles frowned down at her slumped shoulders. She reminded him of a snowdrop, bowed down beneath too much heavy snow.

Harriet took another step backwards, and turned like a fugitive towards the parked Bentley.

'It's not over, Harriet,' he said suddenly, warningly, her name coming from his mouth as if he'd spoken it all his life.

He saw her blonde head turn sharply around. Saw her lovely eyes question his. He smiled. 'I told you before. You haven't won. I'm going to fight you every step of the way.'

For an instant she felt like crying. Did this

man never give up? Then, aware that self-defeatism just wasn't her style, her chin came up. 'Oh? And just how do you plan to do that?' she asked archly.

Giles grinned. He couldn't help it. She was so damned feisty, so sure of herself, and he was so much looking forward to teaching her that she'd taken on the wrong man this time.

'For a start, I'm going to contest the will. The local courts around here . . .' Giles shrugged. 'Well, let's just say, our magistrates know which side their bread is buttered on.' But instead of looking alarmed, Harriet Jensen began to smile again.

The courts . . . Let him try! I'm a blood-relative. Frankie's favourite niece. Frankie's only niece. Oh no, Mr Giles High-And-Mighty Powell. No magistrate in the world would ever take Windrush Shallows away from me. He looked so unbelievably strong, standing there, backed by the family mansion. So incredibly assured. In a way, it seemed almost a pity to rock his foundations. And yet . . . it would be so . . . lovely . . . to bring him to his knees.

She shook her head, as much at her own hitherto unsuspected vicious streak as anything else.

'Oh Giles,' she said softly, feasting her eyes on his male beauty, testing the fine, delicious tremors he sent coursing around her body as she'd test a new wine, sipping it, letting the taste of it settle on her tongue. But that way

70

lay sheer folly.

Oh, but she wanted him so. But no. She had yet to take a lover, and she was not so suicidal as to opt for this man. And yet he was so . . . desirable. So utterly desirable. And so unaware of the true situation.

'You poor, misguided idiot,' she said softly. But whether she was talking to him, or to herself, she had no way of knowing.

Harriet turned and walked resolutely away from him.

CHAPTER FOUR

Vania reached for her fourth slice of toast, and gave Mrs Barrett a broad wink as she did so. The old lady chuckled appreciatively and winked back at her.

Vania always ate her meals in Windrush Shallows' dining room, as did Harriet. They found that it helped create a 'family' atmosphere.

There wasn't anything about her job at Windrush Shallows that Vania didn't enjoy. And she was well aware that it had been the luckiest day of her life when she'd knocked on Harriet's and Frankie's door. Now Vania glanced surreptitiously at her watch, but the eagle-eyed old lady caught her out.

'Where we goin' today then, Vania?' she

asked cheerfully. Mrs. Barrett was one of the many guests staying at the hotel who were constant passengers on 'Vania's charabanc', as it was widely known.

'I thought . . . oh . . .' Vania teased, cocking her head to one side, looking as if she was making up her mind, 'Bourton?'

Harriet came through from the kitchens and hesitated in the doorway, glancing around the dining room that, at eight-thirty in the morning, was beginning to empty. Her eyes passed over Vania and the old lady and she smiled, then spotted a pair of middle-aged tax accountants from Oklahoma, and moved towards them. They were just starting on their cereals, and their faces lit up in welcome as she approached and greeted them.

She was offered a chair in a trice. Vania watched her friend, unaware that her worried look was being quickly and expertly analysed by the eagle-eyed Mrs Barrett.

'She'll be alright,' the old lady said softly, making Vania swing her cat-green gaze in her direction. 'She's still missing her aunt, ain't she?' she added bluntly.

Vania nodded. 'Yes. But . . .' She knew it wasn't that. Ever since she'd come back from the reading of her aunt's will yesterday, Vania had sensed that her friend was in turmoil.

Not that it was obvious. Harriet's loveliness was every bit as effective as a mask. Only those who knew her really well could see behind the

72

charming smile and the light breezy voice, and sense the upset that churned below the calm expression on her face. But Vania wasn't about to discuss such things with a guest. 'Do you suppose all our happy troops are down yet?' she asked the old lady, who finished off the last of her grapefruit and smacked her lips.

'Probably not Mrs Carlson,' Mrs Barrett said promptly.

Vania grinned. Mrs Carlson was always ten minutes behind everyone else. And so it was, that at ten minutes past nine (not nine o'clock as stated on the itinerary) the comfortable, red and cream 1950s charabanc pulled out of the hotel and headed towards Bourton-on-the-Water.

Vania sat at the front, alternately chatting to their regular driver, and commenting aloud for her group, with no idea that her happy, safe, and familiar world was about to crash down around her head.

Vincent White cursed as he found himself driving on the wrong side of the road again, and quickly steered his hired Rover back on to the left-hand side of the road. Why the British had to be different, he didn't know.

But at least he couldn't lose sight of the weird-looking bus even if he wanted to.

He'd had a tip-off from one of his many sources in London that had led him to a little hotel off the beaten track in Oxfordshire. He hadn't really been expecting much from it—

73

but he'd arrived just in time to see a woman who, from a distance, might have been Vania McAllen, so here he was.

Vince yawned. He needed to check Windrush Shallows Hotel employee records first off. Although Vania McAllen definitely wasn't using her real name, he might get a hint . . .

He cursed as the bus in front of him turned sharply right, and he braked, turning into what felt like to him to be oncoming traffic.

In the coach, the passengers were perking up, glancing around them, an excited buzz filling the air. They'd seen the signs that said Bourton-on-the-Water was only half a mile away, and already anticipation was rife. It was all so familiar to her, that Vania smiled gently and took the opportunity to twist in her seat and look back at them.

'Now then,' she said, her strong voice earning her instant silence and attention. 'For those of you who've bothered to read the pamphlets . . .' There was a good-natured groan. '. . . You'll know that there are several attractions to see at Bourton-on-the-Water. We're going to park right next to Birdland. As soon as you get out you'll hear them all screeching—especially the parakeets. There's also a trout farm, and I recommend that you buy some fish pellets to feed to them. It's simply amazing how the big trout snap them up. And some of them *are* big.' Vania held her hands stretched out far apart in wild exaggeration.

There were cat-calls and whistles, especially from the fishermen in the group, as the bus turned into the car park.

'I know some of you don't much care for our feathered friends, so you can also check out the model village, a rustic museum showing how farm life used to be, or a working perfumery. There's plenty of arts-and-crafts shops too. Lots to keep you busy! It's now . . .' she checked her watch, 'nearly ten. We won't be leaving until four. There are plenty of pubs and cafes you can go to for lunch, and it looks like it's going to be another scorching day. Okay gang—everybody out!'

Vincent White, parked by a tree-lined fence, watched the red and cream coach disgorge its passengers. He checked his photograph of Vania McAllen, although, by now, the woman's face was imprinted on his memory, and lifted his binoculars.

Then he froze, his breath catching in his throat, hardly daring to believe his eyes. The brunette was the last to leave, and . . . yes . . . it was Vania McAllen.

'I'll be . . .' Vincent breathed. For nearly six years he'd been trying to find this woman. He'd lost track of the many false leads he'd had, of the times he'd lain in wait, just like this, for a glimpse of his prey, only to find another dark-haired, green-eyed stranger at the end of the long chase.

Now, suddenly, there she was. Vincent grinned, fighting back the urge to holler and shout in triumph. He reached for his ever-ready camera, re-adjusted the telephoto lens, and began clicking away.

'You, young lady,' he muttered, clicking away, 'have been giving me nothing but trouble for years.'

Ringing Brett Carver with the good news was going to be one of the sweetest telephone calls of his life. Even though it meant that the longest-running (and easily the most lucrative) case of his career was now over.

Vania stood in front of a big cage watching two dark and impressive birds of prey—who were themselves watching a passing grouse with eagle-eyed fascination. Birdland was home to birds that were both in cages and flying free. Talking parrots and cockatoos especially were free to roam at will, and liked having their feathers stroked.

At first, the guests had stayed close to her, but soon, gaining more confidence and enchanted by the birds and the big, greedy rainbow trout, they'd gradually wandered off by themselves, allowing Vania some pleasant time alone.

Standing by an ice-cream stand, out of the way and unobserved, Vince White held his breath as he watched his quarry stick her pale fingers near the big bird of prey. Was she out of her cotton-pickin' mind? Then he whistled, slow and easy, as he watched the bird take it gently.

'My apologies, little lady,' he muttered under his breath. 'I was underestimating you. Again.'

For, after years of searching for her, Vince had learned a very healthy respect for Miss Vania McAllen.

When he'd first been called in, by Vania's father, he'd expected to have the runaway daughter back within the week. After all, in his experience, seventeen-year-old rich kids weren't that hard to find. They usually went somewhere familiar, and, having no sense of the real value of money, quickly spent all their stockpiled cash. Most kids like Vania McAllen never learned how to get along in the big wide world without the insulation of their parents' wealth. But this woman had been different. And how.

Vince had first begun to understand how different this particular case was going to be when he'd first discovered that she'd managed to get out of the country without passing through any airport or dock, and without using her own passport. That took planning. And courage. And since then, it had been one long hard slog. He'd searched Mexico for her for six months back in '98 without success.

Now, watching her wander around the cages, he had to take his hat off to her. It had been sheer luck on his part that he'd found her at all. It had been on a random sweep by one of his London people, that they'd got on the trail of one green-eyed American who'd worked, for a while, in Oxford. From there they'd tracked down a 'possible'—a tour guide at Windrush Shallows Hotel.

Vincent, aware there'd never be a better time, slipped out of the park and flipped open his mobile.

It was still night in Boston, and Brett Carver came out of a light and restless sleep at the first ring of the telephone. He reached up and switched on the overhead light, rubbing his eyes before lifting the receiver. 'Yeah? Brett Carver.'

'Vincent.'

'Hold on, I'll transfer you to the . . .'

'I've found her.'

Brett, who'd already swung one leg out of bed, froze. In the overhead light, his dark red hair shone with the dull lustre of uncut rubies. 'What did you say?' he said, his voice coming out as little more than a croak.

Even over the thousands of miles separating them, Vincent could hear the sheer disbelief in his voice, and grinned.

He knew how the fella felt. 'Not ten minutes ago,' Vincent said, clearly and precisely, 'I was looking at Vania McAllen.'

Brett's hand tightened so hard on the telephone receiver, he heard the plastic crack.

He slowly leaned back against the headrest, closed his pale grey eyes for a long, thankful second, then slowly opened them again. 'Where is she?'

'She's working as a tour guide at a hotel in the Cotswolds. Got a pen?'

Brett grunted. 'I don't need one. Believe me, I'm not about to forget anything you tell me.'

Not after six years of torment. Not after six years of aching for her. Not after six years of simply existing.

'She's at a place called Windrush Shallows Hotel. It's in a village called . . . oh hell . . . hold on . . .'

Vincent rifled through his small notebook, praying he hadn't been too tired or addled to jot down the name of the small village he'd arrived at only a few hours ago.

He hadn't. 'Rissington Basset.'

In his penthouse, Brett took a deep, ragged breath. 'Right.'

'I haven't had time to find out any of the details yet. The name she's using, how long she's been there . . .'

'Don't worry about it,' Brett said crisply. 'You can do that while I'm flying over.'

Vincent frowned at his mobile. 'You're flying over right away?'

'Damned right I am,' Brett all but snarled. 'I'll catch the first flight out. Do me a favour and book me into this place will you?'

'Right. Er . . . under your own name?'

Brett, who'd tucked the receiver between his ear and one hunched shoulder, and was reaching for his watch on the nightstand, hesitated. 'No,' he said finally. 'Better not. She might see it and bolt again before I get there. Make something up.'

Vince nodded. 'OK. How does Brady Carson sound?' Brett grunted, fastening on his watch, his mind racing. 'OK then,' Vince interpreted the grunt as a 'yes'. 'See you later.'

Brett hung up. For a few seconds he just sat there, staring unseeingly at the floor. The overhead light threw golden light and dark shadows across his broad back and muscular shoulders and arms. His big body was shaking.

Vania. He was going to see Vania again.

He was suddenly aware of how heavily his heart was thundering in his chest—as if he'd just run a marathon.

He swallowed, and his mouth was dry. He got up and walked a little unsteadily into the bathroom. He'd waited for this day for so long . . . Now it was here he felt shattered. But pulling himself ruthlessly together, he stepped beneath the shower, allowing the fierce, powerful spray to hammer on his head and darkly matted chest. Then he dressed, phoned the airline, packed a bag and was gone.

The Brett Carver name and money got him a first-class seat on the next plane out, and he drove the Jaguar at break-neck speed in order

80

to make it to the airport on time. Crossing the Atlantic nowadays was nothing. As he sat back in his seat, watching the lights of the city fall away behind him, he gazed down into the inky blackness of the ocean and forced himself to relax. Even though it was already late morning in England, he'd arrive at the hotel in time for dinner.

And then . . .

Vania tossed a huge handful of fish pellets into the big pond, and watched the rolling mass of rainbow-sided fish thrash in the water. A black swan, who also quite liked the fish pellets, bad-temperedly gave a passing trout a peck, but the fish was still quicker, and the pellets rapidly disappeared. She leaned on the railing, smiling.

How her dad would have loved this place. Her heart gave a painful wince, as it always did, whenever she thought of him.

She'd been working at Windrush for only six months when she saw the notice of her father's death in one of the American papers that the hotel always imported. The papers were always a day old, of course, by the time they got to the U.K., but the guests appreciated the familiarity of the *New York Times*, the *Washington Post* etc. on their breakfast table.

But it meant that Chuck McAllen had already been dead for two days before she knew.

She could still remember that morning—it

81

had started off like so many others. It had been September—late in the season, but still the hotel was three-quarters full. She'd been enjoying one of Maisie's full English breakfasts, when she'd turned the page and seen a picture of her father staring back at her. At first it had given her a great rush of pleasure. She'd missed her dad. Seeing his picture had brought her old life rushing back. She'd smiled.

Then her world had plummeted as she realised she was looking at the obituary section. With the blessed numbness that comes with shock, she'd read about how the 'Car King of the East Coast' had had a sudden and massive coronary at his office and had died before paramedics could reach him. She skipped over the statement that the city rested secure in the knowledge that McAllen's would carry on under the astute leadership of Brett Carver.

All that Vania could think about was that her father was dead. She'd never see him again.

Guilt had almost eaten her alive.

It was only the realisation that, even if she had stayed at home, even if she hadn't run away, her father would still have died too quickly and too suddenly for her to have got to him before he went.

And time had a way of healing. She had grieved for her father, deeply and secretly, and

82

at the end of the process she remembered only that he'd loved her, and she'd loved him. And that they'd both always known that.

She'd written him every month since she'd been gone, so that he'd know she was alright, always careful to make sure that he knew she loved him, and that she hadn't left because of him. At first, she'd enclosed her letters in a second envelope and mailed them to the US postal service for forwarding. But after she arrived at the Shallows, she got into the habit of handing them to returning guests, asking them to mail them when they got home, so that the envelopes always bore a US post mark. That way, no PI hired by Brett could track her down via her correspondence. If her father'd still been alive, she'd now be giving a letter to Mrs Barrett to post for her when she got back to New York. Vania sighed, turning away from the handsome fish and glancing at her watch. Her father would not want her to brood.

As she half expected, her little group were all waiting for her at the exit. 'So,' she called gaily. 'Who's for fish and chips?'

There was a roar of approval. One old lady demurred though. Said she couldn't possibly think of eating fish, not after making friends with the trout. She'd feel too guilty.

Everyone laughed. including Vania. But she wouldn't have laughed quite so long, or so loud, if she'd known that Brett Carver was

83

already winging his way across the Atlantic towards her.

*   *   *

Brett landed at Heathrow airport and made the disorientating time change to his watch.

As the chauffeur turned off the motorway and headed into ever greener, ever quieter depths of the countryside, Brett tried to make himself relax. But it was not easy.

Every mile brought him closer to her. To the woman he'd loved, from the moment he'd first set eyes on her. The woman he had always known he would marry. The woman who'd deserted him, leaving him to suffer in a living hell.

His pulse throbbed. His head pounded. His body ached.

It was one of his deepest regrets, during those long barren years without her, that he'd never made love to her.

But she'd still been so young—not yet eighteen. Now though . . . Now there'd be nothing to hold him back.

And if she thought she was going to get away from him again—well, this time, he'd be right behind her.

CHAPTER FIVE

Giles Powell walked into the Blue Finn Restaurant and nodded at the head waiter, who smiled instantly. His suit was silver-grey Italian silk, the shirt from an Oxford tailor famous in the district.

'Yes sir? May I help you?' the waiter enthused, obviously anticipating a large tip.

'I hope so. I'm meeting Geoffrey Wainwright?'

The older man ran a manicured fingernail down an impressive table reservations book, stopping theatrically halfway down. 'Yes sir. This way, if you please.'

Giles had managed to keep a straight face throughout all these proceedings, and nodded blandly. Although he moved in this sort of world regularly, he didn't much care for it.

Oh, he could talk about wine with the best of them, spoke French, German and Japanese fluently, and was regularly invited to film premiers, first-night parties and gallery openings. But he preferred life in his study, creating computer software, which exercised his brain and allowed him to be outrageously creative. Or driving around his estate with his land agent.

Given a choice right now, on this lovely July evening, he'd rather be out walking in the woods with his dogs, than meeting a bank manager at this fancy, overpriced eatery. But Giles Powell was a man of many parts. And he could play any one of them with practised charm.

Geoffrey Wainwright, a tall, sandy-haired, middle-aged man, stood up as the waiter led Giles to his table.

The two men shook hands as the head waiter snapped his fingers to summon up a wine waiter.

Giles saw Geoffrey wince. As the 'host' he knew Geoffrey was expecting to pay the bill at the end of the evening. Giles turned his gaze on the two waiters. Not a flicker of expression crossed his face, but within moments both waiters had melted away.

Geoffrey watched the performance with a mounting nervousness. He'd heard other people talk about Giles Powell's charisma before but, until this moment, he'd never had a first-row seat at one of his performances.

Now he felt himself begin to sweat a little. What the hell did the man want with him?

It wasn't until the meal was almost over, and Giles had done his best to make the bank manager feel more at ease, that he even attempted to broach the subject that had brought the two of them together. The coffee had arrived, and Giles said casually, 'I understand your bank was responsible for the loan to my aunt . . . for her little hotel?'

Since they'd been talking like old friends for the last half-hour or so, Geoffrey at first didn't even realize that they'd finally got down to the matter in hand. 'That's right. A splendid woman, your Aunt Frances. I was so sorry to hear of her passing.'

Giles gave a grim smile. 'Yes. We're all sorry to lose her. We never were quite sure why she wanted to start up a hotel in the first place,' he mused, for all the world a vaguely puzzled man, chatting about nothing in particular.

Geoffrey shrugged. As Frankie Powell's long-term bank manager, he knew how precarious her bank balance had been. Not that the bank would ever dream of making things difficult for a a aristocrat, and aunt of the richest man in the county! Still . . . business was business.

'Well, she didn't really have much capital, you know,' he murmured, with just a faint hint of caution.

Giles frowned. 'Oh?' He felt a distinct shiver of unease creep up his spine. 'I thought Aunt Frankie's cash flow was fairly . . . liquid.'

Geoffrey, who was into his third port by now, glanced up in surprise. 'Really?' he said. And that one word, spoken with such evident surprise, told Giles everything.

Grimly, he wondered why he hadn't guessed it before.

Apart from the house, his grandfather hadn't left Frankie a great deal. But, like

87

everyone else, it had never even crossed Giles's mind that his aunt might actually be feeling even the slightest financial pinch.

Obviously though, her bank manager knew better.

For the first time ever, it occurred to Giles that Frankie might have gone along with the hotel thing, not simply because she was fond (or, as his grandmother would insist, 'under the thumb') of Harriet Jensen, but because she might actually have needed the money. Dammit, Aunt Frankie, he thought grimly, and with a twinge of guilty pain. Why didn't you come to me? I'd have given you anything you needed.

He glanced down into his own untouched port and shrugged. 'Ah well. My aunt always was an independent soul.'

Geoffrey smiled and relaxed. 'Yes, she was quite something. As was that young friend of hers.'

Giles's hand tightened compulsively on the glass of port, threatening to crack the fine crystal. He remembered only too well the last time he'd seen that 'young friend' of Frankie's. And her mocking, parting words to him. So, she thought him a fool did she? Well. She would learn differently. And soon. He forced himself to push the glass a little around the table and relax.

'Oh yes. Miss Jensen. I understand it was she, more than my aunt, who actually put the hotel package together?' he probed cleverly.

Geoffrey nodded, thinking back to his visit to Powell House, and the beautiful young blonde girl and her clever plans. 'Yes indeed. A charming young woman.'

Giles bit hack a snarl. Good grief, she'd even seduced the bank manager into giving them their loan.

Was there nothing she wouldn't do to get her own way?

'She works like a demon at that hotel, you know,' Geoffrey carried on, unaware of the scorn with which he was currently being regarded. 'Your aunt told me she did all the books and administration. As well as running the day-to-day business.'

Giles snorted in frank disbelief, and when the bank manager blinked and looked at him in evident surprise, quickly smiled.

'Imagine that,' he said smoothly. 'But, since my aunt's death, I must admit I've been a bit . . . concerned.'

Geoffrey, port or no port, suddenly twigged that they were now getting to the crux of the matter. He straightened up a little in his chair. 'Oh?' he said warily.

Giles nodded. 'As you know, my father, Lord Powell,' he began cunningly, 'was a man of honour, as well as practicality. Now he's gone, I'm head of the house, and have done my best to pick up where he left off.'

'Oh, I'm sure you have,' Geoffrey said

hastily, beginning to sweat again.

'Which is why I'm concerned with any . . . bad debts . . . my aunt might have left behind her. So if Windrush Shallows is in trouble, then of course I want to make sure the bank doesn't suffer. I'd like to buy them out, frankly.'

To Giles's surprise and dismay, instead of looking relieved, the bank manager looked only bewildered.

'Bad debts? Oh no, Mr Powell, I assure you . . .' he began, then stopped. Hell, should he have called him 'Lord' Powell? 'Er . . . where was I?'

Giles's lips twisted. 'You were assuring me of something.'

'Oh yes. Windrush Shallows. I assure you, we've never had cause to regret the loan. Far from it. So far, there have been no problems at all with the repayment schedule.'

Giles frowned. 'None? You mean she's making a success of it?' His voice rose a little in surprise.

'Oh yes. Quite. And this last year, with your aunt being . . . well . . . not in the best of health, we've dealt exclusively with Miss Jensen on all matters, and let me put your mind at rest, there have been no problems whatever with her cheques. In fact, by the end of next year, right on schedule, the loan will have been repaid in its entirety.'

Giles swore under his breath. 'I see,' he said

90

urbanely.

He'd been so sure that Windrush Shallows must be in financial difficulty. So sure that Harriet Jensen had seen it only as a meal ticket. Convinced, in fact, that by now the old Powell family home would already be on the market, so she would get the maximum profit and cut and run with it. 'Er . . . she's said nothing to you about perhaps selling Windrush Shallows?' he hazarded quietly.

Giles Powell never gave up. But never.

'No, not that I can recall,' the bank manager said, clearly surprised. 'Why should she? From all accounts, the Hotel is going from strength to strength. I even heard on the grapevine that Sheik Kamil Mohamed is booked in for the entire month of October. Now that, if it's true, is some kind of coup. And, you know, I think it is true. One gets to hear things, in my profession.'

Giles said nothing. He was too busy re-arranging his thinking: 'I see. You know, Geoffrey, you could do me a favour.'

The bank manager, naturally, was very keen to do Mr Giles Powell (or should that be Lord Powell?) of Powell Software a favour. And so, slowly, carefully, stressing the need for secrecy, Giles told Wainwright what he could do for him.

*   *   *

In one of the most expensive suburbs of Boston, a man walked up to a large white house and rang the bell. He was dressed anonymously, in dark clothes. His face, too, had a curiously anonymous look. It was hard to say how old he was. His hair was brown, his eyes the same. His face was utterly 'average'. A major-domo answered the door and silently showed him into a billiard room. The man, a billiard shark of some years standing, lost no time in racking up the balls and potting a few shots. He didn't have much time to play, however, as the owner of the house joined him in only a few minutes. As the door opened, the visitor heard the unmistakable sounds of music and laughter, the tinkling of glasses and the even prettier tinkling of a hired pianist.

Somewhere in the house, a party was going on. Wasn't there always? He glanced up and watched as a handsome blond man approached the table. The visitor quickly stood upright, putting the cue on the green baize table and meeting the blond man's eye. 'Mr Larner,' he said respectfully.

'Carpenter,' James Larner said curtly. 'You have something?'

Vince White would have known who Worrel Carpenter was, had they ever met. They were, roughly speaking, in the same business. But whereas White was a respected member of the Private Investigator's tight-knit community, Carpenter had a less than savoury reputation.

It had been one of the reasons that James Larner, reluctant silent partner first to Chuck McAllen, and now to Brett Carver, had hired him.

'Yes sir. Mr Carver flew out of the country in the middle of last night.'

'Unscheduled?' James Larner snapped sharply.

'Yes sir. One of his secretaries has just told me that he's phoned through with orders for his second-in-command to take over the day-to-day running for the next few weeks.'

James Larner blinked. After years of having Brett Carver's every move carefully monitored, he knew the way the man worked. And he didn't often delegate.

He walked around the table, a slender, blandly good-looking man. There was nothing to suggest why a man like Carpenter should be afraid of him, but the PI was. 'I see,' he said thoughtfully. 'That's not like our Brett,' he murmured. 'Not like him at all. You are going to tell me where he went, and why, aren't you Carpenter?' he asked softly.

The PI nodded quickly. 'Yessir. He went to Heathrow.'

'You have his place bugged, of course?'

'Yessir. Last night Vincent White called him. He told him that he'd found Miss McAllen.' He chose his words very carefully and watched, in half-repulsed, half-intrigued fascination, as the handsome Bostonian

93

blanched.

Socially, James Larner had the reputation of the perennial, blond, handsome, well-educated, all-round American playboy. He broke a few female hearts regularly, but always the right sort of female hearts, and nobody held it against him. He lavished his money wisely. Nobody in his carefully cultivated circle found it all distasteful that it was Brett Carver who earned him all that money. Like everyone else, they assumed James liked it that way. Only James himself, and people like Carpenter, knew different.

'I see,' James Larner said at last.

So Brett Carver had finally succeeded in tracking down the runaway Vania. And she was . . . he did a quick calculation, still only 24. He had a year in which to marry her, before she became 25 and her shares went on to the open market.

James Larner knew all about Chuck McAllen's will.

James had invested wisely over the years. It was a talent that nobody would suspect him of having—including Brett Carver. With money thus kept available, he'd always planned to swoop down on those shares like a hawk, grabbing the lion's share before Carver knew what hit him. Then, then, they would see who ran McAllen's.

James slowly began to pace the room.

When his own father had died, leaving his

shares in McAllen's to his only son, James had been free to act at last. Whereas his father had always been grateful to Chuck McAllen for their millionaire lifestyle, James had always been resentful. He'd schemed for years to take McAllen's away from Brett Carver. And with Vania McAllen's shares on the open market, the opportunity was there, with him in a perfect position to orchestrate a board room coup. Initial contract, or no initial contract.

Possession was still nine tenths of the law.

Now though . . . If Brett Carver succeeded in getting Vania McAllen to marry him, and he got his damned hands on those shares . . . James would never be rid of him. He'd always be the 'sleeping' partner, the leech, the city joke. And that simply could not be permitted to happen.

'Carpenter,' he said softly, turning to look at the PI, 'tell me all about Vania McAllen. Where she is, what's she been doing, who she's been seeing . . .'

*   *   *

Harriet was having a rare night off. She'd left the hotel just after lunch, and was dining with friends in a nearby village.

She'd been so tense lately, that Vania was glad when she'd told her she was taking even this little break from her gruelling workload. She'd hastily reassured her friend that the

95

hotel wouldn't fall down around their ears overnight, and that she could play the gracious hostess for just this once.

Harriet had laughed, and told her she'd probably make a better job of it than herself, and left, for the first time feeling a sense of freedom as she left the hotel behind her.

Now, at eight-thirty, dinner was about to be served downstairs. In her room, Vania checked her appearance one more time in the mirror. Although she always dined with the guests, tonight Harriet wouldn't be there, and she truly would be the hostess for the evening. She was wearing an emerald green dress that matched the colour of her eyes exactly. It was made of Thai silk, and clung to her figure like the hands of a lover, even though it had a modest boat-shaped neckline, and fell to just below her knees. She was wearing sheer silk stockings and a pair of high-heeled matching green sandals to complete the outfit. At her throat was a gold necklace, and matching earrings dangled from her lobes. Her hair was left down, falling in lush, dark, waves to her shoulders. Newly washed and brushed, it shone with a dark luster that glowed in the evening sunlight. Reassured by her reflection, she walked down the staircase into the hall.

Although one of the few alterations to the building had been to install a lift, it was only ever used by those who really needed it, most guests preferring to use the elegant, intricately carved, original wooden staircase. As she walked down it, she was aware of the low hum coming from the dining room, which meant most people were already down.

The foyer-cum-reception area was empty. Huge ferns swayed in the evening breeze, for during the hot weather all the doors and windows were wedged open, allowing a honeysuckle-laden breeze to waft through from the gardens.

As she stepped off the last stair, and turned sharply to her right to head for the dining room, a guest she hadn't noticed suddenly stepped from behind a huge ornamental fern.

She opened her mouth to speak, guessing that he was a new guest who had lost his way, and was already turning towards him. At first, in that initial moment of awareness, her mind took in only that he was tall and solid—very solid.

Although he was wearing the traditional evening dress of black and white, she sensed the danger emanating from him. It was the first sensation of warning she had. As her eyes travelled over broad shoulders and up, up, up, to the face, a weird shivering had started to invade her limbs.

Before she met the familiar grey eyes, her brain was already screaming warnings at her. Hair that deep, dark, red, was a shade she'd only ever seen on one man before. The impression she gained of him was of granite

97

and stone, as if the man had sprung straight from the earth. And she'd only ever thought of one man in those terms before.

And then she was looking at him. Those familiar, startling, light grey eyes were looking into her own. Something leapt between them—like a spirit of the air, unseen, but dancing. Her heart fluttered. The hand, that was still holding onto the banister, went numb. She took a breath, but it didn't seem to reach her lungs.

Brett. No! Impossible. A guest who looked like him. Brett. No. She was dreaming. Back in her bed—it was still morning. Brett. He was moving towards her. And something was wrong with the angle of the room. It was tilting. She saw the two matching ferns kaleidoscope around her. The noise from the dining room roared in her ears, like a wave crashing against rocks, then receded. The black and white tiles of the floor were rushing up to meet her, but then something hard and solid caught her. Not cold, hard tiles, but warm, strong, sinew. Flesh and blood. Her head whirled. She saw his dark head above her. The flashing grey eyes. Then nothing.

*　　*　　*

When she opened her eyes it was the sight of her own ceiling that met her gaze. The pretty green and pink glass lampshade. The spider's web in one corner that the maid who did her room always missed—whether because she was scared of spiders, or had a soft heart. Vania didn't know. And then the ceiling was gone, and his face was taking its place.

Brett. This time her brain insisted, and this time, she had to acknowledge it. It was Brett. 'What . . .' she said, her mouth so dry it came out as little more than a croak.

'It's all right, take it easy. Here, sip some of this.'

That voice, Vania thought, with a rush of happiness so strong it almost made her cry. That voice, straight from the Kansas corn fields. Rolling. Laconic. Relaxed.

And she'd thought she'd never hear it again. She felt one massive hand slip under her neck, cup the back of her skull, and lift her head off the pillows.

Brett held a small glass against her lips. She smelt the brandy fumes, and took a tentative sip. Smooth warm fire slid down her throat and exploded in her stomach, driving away the numbing cold that, until that moment, she hadn't even noticed.

She sighed, took another sip, and then he lowered her head back to the pillow. 'What happened?' she asked vaguely. She felt so . . . disorientated. The fact that he was here, at Windrush Shallows, was almost impossible to believe.

There had been her life before. And there

was her life now. They were never supposed to meet.

'You fainted,' Brett said matter-of-factly. 'Don't worry, nobody else saw. I carried you up here.' Vincent had told him which room was hers.

She looked up at him mutely. The full force of him, so close, felt mothering. And yet . . . she seemed to be drinking him in like a sponge. It had been so long since she'd looked into his eyes . . . 'Oh Brett,' she wailed, 'what are you doing here?'

Brett Carver smiled. 'What do you think?'

For a long second they simply stared at each other. Then he reached out a tender hand and brushed away a lock of her hair. He was leaning over her, so close that she could feel the cool-warm touch of his breath on her face.

'Vania McAllen,' he said simply. 'Surely you knew I'd tear the world apart until I found you again?'

CHAPTER SIX

Geoffrey Wainwright smiled as he was shown to a small table for two near the big open windows. He sometimes took his wife to have dinner at Windrush Shallows, but had never yet called in for a 'business breakfast'.

Thinking of his waistline, he ordered

grapefruit and kippers but made lavish use of the cook's home-made plum, apple, and cherry preserves on his toast.

When Harriet walked in a few moments later, she spotted him easily, and with a smile of welcome, tinged with just a hint of surprise and anxiety, she walked over to join him. She was wearing a floating powder-blue dress but still looked every inch the hotel owner. She stopped on the way to his table to chat to several guests and when she finally reached him, there was not a trace of worry on her face, even though her mind was feverishly wondering why her bank manager had come a-calling!

'Geoffrey, how nice,' she said smoothly, sinking down opposite him. He poured her some tea and they chatted pleasantly. It wasn't until he'd finished his toast, that he finally made his opening gambit.

'I though I'd just call in to see how you're coping now that . . . well, Miss Powell is . . . er . . . gone.'

'Oh, well. You know how it is,' Harriet hedged. She didn't think Geoffrey was there just to offer his condolences.

'Yes. Well. I was thinking,' Geoffrey began, well aware that if he could pull this off, he'd be in Giles Powell's good books for years to come. Which was a very nice place indeed for a bank manager to be. He took a deep breath. 'Now that you've got the responsibility for the

101

hotel resting solely on your shoulders, I wondered if . . . well . . .' Those dark, incredibly violet eyes looked at his steadily, and he coughed nervously. 'Well, if you'd ever given any consideration to selling this place,' he said in a rush, trying not to look too eager.

'Selling?' Harriet echoed blankly.

Geoffrey leaned towards her and lowered his voice tactfully.

'You know, Harriet, you could make a huge profit on the hotel just now,' he began persuasively. 'It's all but out of the woods financially and is proving to be a viable proposition. The leisure industry is on a high at the moment. It a seller's market . . .' The bank manager spread his hands. 'You could make a very tidy sum.'

Harriet slowly leaned back in her chair. Whatever she'd expected Geoffrey to come out with, it hadn't been that. But, now that she thought about it . . . She and Frankie had just spent six years walking a financial knife-edge. It might be nice to have some real security. And with Frankie gone . . . But no. She loved Windrush Shallows. It was hers. Her creation—hers and Frankie's. To sell it was . . .

'In fact,' Geoffrey went on, 'I've already been approached by a potential buyer. He's willing to offer one point five million.'

Harriet blinked. 'What did you say?' she asked faintly. Geoffrey, grinning, repeated the sum.

Harriet shook her head. She knew the hotel was a valuable commodity of course, but not that valuable. A warning bell suddenly sounded in her head. No, that's right, she thought grimly. The hotel wasn't worth that much—except to someone who felt it was rightfully theirs. So what was going on? 'Who is this buyer, Mr Wainwright?' she asked suspiciously.

Geoffrey felt the sweat break out on the back of his neck. 'Oh, I can't say at this stage. But the offer, let me assure you, is a serious one.'

Harriet narrowed her eyes. If somebody wanted her hotel, why didn't they want her to know his or her name? And why was this mysterious buyer willing to pay so much? Unless . . . someone wanted Windrush Shallows desperately.

And who would want it, except perhaps, Lady Grace Powell. Or Giles Powell? Harriet's lips twisted into a grim smile. She had to hand it to him. He never gave up. And approaching a middle-man like Geoffrey had been a stroke of genius. If she really had been the gold-digger he thought her, she'd have snapped at the chance like a greedy trout after a mayfly.

'I'm sorry, Geoffrey, I don't think so. The Shallows isn't for sale,' she said firmly, and watched the bank manager's face fall comically.

'Oh, but, Harriet you know . . . I'm not sure

that's wise,' he said miserably, desperate to change her mind. 'After all, the hotel business is so risky,' he said hastily. 'The hotel's popular now, but one moment you can be the 'in' place to be, and the next . . .' He waved a hand graphically in the air.

Harriet went pale. Was he threatening her? Correction, was Giles Powell threatening her?

For she had no doubt that Geoffrey was only his puppet.

Harriet felt a wave of pure rage wash over her, but she fought to keep her head. She smiled coldly. It was a good bluff, but she didn't see how even the high-and-mighty Giles Powell could make a hotel unpopular overnight. 'I'm sorry, but my hotel just isn't for sale,' she said tightly, and got to her feet. 'I must go and see Chef, but please enjoy your breakfast.'

Geoffrey watched her go miserably. As she walked out, so did his promotion!

*   *   *

Vania, for the first time ever, had to steel herself to walk nonchalantly into the noisily humming dining room. She was unusually late, and hoped Harriet hadn't noticed. But the simple fact was, she wasn't feeling up to this, and that made her angry. Last night was still so raw and fresh in her mind.

After waking up to find Brett Carver in her

room, things had become a mite . . . strained. Following his shattering statement that he'd never stopped looking for her, she'd felt at too much of a disadvantage lying in bed. She'd jumped up and begun to pace the room like a caged lioness. At first she'd tried reasoning with him. Surely he could see that there was no point to his being here? She'd run away from home in order to get a life of her own, and she wasn't about to give it up now, and so she'd informed him, in no uncertain terms. But in response he'd simply told her that if she wanted to, she could go on being a tour guide—back home in Boston. She'd pointed out that she didn't want to marry him—didn't want him in her life. Had forgotten about him. Didn't care if she never saw him again.

And he'd asked her, if that was so, why the sight of him had made her faint? For which, she'd realised, chagrined, there was no answer at all. Eventually she'd demanded he leave her room. And he'd left.

But as she walked into the dining room the next morning she knew damned well that he'd still be there. And he was. She spotted him right away—at the back at a table for two, calmly sipping black coffee. He was dressed in black jeans and a white shirt, open at the cuffs and collar.

He looked . . . She quickly averted her eyes and headed for a table containing five old ladies, all members of a bridge club from

105

Wyoming. They welcomed her with pleasure, but even as she sat in the table's only vacant chair, she was aware of Brett's sardonic gaze watching her every move.

She was dressed in a bright red skirt and jacket, with a green silk blouse underneath the jacket. The blouse matched her eyes, and the whole outfit set off her dark colouring to perfection. She literally brightened up the room.

Brett smiled. There never had been anything of the shrinking violet about Vania. He could still recall, to the very last detail, the moment she'd walked down those stairs last night. It had taken him back to the very first time they'd met—when she'd been coming down the stairs of her father's mansion. He'd taken one look at her then and fallen. He'd taken a second look at her last night, and found he was still right where she'd originally left him—at her feet.

Except that now, she was a woman. Mature, independent and sophisticated—his equal in every way. Gone was the gawky teenager. Whereas before he'd felt a little worried about marrying her, now there was nothing to stop him. And he was going to marry her. *She* might not have accepted the inevitable. But she was going to be his.

He watched her charm the dentures out of the little old ladies and found himself smiling. It just felt so damned good to be able to watch her again. To catch the sound of her voice, above and beyond the sound of the other voices. Good to know that she was there—just a few steps away. His whole body was tingling with satisfaction. There had never been any doubt about it—her absence from his life had been like a raw gaping wound. Now he was being slowly healed.

For the first time, Brett took the time to look around him. Honeysuckle tumbled past the open windows, bouquets of fresh flowers adorned the simple but stiffly expensive white linen tablecloths and he began to understand why the hotel was so popular. It had . . . ambience.

His neighbour at the next table, noticing Brett's interest, grinned. 'Great place, huh?' he said amiably. 'You ought to try the traditional English breakfast,' he advised. 'Home-made sausages like you wouldn't believe.'

'We'll be late,' his wife suddenly piped up. 'Vania's charabanc will be here soon.'

At the mention of her name, Brett came alive. 'Sorry'? What's that?'

His fellow guest's eyes twinkled. 'That little lady you were looking at so hard just now.' He grinned openly, as did Brett. 'She's the tour guide around here. She takes us out on this really cute old bus.'

'If you want to come along, you have to sign up on the list at Reception,' his wife chipped in, and she, too, was smiling the smile of a born match-maker.

Brett's eyes gleamed. 'Is that so? In that case . . . you gotta pen?'

*   *   *

Harriet walked into the office, carefully shutting the door behind her. What she had to say, she didn't want anyone overhearing. She forced herself to walk calmly to her desk, to sit in the swivel chair, and take several deep breaths before she reached for the telephone. She had to look up the number in Frankie's personal telephone book, and as she dialled she was aware of a fine tremor in her hand.

The butler, of course, answered promptly. 'Powell Manor.'

'I want to speak to Mr. Giles Powell please.'

'May I say who's calling?'

'Harriet Jensen.' There was a slight pause, and she could almost sense the butler's surprise, then his voice came once again, smooth and bland as milk. 'Just one moment madam, I'll put you through to his office.' Harriet realised that she was not the only one up and working at eight-thirty in the morning.

'Yes?'

How, Harriet wondered, fuming, did a man manage to put so much arrogance and strength of personality into just one word? She gritted her teeth, then forced the words through them.

'Mr. Powell,' she said smoothly. 'I don't appreciate having bank managers sent to my home to threaten me. Kindly don't do it again.'

And she hung up deftly.

She didn't, however, stir from her chair but stared at the telephone intently. Sure enough, a moment later, it began to ring. She lifted it up. 'Windrush Shallows Hotel,' she chorused sweetly, 'Harriet Jensen here. How may I help you?'

'What the devil are you talking about?' Giles snapped grimly. And, sitting behind his own desk at Powell Manor, he wondered furiously what that idiot Wainwright had said to her.

'Are you saying you're not this mysterious potential buyer, who's willing to spend so much money getting me off Powell property?' she asked coldly.

Giles laughed. 'Of course I am. Who else would want to take that quaint little place off your hands?'

Harriet knew he was baiting her. She knew he was deliberately trying to get under her skin. Even so, she felt furious. 'Well you're not getting it!' she all but shouted into the phone, then put her hand over her mouth. Damn it, why was she doing this? Playing the game his way? Over the line, she heard him laugh. Smugly. 'Oh, but I am, Harriet,' he said softly. 'I really am.'

Harriet closed her eyes for a moment, but

109

there he was, instantly jumping to life behind her closed eyelids—that fall of black hair, those snapping eyes, that exquisitely handsome, patrician, arrogant face . . . Her eyes snapped open again.

'Well, I don't think I have much to worry about,' she said sweetly. 'Not if poor old Geoffrey is the best you can do.'

In his office, Giles sat up suddenly in his chair. Why the scheming . . .' Oh no, sweetheart.' he snarled. 'That was just the opening salvo. Being a gentleman, I felt I had to offer you the easy way out first.'

'A gentleman?' she squeaked, scandalised. But, in spite of herself she felt a tremor of fear along her spine. He sounded so . . . formidable. So utterly domineering. But she was no weak-kneed maiden in distress.

'Oh, go to hell!' she snapped. Unladylike perhaps, but she was at the end of her tether. She hung up on him yet again, but this time the phone did not ring a second time.

She got up and walked restlessly into the hall, surprised to see that Vania was still there. Wasn't she going to Didcot today? Her tour had been due to start fifteen minutes ago.

She walked towards her friend, her eyes going to the guest beside her. He was new, Harriet saw at once. A good looking man with dark red hair and the sort of rugged, chiselled features that reminded her of cigarette advertisements. As she got closer, she could

110

see that Vania was almost red-faced with anger, and her voice was so low she was almost hissing. Harriet was both surprised and alarmed. If the guest had somehow angered her, it was not like Vania to handle it so badly.

'Well, you can't come and that's the end of it,' she heard her friend snap, and blinked in utter surprise.

She hurried forward. 'Is there a problem, Vania?' she asked, in her best cool, 'I'm in charge' voice. Vania snapped to attention and whirled around.

'No,' Vania said hastily. 'No trouble.' The last thing she wanted was to burden Harriet with her personal problems.

Sensing her unease, and taking unscrupulous advantage, Brett turned to the blonde-haired vision in blue. 'I was just telling Miss McAllen here that I hoped I wasn't too late to sign up for today's outing.'

Harriet frowned. 'If there's room on the coach, I'm sure you're not too late, Mr . . . er . . . ?'

'Carson,' Brett lied, and heard Vania hiss in temper beside him.

'After all, you're our guest,' Harriet said, giving Vania a surprised look.

It was not like Vania to let a guest get under her skin. Unless . . . Her eyes sharpened on Mr Carson. Was he making a pest of himself? Vania could usually put off the gropers and those hitting on her with a well-aimed withering word or two. Vania, knowing what she was thinking, sighed. The last thing she wanted was to look unprofessional in front of her boss—even though that boss was Harriet. And Brett, damn him, knew it.

'No, it's OK, honest,' Vania said sweetly, and glanced through the open doors. 'Look, there's the bus. We'd better get going,' she chided, all brightness and light. She smiled at Harriet, shot a fulminating look (behind Harriet's back) at Brett, and waved a hand at the door.

'After you, Mr Carson,' she gritted.

'No, after you, Miss McAllen,' he said, and gave a mocking half-bow in return. Vania stamped off. Brett followed, whistling softly between his teeth. Harriet watched them go, a puzzled look on her lovely face, as she wondered why the new guest was calling Vania Lane 'Miss McAllen'.

CHAPTER SEVEN

The hotel was gloriously quiet. It was approaching eleven o'clock in the morning, and only the staff remained. Harriet was just heading for the open front doors, intending to do a brief tour of the garden to see all was well, when she heard the dulcet tones of Evelyn Grey, the receptionist. 'Yes sir, we have a double room available, but none of our rooms has a private bath.'

Harriet knew this was a familiar phrase for Evelyn, and she smiled, heading towards the curved walnut and rose-wood reception desk. 'Everything all right, Evelyn?' she asked pleasantly, turning her head to glance at the new arrival.

She very rarely cast her eyes over the guest lists these days, as Evelyn was as capable in her own department as Maisie and the temperamental French chef were in theirs. But it didn't hurt to give fresh arrivals the 'personal touch' if she just happened to be passing. The new guest was tall and so blond and good-looking that he wouldn't be out of place on a film set, Harriet thought. By his feet was a flotilla of expensive crocodile-skin luggage.

She saw the man's eyes widen on hers, but she was used to that double take most people gave her. James Larner gave himself a mental shake, and turned towards her, holding out his hand. 'How do you do, Miss—er—I'm James Larner?'

'Jensen,' Harriet smiled, taking the hand and nodding at Evelyn. 'Harriet Jensen. I hope you don't find our lack of private facilities too daunting, Mr Larner. I assure you there is a bathroom no more than three doors from any of the bedrooms, and queues for the bath hardly ever happen!'

113

She grinned disarmingly, and James could feel himself becoming aroused, as his heart did a crazy somersault. He blinked, forcing himself to concentrate on what she was saying, and managed a smile. 'Oh, no, I'm sure it'll be fine. You . . . er . . . work here?' he asked, wondering what had happened to all his famous charm.

Harriet smiled. 'I'm the owner,' she said non-committally.

James flushed. Hell—what a gaffe.

Harriet smiled again, understanding his embarrassment, nodded at both Evelyn and the new arrival, and drifted away towards the open doors, stepping out into yet another glorious summer day.

James watched her go, amazed at the way the summer sunshine courted her hair and literally dazzled his eyes. He registered and went to his room to unpack, still in a daze.

But then it was time to get down to business. He reached into the inside of his jacket pocket and brought out a small personal diary. In it he found the number of a local man recommended to him by his PI and dialled the number. But even as he arranged to meet the owner of the wary voice who answered, his mind was still full of Harriet Jensen. She was gorgeous. And a very pleasant way to pass a few summer weeks.

*　　*　　*

Everyone was beginning to wander back to the bus. Didcot Railway Museum was always a popular stop, especially with the men. Vania winked at two women, who were listening to their husbands arguing about whether the engine No. 4073, the Caerphilly Castle, was better designed than the King class No. 6023. 'Whatever,' one of the men finally huffed, 'I still think that broad gauge Firefly locomotive of 1839 was the best thing in there anyway!'

Her eyes slewed past them, and alighted on Brett Carver. Her smile faltered. 'Very interesting, that,' Brett drawled. 'I now know more about the golden age of steam than I ever dreamed possible.'

'Oh, don't be such a killjoy,' Vania snapped. 'You know you loved it really. All men do.'

Brett had in fact enjoyed the steam trains. But he was enjoying watching Vania more as she climbed aboard the bus.

'The real fun starts this afternoon,' she called out gaily, 'when we actually get to ride on a real steam train that's been fitted out to the height of luxury. It's like experiencing a little slice of the Orient Express, but without the murder.'

As she'd thought, the prospect of a romantic steam-train ride perked them up no end. What was it, Vania wondered dreamily, about sitting back, and listening to the chuff-chuff of steam that was so romantic? Not to mention so deliciously nostalgic?

Dead on time, the charabanc set off for the private line where a steam-train enthusiast ran his lovingly restored steam train over a 31-mile circuit through his own land. As they headed towards the Welsh border, she tried to ignore Brett Carver, who, damn him, had hogged the seat right behind her, but it was impossible. She could hear him talking to the passenger on the other side of the aisle to him, every cadence and timbre of his voice making her stomach vibrate.

Every now and then, when he moved, she felt him bump his knees against the back of her own seat, and her body would erupt into embarrassing flares of heat. At this rate, she'd be lucky if she got through the day with her nerves intact. She already felt frazzled, and the day was only halfway over.

*　　*　　*

James Larner walked into a burger bar in the small town of Bicester and looked around. Near the door, watching him with near-contemptuous eyes, was a hiker. His black helmet sat in the chair beside him. Outside, another biker sat astride a parked Suzuki. The dark glass of his visor made it impossible to see anything of his face. He had to he the contact man's back-up. James smiled to himself. He liked dealing with men who knew their business. Amateur crooks could get you into trouble.

The biker sitting at a table near the window, had done his own reconnaissance, and was watching James carefully. Good. Things looked like they would be going well. Which meant a nice big fat fee for him.

James sat down beside him and leaned back in his chair. The biker was in his early thirties, with reddish-brown hair and hazel eyes. 'Hi,' James said casually. 'A bit hot isn't it? I thought your English summers were always wet and cold?'

The biker nodded. 'You're in the market for some interesting items I hear?' he said, just as casually.

James nodded. He reached into his pocket and slid a sealed brown envelope across the table. The biker picked it up, tested the weight but, surprisingly, didn't bother to look inside. 'What d'ya want?' he asked flatly.

And just as flatly, James told him.

*   *   *

The small privately-owned railway and its steam trains were located well to the west, not far from the Welsh border. As the coach pulled into a small leafy lane and parked in a tiny carpark overlooking a small, uninspiring village, Vania could sense her little gang's surprise and smiled at the resultant mutters of unease.

From where they were sitting, the view didn't look particularly promising, but Vania knew, from long experience, how quickly their opinions would change. 'Right then,' she said, standing up and facing the agitated group. 'This afternoon we're going to get to ride on a train very similar to the ones you've just seen at Didcot. The engine is called 'The Martha Rose' and is quite something, as you'll see.'

She ignored the way Brett leaned back in his seat and tilted his head to one side, but her throat felt dry, and she licked her lips nervously. Damn him! He was doing this on purpose. Just waiting for her to make a mistake!

*　　　*　　　*

'We're due to leave at three o'clock, and the trip takes about an hour, as we stop every so often at the best viewpoints for you to take pictures. The carriages are all individual, which means there are no corridors, so pick your fellow travellers with care!' There were faked moans and groans.

'Now, included in the afternoon's train ride, is a champagne tea.' Vania glanced at her watch. 'The train station is just down the end of that path there.' She pointed to the little footpath and stile off to her left.

Vania got out first and helped the elderly

guests to alight. As Brett Carver walked determinedly towards her, his dark red hair shining in the sun, Vania stepped back, and started to chat to a friendly family from Utah. Much good that did her! Every nerve in her body seemed to stand to attention as he moved past her, amiably following the little straggling line down the footpath to the station.

Vania watched him go, her heart and her body aching for him.

*   *   *

When James Larner returned to the hotel, he felt much better. It was nearly three, and he wandered around the gardens, more in the hope of catching sight of Harriet Jensen than to admire the view. It wasn't until he noticed a small stream of people filing through some open French windows into a mirror-lined, fern-bedecked room, that he realised something was going on.

What was going on was Tea at Windrush Shallows.

He found himself a table and ordered tiny smoked salmon titbits, crustless cucumber sandwiches, and the freshly baked scones and clotted cream that seemed to be almost compulsory.

A pianist played softly in the background. And then, at last, he spotted his hostess coming through the doorway, and smiled with

119

satisfaction. Although Harriet did little more than toss a bland smile in his direction as she passed, James was contented. As soon as he'd cooked Brett Carver's goose once and for all, he'd start giving Miss Harriet Jensen the serious attention that she deserved.

He helped himself to another scone and watched her go.

Harriet, well aware of his scrutiny, cast him a final look over her shoulder as she stepped up to the French doors. She'd checked his details in the register—James Larner. He apparently owned some kind of car dealership in Boston, and if he asked her out, she would accept. That was the decision she'd spent the whole of the afternoon agonising over.

Although she'd never dated a hotel guest before, something told her it was about time that she started to take a proper interest in men. After all, at twenty-four, she was ridiculously old to be so inexperienced. And not for all the tea in China was she willing to admit to herself that it was Giles Powell's dark, fulminating, utterly male presence in her life that had something to do with her sudden interest in handsome blond hotel guests. Besides, she didn't doubt for a moment that Giles Powell had a string of beautiful women just waiting for him to call. And without some admirers of her own to fall back on, she felt, for some obscure, worrying reason, just a tad vulnerable.

120

*　　*　　*

'OK, there's the final whistle,' Vania called, looking down the platform that was bedecked with hanging baskets of scarlet and blue flowers. 'All aboard!' she yelled gaily at the top of her lungs. She walked to the carriage she'd arranged to share with the family from Utah, but it was empty. She craned her neck to look along the platform—but it too was reassuringly empty. The family must have buddied up with someone else. Which meant that she had the carriage with its delicious tea that was set out on the window table all to herself. And on a day like this, she was glad of the privacy.

She walked to the row of three seats and sat down.

The carriages were indeed the last word in luxury, each one having its own colour scheme—this particular one was mint green with touches of gold and cream. Vania kicked off her shoes and brushed her dark hair back off her face.

Just as the train gave the familiar starting-off lurch, she stood, reached up and pulled down the old-fashioned window, letting the warm July air rush into the carriage. She heard the door behind her open and close, and turned around in surprise, her mouth falling open in shock and dismay as she saw—not the family from Utah, but Brett Carver standing

121

before her, his hand still on the door-handle, his grey eyes gleaming.

'Almost missed it,' he said.

Vania, of course, didn't believe a single word.

'Almost missed it like hell,' she snapped. 'You arranged this!' Her hands clenched into fists by her side. 'What did you do with that nice family? Bribe them?'

'Hell no,' Brett drawled, leaning back against the carriage wall and crossing his arms across his broad chest as he looked at her thoughtfully. 'All I had to do,' he explained with that seductively lazy Kansas drawl of his, 'was tell them my predicament, and they offered to join up with another family, leaving us with this all to ourselves. Now wasn't that nice of them?' he purred, attractive crinkles appearing at the corners of his eyes as he smiled.

Vania's jaw clenched. 'What do you mean? What predicament?'

Brett shrugged and crossed one ankle over the other. Leaning against the wall like that, his big body easily swaying with the gentle motion of the steam train, he looked the picture of easy-going male reasonableness.

Vania, every inch the unreasonable female, longed to hit him!

'I just told them that I wanted some time alone with our gorgeous tour guide, and they sympathised completely.'

Vania snarled. 'Bah!'

'No, it's true, I swear,' Brett held up one hand in a gesture of peace. 'I told them I'd fallen in love with you at first sight, and the wife especially fell over herself to help me think up a plan to spend some time alone with you.'

'I'll just bet she did!' Vania knew to her cost that, when he tried, Brett could charm the tail feathers off a peacock in mating season. 'Lies come easy to you then?' she asked, tossing her head back. Wishing her heart wouldn't thump quite so loudly.

'I didn't lie,' Brett said, suddenly all sense of teasing, all sense of fun, gone. Vania sensed the very air in the carriage change—become thicker—and swallowed nervously.

'Don't,' she said sharply, and sat back down in her seat, staring at the laden table, with its bottle of champagne nestling in the ice bucket, and its attractive plate of cakes, tiny quiches, cheese, grapes and biscuits.

She sensed him move away from the door, but instead of sitting opposite her, he sat on the seat next to her. As his jeans-clad thigh brushed against hers, she scooted over—pretty damn quick—to the window seat, and stared out mutinously at the passing scenery. There was nothing more beautiful than English pastoral countryside at its best, she reminded herself firmly, and Vania stared at it all with a determined intensity that hurt her eyes. She heard him sigh. 'You don't believe I fell in love with you the moment your father introduced us?' Brett asked quietly.

Vania's heart stalled. She made a quick, distressed gesture, then nervously licked lips that were so dry she impatiently reached for the champagne.

She struggled with the cork, growing more and more exasperated, and when he patiently reached out and took it from her, twisting off the wire and deftly popping the cork, she made no demure. He poured her a glass and handed it to her, and she took a long quick gulp.

He watched her, smiling. 'Another?' he asked, as she drained the delicate fluted glass with a second gulp.

She shot him a quick snapping glance. 'Are you trying to get me drunk?'

Brett stared at her blankly for a second, then threw his head back and laughed. 'Oh Vania, you're priceless.'

Vania bit her lip and turned back to the window. It was so much easier than looking at him. But with every mile that crawled past, she became more and more attuned to his body next to hers. The way they swayed in unison as the train turned a bend on the line. The scent of his aftershave, mingling with that of the opened champagne and the country air wafting in through the windows. It seemed as if the very heat from his skin reached out to her across the space of the seat that separated them. She was utterly aware that all she needed to do was lift her hand from her lap and move it just a few inches, and she could rest on his thigh. She knew that if she did so, he would drag his breath in a quick male hiss. She knew she'd feel his muscles clench instinctively at her touch. Knew he'd get a tight, sensual look on his face. Knew his eyes would darken a shade. And yet, in all her life, she'd never so much as touched him. Never seen those things happen. She just knew that they would.

'What do you want Brett?' she asked at last, her voice a mixture of despair and anger. He waited in silence, forcing her to turn and look at him before he spoke.

'I want you, Vania,' he said simply. 'I always have.'

Vania smiled grimly. 'You want my shares you mean. You think I don't know how Dad left his will?'

Brett shook his head. 'I don't care how Chuck left his will,' he said flatly. 'From the moment I watched you come down those stairs back in Boston, I've wanted you. And nothing but you.'

But Vania didn't believe him. Or, perhaps to be more accurate, didn't dare let herself believe him. Once she started to believe in him, she was on the highway to nowhere.

Brett saw the dark spear of pain flicker in her cat-green eyes and opened his mouth, on

125

the verge of telling her that he was about to pull off a deal that would prove to her once and for all that he didn't give a damn about her money. Soon now he would have an empire distinct and separate from the McAllen car dealership. A company all of his own, worth tens of millions.

But, in the end, he closed his mouth again, the words left unsaid. Until he could prove to her that he loved the woman, and not the power and wealth behind her, he knew he was going to have an uphill battle. Vania, he knew to his cost, was a stubborn opponent. But he was a born fighter.

So instead he moved closer, putting a firm finger under her chin and turning her to face him. Her cat-green eyes made his heart leap. Her large, generous mouth fell open and he felt his whole body, his entire being, surge into life.

'I've missed you,' he said gruffly. 'Oh, Vania, how I've missed you.' And then his lips were on hers. Even though she meant the world to him, he'd never kissed her before.

Vania groaned at the touch of his lips, which were like the man himself, so hard and yet so gentle. She felt her head fall back against the headrest, as if her neck could no longer support the weight of it, and then he was moving across her, pushing her back, their bodies clinging together. She felt the touch of his hands on the side of her face, and her skin flared at that touch. Their legs entwined, their knees coming together. Her breasts were pressing against his hard chest. She could feel, smell, taste, hear, see only him. She closed her eyes, lost.

And then she felt the wonderful pressure of his lips ease, and her eyes snapped open as his mouth slowly left hers, leaving her so bereft it was terrifying. One kiss, she thought in despair. Just one kiss, and the victory was all his?

She felt the train shudder to a gentle stop, and knew that they'd made their first stop. Outside, a picturesque bridge over a winding river, beside a small copse of oak trees.

Suddenly her brain leapt into action. Escape!

She pushed against him with all her strength, her hands flat against his muscular shoulders, but it was only because he obeyed her unspoken command to back off that he moved away.

She slipped underneath him, lithely slipping around the side of the seat and rushing for the door. She barely had time to get out and clamber into the carriage next door before the train pulled away again. Luckily for her, it contained the five bridge-playing widows from Wyoming, who were only too happy to have her share their tea.

But for the rest of the journey, as they chattered all around her, Vania could only

remember the touch of Brett's lips against hers
. . . Could only think about the way it had felt
to finally—oh so finally—be in his arms.

CHAPTER EIGHT

Giles smiled as the red-headed receptionist
rose from her desk and walked to her boss's
door. He smiled as she tossed her head back
and opened the door. 'There's a Mr Giles
Powell to see you, Mr Keeler,' she sing-songed
cheerfully.

Giles took the chair, crossing one leg
elegantly across his knee, and casting a casual
but all-seeing glance around the room. He'd
never been to his aunt's solicitors before.

'So, Giles,' Gordon Keeler said, anxious not
to prolong the agony. 'What can I do for you?'

Giles smiled, understanding the man's
hurry. 'Nothing specific,' he said blandly.
'This is more of a courtesy call than anything
else. I just wanted to inform you, before
the paperwork comes through, that my
grandmother and I are going to contest my
aunt's will.'

In fact, he hadn't yet approached his own
solicitors, just wanted to test the water with
Gordon before he did so. Gordon's face
remained utterly blank. 'I see,' he said flatly.

Giles leaned an elbow on the edge of the

desk and thoughtfully rubbed his chin. 'You don't seem particularly surprised,' he mused, baiting the hook skillfully.

Gordon shrugged one shoulder casually. 'Not particularly, no. After your reaction at the reading of the will it seemed . . . likely, that something like this might occur.'

Gordon was unwilling to play cat-and-mouse with a man who always took on the role of cat. Besides, he liked Giles Powell—he always had. He was Frankie's favourite person in her family, too. As an adopted son, he'd had to run the gauntlet, at first, of Grace Powell's formidable displeasure. And instead of turning out like a spoilt brat, or a nervous wreck, he'd emerged strong, trustworthy, and likeable. Giles Powell was one of the few men Gordon would trust with either his life or his wife.

Now he sighed. He knew that Frankie wouldn't have wanted Gordon to be anything but be straight with Giles. 'Look, if you bring a lawsuit against Harriet Jensen you're going to lose,' Gordon said flatly, and with such assurance that Giles, in spite of himself, felt suddenly uneasy.

'Oh?' he asked, letting one dark eyebrow rise in surprise, and uncrossing his leg to sit a little straighter in the chair. 'You seem so sure?'

'I am. For a start, the will was dated nearly four years ago, so if you're going to try and convince the judge that Harriet exerted 'undue 'influence' on your aunt during her final illness, you won't have a leg to stand on.'

Giles nodded. 'Nevertheless,' he said smoothly, 'leaving all that property outside of the family, to a woman who was a stranger only a while ago . . . You know as well as I do Gordon, that if we get a sympathetic judge . . .'

Gordon sighed. How he wished Harriet would let him tell her family that she was Mark's daughter. 'I'm afraid, Giles,' he said quickly, 'that all a magistrate will want to know is whether or not Frankie was of sound mind when she made the will. Which means, if you're to have any chance of winning, you'll have to try to get her doctor to testify that she wasn't. Now can you see old Doc Matthews doing that?'

Giles couldn't. Besides, the thought of having his aunt's reputation dragged through the mud like that . . . Gordon easily read the pained expression on his face and shook his head. 'Look, Giles, why can't you just accept the fact that Frankie was free to leave her money and property where she wanted to? And that she wanted to leave everything to Harriet?'

Giles smiled mirthlessly. 'You think I want Frankie's money, Gordon?'

Gordon laughed. Frankie's inheritance was peanuts to a man like this. 'No. I think you're doing this mainly for your grandmother's sake. She's the one who has the real problem with

Harriet inheriting, isn't she?'

Giles's face became utterly still. The solicitor had just touched him on a raw spot. The truth was, he was becoming more and more worried about Grace's state of mental health. Every time she talked about Harriet Jensen now, she practically raved.

'Giles, I can guarantee that if you take Harriet to court, you'll lose,' Gordon said harshly. 'And that won't help Lady Grace at all, will it?'

Giles's eyes flickered. So he wasn't the only one who'd noticed his grandmother's faculties were beginning to fail her. For a long second the two men looked at one another. Finally Giles rose. He held out his hand. 'Thanks Gordon. I appreciate your candour,' he said simply. Gordon sighed with relief, and happily shook the man's hand. But as he watched him leave, his eyes were worried. He would have liked to think it was all over—Harriet, after all, had had enough worries in her life.

But somehow he didn't think they were out of the woods yet.

*   *   *

'The man's besotted with the money-grabbing baggage,' Grace Powell hissed. 'I thought as much at the will reading.' Sitting in her favourite chair, reading a Jane Austen classic, his grandmother looked ferociously over her spectacles at him.

Giles sighed. 'I don't think that's the whole story, somehow,' he said, careful to keep his voice level. 'Look, Grandmother,' he said softly, coming to sit beside her on the sofa, 'it's not over yet. I've made an offer for the hotel, and you and I both know she won't be able to resist that.'

Even as he said it, he knew he wasn't being utterly honest—either with himself or with his grandmother. But, right now, he needed to give his grandmother some hope. This outright hatred she was developing for Frankie's protégée was beginning to seriously alarm him.

Almost as if reading his thoughts, Grace suddenly shrugged. She reached out and patted one of his hands with her own. 'You're quite right, Giles,' she said, her old and wavering voice gentle once more. 'And no doubt you'll get your way. You're like me in that respect.'

Giles smiled, relieved she was taking it so well. 'Right. And, anyway, I've decided to do a little . . . let's call it, field-work.'

Grace looked at him, her pale eyes glittering. 'Oh?'

Giles grinned. 'I've just checked into Windrush Shallows by telephone. Under the name K. Browning. I think it's about time I had a look at the place myself.'

'That's the spirit, boy,' Grace said at last, and gave a harsh laugh. ' "Know thine enemy".

Right?'

Giles smiled uneasily. 'Right. So leave it all to me, all right Grandmother?' he urged her anxiously. 'And as soon as I've found where her real weaknesses are, I'm sure she'll be more reasonable,' he added softly. But his eyes were guarded.

The thought of tackling Harriet Jensen on what she considered to be her home territory was breathtakingly exciting. Grace saw the predatory look in his eyes and nodded. Good. The Jensen girl hadn't fooled her grandson.

'Well, I'd better be going,' Giles said. 'I want to question as many of the hotel staff as I can before dinner.'

Grace nodded, hiding a secret smile behind her book. 'Good luck boy.' She watched him leave the room, then impatiently tossed the book aside. When you wanted a job done, you did it yourself, that was her motto. Slowly, she began to smile. 'So the will can't be broken, hum?' she muttered to herself. And began to laugh again.

There were more ways than one to skin a cat—or should that be a *rat*?

*　　　*　　　*

Giles turned the bottle-green Ferrari into the familiar drive of his aunt's house, and slowed to a crawl, a surprised but pleased expression flitting across his face.

133

It looked just the same. He'd expected an ugly glass portico to have been added, perhaps even an ugly car park where the rose gardens used to be. Instead, the house looked exactly as it always had. Well, not exactly. The gardens had been restored to their former glory. The stonework had been cleaned, the window-frames repainted. The house looked . . . prosperous, and pleased with itself.

He frowned, following the arrows towards the old stable blocks and found the car park. It was nearly empty—hardly surprising at four o'clock in the afternoon. But he doubted it was ever really full. He parked and walked the familiar route to the front of the house, noting the manicured lawns, the well-pruned roses, the rejuvenated fountain, and feeling guilty that he'd never had these things done himself.

Stepping into the hall, he was prepared for a transformation. But apart from the addition of a curved reception desk, and a big bulletin board on one wall, the hall was exactly the same as ever. It still felt like coming home.

As a boy, he'd spent many summer holidays here, catching minnows at the bottom of the garden, where the river ran shallow. Then he heard, 'Can I help you sir?' and suddenly pulled himself together. This was no longer his home away from home. This was Windrush Shallows Hotel—and it belonged to a beautiful blonde usurper who had no right to it.

He smiled and approached the receptionist.

134

'Yes. I'm Mr Browning. I telephoned earlier.'

'Oh, yes sir. You were lucky—we had a cancellation.'

That old chestnut, he thought, suppressing a smile. As Giles approached, he saw the long list of names already signed in—the place really was full! He signed, glancing up in surprise as the woman came from behind the desk and picked up one of his cases. 'Room twelve is on the second floor sir, if you'd like to follow me.'

'No, please, I insist,' Giles said, taking the case back from her. The receptionist smiled her thanks. What, no smartly uniformed bell-boys? he mused, not sure whether to be disappointed or approving. And instead of leading him to an out-of-place lift, she preceded him up the newly-carpeted staircase, and towards a room at the rear of the house, with a view over the river and woods.

The receptionist opened one of the doors and handed him the keys. 'I hope you have a pleasant stay sir,' she smiled, walking in to push open a window and do a quick visual check that all was as it should he. 'The bathroom is just two doors down the hall, and clearly marked.'

With a start, Giles glanced around, and realised there was no adjoining bathroom. In fact, he recognized this room now—it was one of the unused bedrooms that had always been covered in dust sheets. And nothing in it had

135

changed—the same big comfortable bed still stood against one wall. Even the wallpaper was the same. It just looked . . . cleaner, brighter, more welcoming somehow. Lived in.

'I see,' he said. 'How . . . novel.'

Evelyn Grey smiled. 'Yes sir, a lot of people think so. The original owner wanted to keep the atmosphere of the original house as much as possible, and Miss Jensen has kept everything just the same. All of our guests remark on the atmosphere. They find it so calming and restful.'

Yes, Giles thought grimly. 'I'm sure they do. Of course, it would have kept down the costs,' he added, nodding his head. How very clever you are, Harriet Jensen. 'After all, not having to do any major remodeling must have been a very cheap option.' Evelyn looked puzzled for one moment. The new guest had sounded almost . . . bitter.

'The whole idea of Windrush Shallows is to offer guests a slice of real English country living sir,' she murmured.

Giles, aware that he was alienating her, smiled dazzlingly. 'Oh yes, I can see that,' he said smoothly. 'I was just admiring the owner's . . . vision. She must have had good advisors.'

'Oh, Miss Jensen drew up all the plans herself sir,' Evelyn said. Like all the staff, she was fiercely loyal to Harriet. 'She and Miss Powell, her late business partner, did everything themselves.'

136

Giles looked at her quickly. She actually sounded sincere. 'But surely,' he said quietly, 'Miss Jensen has a manager to run the place for her?'

'Oh, no sir. Miss Jensen is the manager *and* the owner.'

Giles smiled disbelieving. 'I see.' And, indeed, a few hours later, he really did begin to see. By carefully charming the maids and getting them to chat, he started to learn all there was to know about Windrush Shallows. And by striking up a conversation with another guest in the small bar, he began to understand the nature of the clientele the hotel attracted. And the more he learned, the more puzzled he became. For, as crazy as it seemed, he was being forced to admit that Harriet Jensen really seemed to have worked like a demon to make the hotel a success. Apparently she still worked twelve-hour days, even now that the hotel could almost run itself.

The staff—locals all of them—did nothing but sing her praises. The guests were delighted with the place. It was, without doubt, a well-run establishment. When the hour came for changing for dinner, Giles Powell was not a happy bunny.

*　　　*　　　*

Harriet, through nothing more than sheer bad luck, had yet to realise that the enemy had booked himself into her hotel.

She'd been working flat out in the office all afternoon on the idea of holding an annual Autumn Ball, as an added attraction to help keep the hotel full in the off-peak season.

So it was, that as she walked upstairs to her own room, she actually passed Giles Powell's door, little knowing that he was at that moment inside and slipping into a dinner jacket.

In her own room she quickly showered, and as she finished and wrapped the towel around her, she heard the charabanc pull up outside. She smiled as she heard the trooping of feet passing her door, and from the guests' excited and happy chatter, the day had obviously gone well.

She brushed her silvery hair into a shining silken curtain, and on the spur of the moment, decided to leave it loose for a change, so that it hung to just below her shoulder-blades. Next, she walked to her wardrobe, just in the mood to make an extra effort. After a moment's thought, she reached for a pale silver-and-lilac evening gown with spaghetti straps, and a matching pair of strappy, silver high heeled shoes. The gown was all but backless, with just six thin strips of material criss-crossing her back. A deep V-neck at the front was mirrored by a V at the back, that stopped just above her delicately rounded buttocks.

The material was of a shimmering silk, so

pure that it looked as if it should be transparent. With it, of course, Harriet couldn't wear a bra, but she had always been slim and her well-shaped breasts had nothing to fear from the clinging touch of the gown. After gathering at her tiny waist, the dress fell to just below her calves, leaving the strappy silver sandals to show off to perfection her shapely ankles. Harriet needed only to add a silver and amethyst necklace to complete the outfit. She kept her make-up light, merely adding a touch of colour to her cheekbones and lips, a light frosty eyeshadow to her lids, and a touch of mascara to darken her lashes. With her creamy white shoulders (she never could tan properly), perfectly enhanced by the colour of her dress, she looked utterly spectacular.

As she passed, she tapped on Vania's door and popped her head in. 'Everything go OK?' she asked.

Vania, in the midst of putting on stockings glanced up and managed a big smile. 'You bet. They'll be talking about nothing but steam trains throughout dinner, though, so be prepared. Wow, you look great! Special occasion?'

Harriet shook her head. 'Nope. Just in the mood for a bit of glamour, that's all. See you downstairs in a bit then.'

Vania nodded, and watched her go. Then she sighed, sinking back down on to the bed.

Hell, she felt like a wreck. And she still had dinner to get through. She'd just have to make damned sure that she got down late, and wherever Brett Carver was sitting, she'd sit somewhere else! After that fiasco on the train, it had been sheer torture in the bus, knowing he was right behind her.

Her peace of mind was shot to hell and back!

Harriet, unaware of Vania's turmoil—and unaware that she had turmoil of her own still to come—made her way downstairs.

Some of the guests were already at the bar or making their way into the dining room. One of these was James Larner. He was just crossing the hall towards the dining room, when the vision in silver and lilac stopped him dead. His reaction to this woman both scared and intrigued him.

Harriet saw him stop and knew that he was waiting for her to catch him up. 'Miss Jensen. Would you like a drink before dinner?' he asked, glad that his voice came out even, and not in the schoolboy-with-a-crush squeak he was half expecting.

'Please, call me Harriet,' she said, her English accent pouring over him like fine wine. 'And a drink would be nice.'

James took her arm in the lightest of grips as he led her through the door to the small, discreet bar. But to the man sitting at the bar, drinking a fine malt whisky, the touch looked

140

proprietorial in the extreme. Giles Powell, faced with Harriet Jensen dressed to kill, with a handsome suitor on one arm, gritted his teeth.

Harriet smiled at Bill, the bartender, and without asking, he poured her usual—a lemonade, topped with lime cordial and loaded with ice. She never drank alcohol in the Shallows, and both James Larner and Giles Powell noted it, but with vastly different reactions. James though it sweet. Giles, once again, had to re-adjust his misconceptions. He'd have thought Harriet Jensen would drink nothing but champagne.

James ordered a Manhattan for himself, and when it was served, clinked his glass against hers. 'Cheers,' he said softly. His smoky blue eyes narrowed at the sight of her lips touching the glass.

Giles felt his hackles rise and sneered ferociously. How smooth. How polished. How artificial.

At that moment, the husband and wife sitting between them slipped away towards the dining room, and Harriet, half-seeing another man out of the corner of her eye, suddenly swung her head around in his direction. Her eyes widened at the sight of him. Her heart leapt; the drink in her hand shook. What was he doing here? Suddenly the man beside her was no longer good-looking, or even there. There was only the two of them—her and

Giles.

Mockingly, Giles held up his own glass. '*Salut*,' he murmured.

Harriet took a deep breath, dragging herself back to the land called 'reality'. Grimly, she told herself that he was probably only here for dinner. Just to make a nuisance of himself. Her eyes flickered, then she deliberately turned her back on him. She smiled dazzlingly at James, who actually blushed. Giles stared at the curve of her creamy spine, where the thin lilac straps criss-crossed. The indent where her buttocks met the clinging silk. He wanted to lean forward and plant a kiss just . . .

'Shall we eat?' she murmured. 'Chef has promised us something really special tonight.' She pitched her voice so that it became a seductive pun which was bound to carry to the man sitting behind her. James took her arm again, looking as smitten as he was. Giles watched them go, his face a mask of fury.

As they crossed the hall, Harriet noticed that Vania and the new guest, the one she'd been arguing with that morning, were coming down the stairs together. Harriet glanced up at them casually, as did James. Suddenly, James stopped dead, and Vania's companion also came to an immediate halt on the stairs. For a second, both women were aware of the antipathy flashing between the men. Then James was all smiles again, and leading Harriet onward. In the door-way to the bar, Giles

Powell, too, had noticed the small, puzzling exchange and glanced at the red-haired man quizzically.

Vania, who knew James Larner on sight, said nothing at all as Brett escorted her into the dining room. He'd been waiting outside her door for her, knowing her well enough to guess the kind of tricks she might try and pull to get out of sitting with him at dinner.

Soon the dining room was alive with chatter.

Harriet, who'd deliberately opted for a table for two, was aware of the other guests' speculative glances in her direction. It wasn't often the lovely owner of the hotel dined *à deux* with a guest. And with such a good-looking one too. Many women remarked to one another what a striking pair the two blondes made. Overhearing one such conversation, Giles Powell found it all he could do not to walk out in disgust.

So, she liked to prey on the more wealthy guests, did she? Why was he so surprised? For a woman like her, snaring a rich husband had to be a top priority—and Windrush Shallows was the obvious and perfect place in which to do it.

At another table, Brett Carver wondered what James Larner was doing there, whilst at the same time finding it hard to care. All he could remember was that kiss he and Vania had shared earlier.

Opposite him, Vania was doing her best to

143

forget it.

Harriet, sampling the cold watercress soup, glanced at James and smiled. 'That other guest you met on the stairs, do you know each other?'

James smiled. 'Yes. Sorry about that. We're . . . fellow board members on the same company.'

'You don't seem to like each other,' she murmured in massive understatement.

James laughed. 'No. We both want control of the same firm.'

Harriet shrugged, not really interested in boardroom battles and tales of high finance. Then she realised that Giles Powell's eyes were boring into her like twin lasers. She reached across and gently lowered her hand over James's, gently stroking the side of his wrist with one finger. James flushed. This woman was driving him crazy. 'Don't let it ruin your holiday,' she said softly.

James caught his breath. 'Don't worry. I won't.'

Giles Powell spent the evening glowering. Harriet flirted. James Larner fell reluctantly in love. Vania panicked. Brett Carver smiled, happy to be with the woman he loved.

All in all, it was a memorable dinner for everyone involved.

CHAPTER NINE

Grace Powell smiled graciously at the plump, dark-haired and extremely nervous girl in front of her. 'More tea, Lydia?'

'Oh, no thank you, Lady Grace,' Lydia Brack said nervously.

Grace smiled again. She knew the young girl was as nervous as a cat on a hot tin roof, and who could blame her? For a girl like this to get an invitation to Powell House was bound to be exciting. 'You know, Lydia,' Grace said, leaning back in her chair. 'I have really fond memories of your grandmother.'

That was a lie—she couldn't bring to mind the face of Lydia Brack's grandmother at all, but she knew that a maid by the name of Mary Brack had once worked here and that was all that mattered.

Lydia smiled. 'Really? Granny always spoke of you with real . . . *terror* . . . er . . . affection,' she gushed.

Her grandmother, dead now for many years, had indeed regaled her goggle-eyed grandchildren with tales about how she used to work for the fine 'Lady' up at the 'Big House'. And now Lydia was a chambermaid at Windrush Shallows. Which wasn't the same thing at all, Lydia reminded herself firmly. She got paid good wages, and wasn't treated as a skivvy.

So when she'd received an embossed cream envelope inviting her to 'tea' at Powell House, she'd been flabbergasted. But, of course, far too curious not to come. And, in spite of her modern twenty-first-century outlook on life, the house, the butler, and most of all, Lady Grace herself, were making her feel like her grandmother must have felt, when she'd first come to this house all those years ago.

She stared nervously down into her tea-cup, wondering what this was all about. And Grace watched her and hid a smile. The girl was perfect. Unsure of herself and eager to please. 'Well, Lydia, I hear that you've been working for my daughter for a while now,' she said, and Lydia glanced up uncertainly.

'Er . . . yes, Lady Grace.' For a moment she wondered, with a spasm of panic, if the poor old lady knew that Frankie was dead.

'Do you like working at Powell Manor?' Grace asked, reaching for her own tea-cup and taking a genteel sip.

'Oh yes, Lady Grace,' Lydia said avidly. 'Harriet's really nice.' Grace Powell frowned. Aware that she'd done or said something wrong, but not having the faintest idea of what it could be, Lydia shrank a little in the exquisite chair.

'You know, Lydia, in a way I feel responsible for you,' Grace ignored the way the girl started and looked at her in open-mouthed

146

astonishment. 'In the old days, we looked after our people. They relied on us, you see. So that's why I was glad to hear that *you* were still working for the family.'

Lydia blinked. 'Oh . . . er, thank you,' she stammered.

'That's why I want you to . . . keep me informed, about what goes on in my daughter's house. You wouldn't mind doing that for me, would you Lydia?' Grace forced herself to smile. 'You see, since my daughter's death I feel I have a duty to keep my finger on the pulse, as it were. To make sure that all is . . . well.'

Lydia beamed. So that's what all this was about? The old duck was worried that Harriet couldn't cope. 'Oh, don't you worry about that, your Ladyship,' Lydia said brightly.

'Yes. But I would like to know what's going on, you see,' Grace pressed encouragingly. 'I feel so cut off, here at Powell House. You will telephone or write to me, won't you Lydia, telling me how things are?'

Lydia smiled. Poor old girl. She was just lonely. 'Of course I will, Lady Grace, if you want me to.'

'Feel free to tell me anything and everything that happens at . . . Windrush Shallows. If you have any trouble with the staff, the names of any really important guests, and so on. Even what happens during the general day-to-day running. I'm sure I'll be fascinated,' she gritted.

Lydia bit into a cake happily and nodded. 'Of course I will, Lady Grace. I promise.'

Grace nodded, too, well satisfied. With an unsuspecting spy in the camp, she was sure that the opportunity would come to put a spoke into Miss Harriet Jensen's wheels. All she had to do was wait for the right time to strike. 'Another cup of Darjeeling, Lydia?'

*   *   *

James Larner slipped open his door and glanced down the corridor. It was ten o'clock, and that ridiculous red and cream bus had left for Warwick Castle an hour ago. As he'd expected, Brett Carver had been on it. Wherever Vania McAllen went, he was sure to follow, on that much James could rely.

Good. The maids were cleaning the rooms. That meant, on the next floor up, another girl had either done Brett Carver's room, or hadn't got around to it yet . . .

In his hand was a large, plain brown envelope. He walked towards the stairs, careful to hold the envelope close to his side, where it was inconspicuous, but he got to the third floor unseen and paused to check that all was quiet. As he'd expected, several doors were open, and the sounds of maids working, cheerfully chatting as they changed sheets and dusted, wafted through them as he passed.

He'd discovered from the register that Brett Carver was in room eighteen, and when he tried the handle the door opened, so he quickly slipped inside.

The bed was freshly made, everything shone, and there was a pleasant smell of lavender polish in the room. He quickly looked around the room for a suitable hiding place for the envelope. Inside it were the forged documents he'd asked his biker contact to supply for him.

He walked to the set of drawers, opening them until he came to the bottom one, where only a few shirts, still in their polythene wrappers, lay inside. He smiled. He doubted that Brett Carver would be going into that drawer very often. Very carefully he slipped the big brown envelope inside. It was, quite simply, a time-bomb just waiting to explode in Brett's face. For inside was a very genuine-looking, pre-nuptial agreement, drawn up and already 'signed' by one Brett Carver. Its terms were simple—in the event of Brett Carver and Vania McAllen divorcing, she would get a very generous settlement—but he would get to keep the precious McAllen shares that she'd brought into the marriage.

He'd planned those documents carefully. The very generous settlement outlined made it ring true because Brett Carver was known to be an extremely fair-minded man. And that pre-nup made it very clear that all he wanted was the shares. Oh yes. Vania McAllen would have no trouble believing it to be all his own work.

James grinned widely and stepped back to the door. Sure that the coast was clear he slipped out and walked down the corridor, whistling jauntily. All he had to do now was to make sure that Vania McAllen found the envelope. Surely not too hard, for a man of his manipulative skills?

*   *   *

Harriet walked into the tea-room, glancing at the pianist as she did so. A hauntingly beautiful piece of Rachmaninov that was a particular favourite of hers, was wafting through the air.

She was early, and one of the waiters was fussing over the room's few customers. She glanced at her watch, checking the time. Only ten past three. She was just about to turn around and retreat, when a flash of gold caught her eye. She turned her head a few degrees, seeing a strong, square hand, framed by an immaculately white cuff and sporting an expensive gold watch, lift one of their delicate Royal Doulton tea-cups, and disappear out of sight behind a big blue vase.

She wasn't sure what made her walk around the vase for a better view of the owner of that hand. But for some reason, she wasn't at all

150

surprised by the mocking dark eyes or devastatingly handsome features.

'A charming room this,' Giles said smoothly. 'I've always thought so. When I was a boy, I used to bring snails in here and race them. Frankie made bets with me. When I won she always paid up, but when I lost, she never took my money. She was like that.'

Harriet had a sudden vision of Frankie, lying on the floor watching the snails and her nephew's rapt face, and couldn't help but smile. Yes. It sounded just like her.

Giles found himself utterly wrong-footed by the affectionate smile on her face—and realised, with a nasty jolt, that she just couldn't be acting. 'You really loved Frankie, didn't you?' he asked, his voice barely more than a whisper.

Harriet looked into his shocked eyes, and laughed bitterly. 'Sorry to disappoint you, Giles, but yes I did. And why are you still here?' she added abruptly.

Giles shrugged one elegant, arrogant shoulder. 'Why shouldn't I be? I've booked in for the fortnight, and I understand afternoon tea is part and parcel of the package.'

Harriet's jaw dropped. 'You've booked in?'

Without another word she turned smartly on her heel and marched to the reception desk, where a disconcerted Evelyn Grey watched her feverishly check the register.

When she returned her colour was high.

'You're a liar,' she hissed, and was suddenly aware that the waiter, passing with a tray of dainty white-chocolate confections, shot her an astonished look.

Harriet glanced around, her colour rising even higher as she realised that several guests were looking at her openly.

She turned back to Giles, who was grinning widely and thoroughly enjoying himself. 'We'd better continue this in my office,' she gritted, her voice like gravel. He stood up, gave a mock bow, and followed her from the room. Her chin was so high in the air that he was surprised she didn't hit her nose on the chandelier in the hall as she passed!

'Very . . . business-like,' Giles drawled, looking around the office, noting the workman-like computer, the simple wooden filing cabinets, the plethora of stationary on her desk.

'You're not booked in here, so I'm going to have to ask you to leave,' Harriet hissed, spinning around, and getting right to the point. She was wearing a dark blue skirt and jacket, and a crisp white blouse underneath. Her hair was pinned back in a French pleat, but Giles couldn't help but remember it as it had been last night—loose, and covering her shoulders and arms like a silver, silken curtain.

'Oh, but I am. You probably missed it. Whenever I travel, I always use the name Browning,' he helped her out suavely. 'He was my favourite poet when I was at school. Vastly underrated in my opinion. His wife got all the glory.' He smiled. ' 'Twas ever thus.'

'Whenever you travel?' Harriet hissed, dumbstruck, ignoring his poetic musings. 'You're not twenty miles from home!'

'Ah, I prefer anonymity at all times,' he said, pushing his hands into his trouser pockets, the gesture only adding to his indolent charm. 'I'm on holiday after all, and if some of your guests know I own Powell Software . . . well, they'll be trying to make deals with me all day long.' There was just enough truth in that to make Harriet want to spit tin-tacks.

'I see,' she said flatly.

Giles shrugged. 'So sue me.'

'I have no wish to do that, Mr Powell,' she responded sweetly, and Giles winced. So Gordon had rung and warned her he was thinking of taking her to court, had he? Damn! 'But I am perfectly within my rights to ask you to leave,' she added, watching the smile leave his lips.

She moved around her desk and fiddled with some papers. 'The management always reserves the right to ask any guest that it feels . . . undesirable . . . to leave the premises,' she clarified sweetly. 'I shall, of course, give you a full refund,' she added, so magnanimously that Giles almost growled.

'What's the matter, Harriet? Scared to have me around?'

153

At that, as he'd expected, her head shot up. 'Scared!' she yelped. 'Me? What have I to be scared of?' she asked scornfully. 'Certainly not you.'

Something in the way she said it, so full of dismissive scorn, hit him like a brick, right between the eyes. 'Oh? Is that so?' he said softly.

Suddenly, Harriet became aware of the danger. She was alone in the office. She could hardly call for help—it would be far too embarrassing. Giles took a step around the desk. 'What are you doing?' she squeaked. He took another step towards her. Nervously, she began to back off.

'Not so confident as you seem, hmm, Harriet?' he asked softly. 'Not worried, surely, that if I stay on I might discover something not quite—how shall I put it—right, with the set up here?'

Harriet's chin lifted and her eyes flashed. 'There's nothing wrong here,' she said, a slight emphasis on the word 'here' making his eyes narrow.

'No, Harriet?'

'No!' She had her back to the wall now—literally—and had run out of places to go. Giles closed in on her as she watched him, like a rabbit hypnotized by a snake. Slowly, slowly, he approached her, filling her vision, and then leaned one hand against the wall, just to the left of her face. He was so close her cheek was

154

nearly touching his sleeve.

Her breathing stalled. His jacket had fallen open as he leaned forward, and with his face lowered to within an inch of hers she felt the heat of him all around her, in stark contrast to the cold plaster of the wall against her back.

'Then you've no objection to my staying?' he mocked.

Harriet swallowed. 'No.' She cleared her throat and tried again. 'No,' she said more firmly. And reached out a hand to push her palm against his chest. 'Now get away from me.'

Her skin, where it touched his, burned. Molten heat raced through her veins, shooting up her arm and lodging in her breast. To her utter consternation, she felt her nipples tingle and begin to ache. She quickly snatched her hand away.

Giles's eyes slowly dropped from her own. Ran down the length of her creamy neck, to the delicate blue-veined pulse by her sternum and dropped even lower, crossing the dazzlingly white satin blouse until his eyes saw the thrusting buttons of her flesh pressing against her jacket.

He looked back at her, his eyes darkening to midnight, his pulse throbbing at the look in her eyes. Reluctant desire. Puzzled passion. Helpless need. Slowly, with his other hand, he pushed her blue jacket aside. Harriet gave a shuddering gasp, but couldn't seem to move.

Her legs seemed to have turned to iron, pinning her to the spot. Slowly, oh so slowly it was like torture, he lifted his hand to cover the space between them, and cupped her breast in his palm.

Harriet's dark lashes feathered closed, and a brief, inescapable moan sighed between her lips. Giles felt a moment of utter triumph, then heard a deep, resonating sound. An answering moan from his own mouth. It was raw. Primordial. And quivered between them, like the aftermath of a storm. Harriet's eyes shot open. Giles, too, felt unbearably tense. Everything in him was on the alert. But was he the hunter, or the hunted?

When the explosion came, it surprised them both.

Suddenly their lips were together, clinging, fusing, melting. Her hands were around his waist, pulling him closer, and every inch of their bodies was touching—her breasts were flattened against his chest, her knees between his, thighs pressing together, arms entangling . . .

Harriet had never felt anything like it. And even though she was inexperienced in the ways of sex, she knew that this was something special. This connection, this complete meeting of mind and body was something that could only happen to a woman when the right man touched her, claimed her, loved her.

Right man? Giles Powell? She moaned

again, this time the sound distinctly that of despair. Giles barely heard her above the pounding of his own heart, the fury of passion in his veins. Everything in him was demanding both domination and surrender. Her perfume was making him dizzy. Her soft skin was seducing him. The small sounds she made, the movement of her body when she breathed, everything about her was dragging him closer, closer . . .

From the first instant he'd set eyes on her, this moment had been inevitable, but his subconscious was only now letting him in on that devastating little secret.

He felt her pushing against him, and some answering sense of panic in his own brain had him moving back. No. This was dangerous. Unbelievably, incredibly dangerous.

He'd promised himself, after his divorce, that he'd never again let beauty blind him to truth. But, oh, how he wanted her back in his arms. With a groan, he all but threw himself back, and away from her.

If it hadn't been for the wall, Harriet knew that she'd be a mere heap on the floor now.

For a second, which seemed like eternity, they stared at each other, breathless, wild-eyed and bewildered. Then Giles shook his head, smiled determinedly, wiped her lipstick from his mouth with the back of his hand and shook his head.

'No way, lady,' he said grimly. 'Oh no! No

way. You don't get to me that way. Not like this!'

And with that, he turned and slammed out of the room. Harriet simply stared after him, too stunned to even think.

CHAPTER TEN

James was thinking about Harriet as he ate his breakfast. An English rose, to be sure. But one with thorns, of that he was also sure. James had never believed in love. He didn't want to be in love. It made men vulnerable. He only had to look at his worst enemy to see that. Brett Carver had always been someone to be feared and admired. And yet here he was tied up in knots over Vania McAllen. To the point where nothing mattered to him but her. Just like James now longed for Harriet to come down so that he could be near her.

James sighed grimly. And yet . . . the thought of marrying her, and taking her back to Boston, of showing her off to his friends, of decking her in silk and diamonds . . . It was a heady, lovely, wonderful thought . . .

A maid opened the dining room door and three inveterate early risers were already waiting when Vania came into the room barely five minutes later. 'Hello, George. Going fishin'?' she asked one middle-aged man who hadn't spent a single daylight hour of his holiday doing anything but.

'You betcha, honey.'

Vania settled herself down at an empty table, glad to have a few moments to herself. Yesterday had been a nightmare—a wonderful nightmare. Brett wasn't going to give up. She knew that now. He'd keep on telling her he loved her until she gave in. And she was so desperate to believe him. But, unlike before, this time she didn't have the option of running away.

She looked up in fearful longing as a man sat down beside her, but it wasn't Brett. Vania felt her face fall into cool, neutral lines. 'Hello, Mr Larner,' she said smoothly.

James smiled. 'You don't have to be civil if you don't want to be, Miss McAllen,' he said wearily. 'I dare say you've been raised to think of me as the enemy.'

Vania hadn't. Her father had rarely talked of his erstwhile business partner or his son. James sighed. 'The thing is . . . I need to tell you something . . . and I know you're not going to like it. Or believe it. It's just that . . .' he sighed again, and ran a hand through his hair, the picture of a man with a difficult task in front of him.

Vania's eyes sharpened on him, even as pinpricks of fear and foreboding raised goosebumps all along her arms. 'In that case, I suggest you just get on with it,' she said. 'It's

159

always a good idea to get unpleasant things over with fast.'

James looked at her quickly, sensing no antipathy in her, despite the fighting words. 'All right. I . . . know . . . Brett Carver, much better than you might think,' James began, deliberately stumbling clumsily over his words. 'We're rivals, you know that, and I won't deny it, but I know the man himself, the kind of man he is. I know . . . how ruthless he is. How single-minded.' He paused for breath.

'Surely you're not here to give a character reference, Mr Larner,' Vania said coldly.

'No. I'm just trying to explain why . . . I keep an eye on him,' James said, swallowing hard and looking a shade shame-faced. He saw her eyes sharpen in interest and knew she was hooked. 'When . . . when I heard that you'd been found . . .'

'You're very well informed it seems,' Vania couldn't help but cut in, and James laughed grimly.

'Yes, Miss McAllen, I am,' he said, the epitome of honesty. 'I've found it pays to be. Which is why I know that, after being informed of your whereabouts, Brett Carver had his lawyer meet him at the airport. With papers of some kind.'

Vania shrugged. 'So what? I imagine Brett meets with his lawyers a lot—my father always did.'

'Yes. I know. But, Miss McAllen, I don't

160

think you understand the kind of man you're dealing with. Please don't do anything rash. I know that he can be very persuasive.'

Vania's eyes glittered angrily. 'Be careful, Mr Larner,' she said softly. 'Be very careful.' You're talking about the man I love. But don't trust. Or trust myself with.

James shook his head. 'I knew this would be pointless. But I had to try and warn you. Forget it,' he said abruptly. 'Just . . . forget I ever said anything,' he added, his face a picture of misery. But as he turned and walked away from her, he was feeling anything but miserable.

Vania watched him go, oddly puzzled. So that was James Larner. Somehow, she'd imagined someone more devious. Instead he'd actually seemed remarkably upfront.

She tried to forget his words. But as she climbed aboard the bus an hour later, she was still trying to put the memory of the encounter to one side.

But it just wasn't possible.

When, an hour later, Brett took her hand in his, she still hadn't been able to forget it. As his grey eyes caressed her, wherever she went, she could think only of James Larner's words. I don't think you understand the kind of man you're dealing with. But how could she understand him, when all she wanted to do was believe that he loved her, no matter what?

Oh, she could fight him, yes. Struggle to

keep him at arms' length. And she could also fight herself—make herself not give in. But she didn't think it was going to be possible to fight both Brett Carver and herself at the same time. Harriet took a deep breath as she walked into Frankie's room and closed the door behind her. She'd been putting this moment off for weeks. Now that her 'flu had definitely gone, and work was back to normal, she had no more excuses. She simply had to go through Frankie's things and pack them away.

She started with the clothes first. She knew Frankie had always supported the Salvation Army, so they were no problem. Frankie's books could migrate to the library. Her few ornaments, likewise, would be placed strategically in the public rooms, as a reminder of her. After nearly two hours, the room was all but cleared, and stacks of neatly packed cardboard boxes lined the walls. Harriet sighed and sat on the bed. There was only the little bedside cabinet left to do.

As she lifted out the small box of Frankie's jewellery, she opened it, smiling at the cameo brooch, the few good rings, the gold and sapphire bracelet. Frankie hadn't been much for jewellery. She wondered if she should send them to Powell House. Perhaps it was time to try and bury the hatchet? Harriet sighed and put them to one side. Later. She'd decide later.

She reached into the drawer and

encountered the dry, dusty feeling of paper and pulled out a bundle of letters.

At first her heart hammered, thinking they might be old love-letters, but they were nothing so romantic. Most of them were letters from old, old friends. Some were of a more business-like nature and these she put aside to send on to Gordon Keeler. Then, at the bottom of the pile was a letter that, as soon as she began to read it, sent chills down her spine. It was from her grandfather. The long-dead Lord Powell. Harriet read it quickly, anxious to get it over with.

'My Dear Frankie,

I just thought I'd write to let you know that I'm feeling a bit better after my latest little flirtation with death. I tell you, my dear; there's nothing like a heart attack to get you thinking straight.

And, because I have begun to think straight once more, I've decided to reinstate Mark into my will.'

Here Harriet broke off with a gasp. Of course, her grandfather had died several months before her own father, Mark, was killed. Quickly she read on.

I've had Fanshawe draw up another will, leaving the estates to Arthur—as is only right— but half of the money to Mark. No matter what Grace says, it's only fair. But, speaking of your mother, I haven't told her about this new will, and I must ask you not to do so either, Frankie.

You know your mother. My life, what's left of it, won't be worth living if you do.

I got two of the gardener's lads to witness it, and I've annoyed Fanshawe by insisting on only one copy. I've hidden it very carefully in the Library, and I'll give it to you to keep safe for me, when you next come over. But I'll give you a clue now and advise you to "ask not for whom the bell tolls".

See, your old father still has a sense of humour and adventure left in him!

See you soon, darling daughter,'

It had been signed with an indecipherable flourish.

Harriet let out a long, pent-up breath, hardly aware, until then, that she'd been holding it. What did this all mean? Why had her mother never claimed the inheritance she was due?

Her hand dropped onto her lap, and as it did so, the letter in her hand worked loose and fluttered to the floor. She reached down to pick it up, and saw that on the back, in blue biro, were a few scribbled words in a different hand-writing altogether. Frankie's writing. Quickly, Harriet picked it up and read it. It was just a few disjointed sentences, but Harriet quickly made sense of them.

'Poor Dad—the second heart attack came too soon. The Hemingway novel is there—but no will. Mother must have destroyed it.'

Harriet blinked back tears.

Like herself, Frankie had realised that 'For Whom the Bell Tolls' was a famous novel by Ernest Hemingway, and was where Lord Powell had hidden the new will. She must have gone to the library for it after her father's death and found it gone.

Knowing how bitter Grace Powell was about her youngest son's desertion . . . yes, she would destroy it in a fit of temper.

For a few moments, Harriet was violently angry, but the feeling didn't last long. At least her grandfather had loved her father, and had meant to make it up to him. That was something. But Harriet was only human, and it rankled that a bitter old woman like Lady Grace had robbed her of her father's inheritance. But if the will was destroyed . . . With a sigh, Harriet continued to clear away her aunt's things. But the phrase, 'ask not for whom the bell tolls' kept coming back to her, time and time again. Perhaps it wouldn't hurt, if she could wangle it, to try and search for the will herself? It would be such a good hold to have over Giles Powell, if nothing else.

And, after that devastating kiss of yesterday, she was beginning to think that she'd need all the ammunition she could get. That man was just so much walking dynamite.

Perhaps there was more than one copy of the Hemingway novel in the Powell family library? Perhaps a first edition—kept safely locked away? Harriet shrugged. She'd give it a shot. What did she have to lose?

*   *   *

Vania avoided the packed dining room, unaware that Brett Carver was watching her from the entrance to the bar. She moved quickly up the stairs, hesitating at the turning to her own room. After a grim battle with herself, she carried on up the stairs to the top floor and made her way to Brett's room.

In her pocket she had the pass-key. She didn't usually carry one, but she knew where they were kept, and had helped herself, feeling at once both guilty and fatalistic.

But, once and for all, she had to know . . .

She opened his locked door and walked inside. Instantly, she was aware of him—the tang of his aftershave, the smell of his clothes, the set of shaving things on the dresser.

She walked to the wardrobe first and opened it, delving into all the jacket and trouser pockets, but came up only with an extra wallet and the stub of a airline ticket. She tried the dresser next, blushing over the briefs she found there. Her hands seemed to tingle as they probed through the underwear, but there was nothing but plain white cotton. The next drawer down was a similar story—clothes and nothing but clothes.

She was beginning to feel foolish. Like some kind of overgrown Nancy Drew or junior

Miss Marple. Nevertheless, she felt compelled to check. All her adult life, she'd loved Brett Carver, and believed she could never have him. And so, even as she hated herself for it, she continued to search.

Outside, Brett reached the top of the stairs and walked towards his room. He was a different man from the one who'd arrived at the hotel just a few short days ago. Gone was the tight-skinned look of a haunted man. In his place was a man who whistled under his breath. A man who lived again.

As he walked to the door, he fished in his jeans pocket for a key, anticipating this afternoon. Perhaps, if he could find a little shady nook somewhere, he might steal another kiss . . .

He didn't care how long it took to win her. How often he had to follow where she led. How much patience it needed. He had her in his sights now and he was never going to . . .

He put the key in the lock, turned it, and pushed open the door. And there she was. Waiting for him in his room. Sat on his bed. The sight of her dark-haired vitality zinged into his veins. 'Vania!' he said softly.

Vania lifted her head, her cat-green eyes strangely cloudy. It was only then that he noticed she had some papers on her lap, and that a big brown envelope lay discarded on the carpet at her feet. He frowned, sensing danger, as he carefully shut the door behind him and

167

walked up to her. He was dressed in blue denim jeans and a tight-fitting white T-shirt. The morning had been warm, he smelt of clean maleness and the outdoors.

'You were so sure of me then?' Vania said flatly, and saw him frown. He hunkered down in front of her, resting his hands on his powerful thighs, and Vania quickly looked away. The grey eyes darkened. 'What are you talking about?' he asked quietly, reaching out and taking her icy hands into his own.

'This, Brett,' Vania said, her voice utterly weary and with a tone of defeat in it that Brett had never heard before. He didn't like it—not one bit. This was not like her. Where was the firebrand he loved and understood so well?

'What?' he asked softly, taking the papers from her unresisting fingers. He bent his head and read them rapidly.

As he did so, Vania devoured every expression on his face hungrily. She saw surprise, then anger. No doubt he was angry that she'd found them. What had he planned to do—propose and then drop those papers into her lap as an afterthought on the eve of their wedding? And why couldn't she even feel angry? Even after reading that pre-nup, all she wanted to do was reach out and run her forgers through that dark red hair. Wanted to feel the caress of those grey eyes on her. Wanted him to run his hands over her, stripping her, touching her . . .

She closed her eyes briefly, and when she opened them again, he was looking at her. 'Vania,' he said simply, 'I've never seen these papers before. I didn't have them drawn up. That isn't my signature. I'll send them away to an expert, and prove it to you.' His voice was grim and cold, and yet oddly desperate.

Vania shook her head. Oh, what did it matter? Oh Brett, she thought, agonized. If I could just give you those shares, I would. I don't want them. I never did. And I love you so much I'd give you the moon, if that's what you wanted, and it was mine to give. It's just our tragedy that we have to marry in order for you to get what you want. And that's the one thing I won't do.

'Vania?'

She blinked. 'What?'

You know who's behind this, don't you?' Brett said urgently, shaking the papers in his hand. 'James Larner.'

Vania nodded, but she didn't really believe him, and she didn't care. She was so tired and so much in love.

'Think, Vania,' Brett said, clutching her hands in his own, almost hurting her. 'I came straight here the moment I heard where you were in England. When would I have had time to get these papers drawn up?' His eyes beseeched her. His voice shook in an effort to convince her.

Vania smiled. Poor Brett. He must think she

169

was really gullible if he thought that she couldn't figure out for herself that he'd probably had those papers ready for years—ready for when he found her. And still it didn't matter . . . What they said about women in love is true after all, Vania thought in a daze. They could forgive anything.

And she *did* love him. And need him. And want him . . . And why shouldn't she have him? A militant voice began to make itself heard. She was free, and over twenty-one. Why shouldn't she just have him? This time she didn't fight the urge to reach out to touch him. In fact, she felt that if she didn't touch him she'd perish, on the spot.

His hair was still warm, retaining the heat from the sun outside as she ran her fingers through it at his temples. His cheekbones were hard beneath her fingers. His jaw just slightly prickly—he needed a shave. It was like learning his face all over again—this time by feel, not by sight. Her eyes were avid as they followed the path of her fingertips. Brett froze, his every sense quiveringly alert. Her fingers felt like soft velvet against him. He closed his eyes, his lips opening on a sigh, as she tenderly cupped his face in one palm.

'Oh Brett,' she quavered. 'Oh Brett, I wish . . .' Wish you wanted me as much as I want you. No. No, not even that, she thought, with a blaze of self-revelation. For centuries, women had loved men, knowing that the intensity of

170

their feelings weren't being matched. All she wished for, really, was that he wanted her more than he wanted her shares.

Brett, lost in a sensual dream, opened his eyes. 'What, Vania?' he breathed. 'What do you wish . . .' He'd hoped for this moment for so long. Wanted it so much. Vania, touching him, of her own free will. Vania, looking at him as she was looking at him now, her green eyes glowing with love. He'd give her anything . . .

'Make love to me, Brett,' Vania said simply.

* * *

He let his breath out in a huge sigh, and before his brain had even processed her words properly, his body was reacting. He was already moving up, pushing her back onto the bed, lying on top of her, aware of her harsh, answering, echoing cry of passion ringing in his ears at his sudden, tender assault. Feverishly, and yet taking infinite care, he unfastened the pearly buttons of her lemon yellow dress. His lips followed the path of his fingers, depositing tiny kisses on her tanned skin, his big body shaking hard with the release of so much tension.

Vania ran her hands across his head, crying out as he pushed aside the dress and fastened his mouth on to one, aching, pulsating nipple. Her back arched off the bed, her long dark hair splaying out across the pillows. She pulled

171

on his T-shirt, and he lifted his hands obediently above his head to help her take it off. Instantly, her fingers sought out the dark red hair on his chest, the coarseness of it tickling her sensitive fingertips.

Brett gasped, his head going back, revealing the taut line of the strong column of his neck. Quickly, Vania reached up to kiss him there, loving the way he swallowed hard at the touch of her lips, following the movement of the Adam's Apple in his throat. A hard, hot, pulsating volcano of desire buried deep within her sent red-hot fingers of passion racing outwards, spiralling into a dizzying, obliterating explosion. She dipped her head, kissing the indentations in his shoulders. Then he pushed her back, stripping the dress and panties from her, his big, strong, calloused hands surprisingly gentle on her clothes and on her body.

The buckle of his belt dug into her as he lay across her again, and she quickly slipped her hand down to unbuckle it, her fingers grazing against the hard pulsating bulge of him as she did so. Brett gave a groan and fell back. Vania was like a tigress, wrenching at his belt buckle, yanking the jeans down, pausing only fractionally to admire the primitive pulsating power that was all Brett. He looked just as she'd always known he would look. An aching, empty place deep inside her longed to be filled. She moved atop him, and without

172

hesitation speared herself, crying out as a brief flash of pain, followed by the ultimate satisfaction, crashed over her, through her, around her, carrying her to a place she'd never been before . . . a haven for lovers.

Brett cried out, reaching convulsively to grab the pillows either side of her, clutching the soft feathers in a grip that could have bent iron.

'Vania!' he cried her name as she rode him, giving of himself without a single thought of holding back, as Vania McAllen finally claimed the man she loved.

She thought she would die from the ecstasy of it, but eventually, long moments later, she discovered that she was cradled in his arms, her whole body pulsating in the afterglow of climax. The world came back only slowly. But it was a world changed forever by the touch of one man.

CHAPTER ELEVEN

Harriet sighed as she sorted through the afternoon mail. It had been a hectic day, and Vania too, she noticed, was beginning to look a little wilted around the edges. She glanced up as the door opened. 'Yes, Lydia? No crisis with Chef's snails I hope?'

Lydia grinned. 'Nothing like that, Harriet. I

just wondered if you'd like a cup of tea?'

'Bless you,' Harriet smiled and began to open the mail. Vania came in a moment or two later, and slumped in the chair opposite her. 'Hi.'

Harriet frowned. 'You look like death warmed over,' she said bluntly, and Vania grinned widely.

'Thanks a lot! I'm just having a bad day, that's all.'

Harriet nodded sympathetically. 'We all get them once in a while,' she agreed. And thought about Giles Powell.

'Oh no!' Harriet wailed, just as Lydia Brack came in with the cup of tea. She was reading a neatly typed letter and shaking her head woefully. 'This is all I need. The annual health inspector's visit is scheduled for next Thursday.'

'Never mind,' Lydia piped up. 'You know we never have any trouble with inspections.'

Harriet sighed. 'Better inform the staff, Lydia. Thursday is D-day.' But Lydia was right—she wasn't really worried about the health inspector's visit. It was just one more hassle that she could do without right now . . .

*   *   *

James Larner looked across the river and thrust his hands into his pockets. Harriet certainly had a nice little place here. They'd

174

have to find someone competent to run it for them, when they left for the States. For James had no doubts that when he left here, Harriet would be coming with him.

And, thinking of Harriet, he'd have to find her and invite her to the big ball he'd been hearing so much about, due to be held this Saturday in Oxford. He was just moving past one of the open windows, when the sound of Harriet's voice made him hesitate. He peered into the nearest room and saw Vania McAllen get up and walk to the door.

'OK. Have a bath and relax for a bit,' he heard Harriet say. 'If you want—have dinner in your room.'

'Thanks, I think I'll take you up on that. You're a pal,' Vania called, disappearing out the door. Harriet continued to sort through some papers, and all he could see of her was the top of her platinum-blonde head.

Suddenly, out of the corner of his eye, he saw a familiar figure walking through the rose garden. Instantly, James seized the advantage. He moved just far enough away from the window so that Harriet couldn't overhear him, and stepped deliberately in front of Brett Carver as he walked along the gravel path that skirted the hotel.

'Hi Carver. How's it going?' he asked cheerfully.

'Things are fine, thanks James,' Brett said coolly.

175

'Oh? I thought Vania looked a little . . . distracted this afternoon.'

Brett's hands clenched into fists by his sides, and he forced them slowly open again. 'Miss McAllen to you, Larner,' Brett said, his lazy Kansas drawl as hard-edged as a knife.

James laughed. 'Oh come on, Brett. Vania and I aren't so formal. Why, we're almost friends now.'

Brett took a quick step towards the other man. He couldn't help it. He'd always been ultra-protective where Vania was concerned.

'You leave Vania alone, Larner,' Brett gritted.

Deliberately leading Brett towards the open window, James strolled along beside him, his hands slipped casually into his trouser pockets. He only hoped Harriet was still inside. 'Oh? Don't you think that's up to her, chum?'

Brett took a few steps closer to him. 'Don't think I don't know about that little scam with the forged pre-nup you hid in my room,' Brett snarled. If you try anything else like that—I'll haul your sorry ass into court.'

James made sure a particularly confident smile crossed his face. 'I'm sorry,' he grinned tauntingly in Brett's face, even though his voice sounded genuinely placatory, 'but I don't know what you're talking about.' And he reached up and prodded Brett in the chest with one hard finger. 'Chum.'

Brett snarled, grabbing James by the lapels

and thrusting him back. 'Listen to me, you sickening little leech. If you don't keep away from me and Vania I'll . . .!'

* * *

'What on earth's going on here?' The cold, hard, utterly English voice cut through the afternoon air like a knife.

Brett's eyes flickered in surprise and looked past James Larner's taunting face to find those of the beautiful blonde owner of the hotel looking back at him. Her violet eyes were distinctly hostile. 'Mr Carson,' she said primly, 'I don't appreciate brawls in my hotel. Kindly let go of Mr Larner, this instant.'

With his back to her, James was free to grin jauntily at Brett. Brett's eyes narrowed. His grip on James's lapels tightened ominously, but then he released them. And forced a small smile on to his face. 'I apologise Miss Jensen,' he said smoothly. 'And I assure you that whatever differences Mr Larner and myself have, will soon be sorted out.' The look in his grey eyes as he smiled made James gulp.

'Good,' Harriet said briskly. 'In the meantime, I'd appreciate it if you could act in a more restrained manner.'

Brett looked at her, and couldn't help but smile. She sounded so coolly fierce. He could understand why Vania liked her so much. Harriet blinked, surprised by the sudden

177

friendly warmth in his eyes. Once again, her instincts told her that, in spite of the evidence to the contrary, this was the sort of man you could trust. But, unless she was mistaken, there was something very . . . interesting, going on between her friend and this complex, puzzling man. But it was none of her business, and she'd wait until Vania decided to confide in her.

She inclined her head graciously. 'Very well. We'll say no more about it.'

James Larner watched Brett walk away, then turned back to the window, rubbing his neck wryly. 'Sorry about that. And I hardly came off looking like a he-man, did I?' He sounded like a rueful small boy. He knew most women were against violence, and was hoping against hope that that little show would have made Harriet warm to him.

Harriet smiled. 'I don't think many men would come out looking good when compared to Mr Carson,' she said honestly, pleasing James not at all. Except Giles, she thought suddenly.

Annoyed at herself for not wanting to believe the worst of the red-headed American, and even more annoyed at herself for the way her mind used even the slightest excuse to dwell upon Giles Powell, Harriet smiled winningly at James. 'Come on. You look like you could do with a drink.'

His eyes lit up as Harriet joined him. He

178

reached out a hand for her as she approached, and after the merest hesitation, she took it. So it was that they were hand-in-hand as they walked into the bar.

Giles Powell watched them enter, his dark eyes turning almost black at the sight of their carefree but intimate handholding. He lifted his drink to his lips and took a healthy swallow, as he shot James Larner a glowering look.

He was still feeling wrong-footed from yesterday.

What the hell had possessed him to kiss her like that? He, above all men, should know about gold-diggers. They wanted the good life, but didn't want to work for it. And that meant netting a rich man.

But, a little voice piped up, she does work darned hard here at the hotel. Even so, if Harriet Jensen thought she could seduce him into surrendering his rights to Windrush Shallows, she was damned well mistaken. Except . . .

Surely, she hadn't instigated yesterday's fiasco? No. If she were out to get him, she'd hardly be concentrating on the American now. Unless she was trying to make him jealous, he thought savagely. Hah! Fat chance of that.

Just then, James leaned closer to Harriet and said something to her that made her laugh, and the hand holding Giles's vodka and tonic shook. Slowly he stood up and moved closer.

179

'I was wondering if you were going to this dance I keep hearing about?' he heard James Larner say.

Giles knew about the Summer Ball—he'd already bought two tickets and had been waiting for the right opportunity to ask Harriet to go with him.

'Well, I'd like to,' Harriet said hesitatingly, 'but I don't have a ticket—I think they're all sold out.'

James smiled and reached into his jacket pocket. 'Tah-dah!' he whipped out two tickets like a conjurer. Harriet laughed.

What a poser, Giles thought savagely as he walked past the American. Harriet glanced up, her face freezing, as her wide dark eyes encountered those of Giles, who gave her a mocking look.

Then, for what felt like an eternity, neither of them could look away from each other. Harriet felt the whole world disappear—the bar, the chatter, the clink of glasses, James—everything just receded and no longer mattered. All that she could see were Giles's dark eyes. The mocking curve of his lips. The tall, elegant, solid male form standing just inches from her. Her breath faltered.

Giles. for his part, found himself swaying towards her. Memories of the way her lips had felt under his rushed into his mind, chasing every other thought out of his mind.

In a single instant, one thought fused them

together.

I love him, Harriet told herself. I love her, Giles realised.

With a wrench of loss, Giles turned away and carried on walking. Harriet hunched over her drink, as if seeking its protection, for she realised, her whole world had changed in the winking of an eye, and nobody else, including James, had noticed.

'So, would you do me the honour of coming to the Ball with me?' James asked cheerfully.

'What?' she replied numbly. 'Oh. Yes, of course,' she said. Was she smiling? She hoped so. 'Yes, I'd be glad to,' she confirmed, her voice, amazingly, sounding cheerful and carefree.

What *was* she going to do!

*　　　*　　　*

In her room, Lydia Brack pulled out a ruled notepad and reached for a biro. She wasn't much of a letter writer, but Lady Grace had asked her to keep in touch. It wasn't much to ask, Lydia thought, after all the poor old soul seemed really concerned about everyone at the hotel. As she came to the end of her rambling note, she remembered Harriet's comment about the health inspector's visit. With a small grunt, she bent down and laboriously added a postscript.

P.S. The health inspector's coming next

Thursday, so I expect we'll all have to give everything a bit of extra spit and polish. Still, it means I'll get some overtime, and that always comes in handy, don't it? Miss Jensen's really generous with things like that, so I never complain.

She'd post it on her way home and hope it cheered the old duck up.

In his room, Giles Powell paced, ignoring the sounds of gaiety and laughter emanating from downstairs. He'd skipped dinner, having suddenly lost his appetite, and as he walked to the window and pulled aside the curtain, watching the rising moonlight shimmering on the River Windrush below, he shook his head. He didn't love her. Of course he didn't.

It had just seemed, in that one moment . . . but it was only her beauty, her extraordinary, damned beauty, which had made him feel so stunned. Who was he kidding? The woman had him hooked. He was just wriggling around, trying to escape. But that didn't mean the game was over yet. Like hell it was! And if she thought otherwise, she was in for a surprise!

He walked to the phone and grimly dialled a number. Harriet Jensen wasn't the only beautiful woman he knew. And she was not the only one who'd be going to the Oxford Summer Ball with a partner on her arm. 'Hello? Laura? Yes, it's me. What are you doing on Saturday night?'

CHAPTER TWELVE

When Vania had first arrived, Harriet had often gone on some of the jaunts she'd organized, just to check out for herself the quality of the tours, and to make sure that the 'entertainments' the hotel provided were adequate.

Nowadays, of course, she rarely ever went out on the charabanc. But that Friday morning she awoke with the unusual but strong need to get away from the hotel for a little while. The weather looked set for another blazing day, so she reached for a feather-light white dress, and teamed it with simple sandals. She quickly put her hair up in a French pleat, and added the merest touch of make-up. A few moments later she tapped on Vania's door and found her friend dressed and ready. 'Mind if I tag along today?' Harriet asked. 'I feel like a day out.'

'Sure,' Vania said at once. She too was feeling restless.

'Vania,' Harriet asked quietly. 'Is there something I should know about our red-haired guest from Boston?'

Vania dropped the make-up bag she was holding and the contents scattered everywhere. Harriet watched the other girl's face and could have kicked herself. 'I'm not

183

trying to pry,' she added quickly. 'Really I'm not. But last night I had to break up a fight between him and James Larner.'

Vania's head shot up. 'A fight? You mean they were quarrelling.'

Harriet smiled grimly. 'No. I mean your red-headed Mr Carson or Carver or whatever his name is, had James by the throat, and he looked, well, the only way I can describe it is murderous.'

Vania shook her head. 'Of all the stupid . . .'

'Am I wrong,' Harriet murmured, 'or did you know Brett before you came to England?'

Vania grinned wearily. 'Spot on.'

'Things didn't work out?' she asked sympathetically.

Vania began to laugh. She couldn't help it, but she quickly brought herself under control. 'You could say that,' she said drolly.

Harriet, who wasn't fooled by that laughter, sighed. 'Men,' she said flatly.

At that, Vania glanced up quickly. 'Now that sounds familiar. A touch of despair, mixed with a splash of anger, iced with bitterness, with a just a shake of need, rounded off in a glass full of wistfulness.'

Harriet smiled. 'Quite a cocktail, isn't it?' she said.

Vania shrugged. 'Mine's called a Brett Special. What's yours called?'

'A Giles Sling.'

Vania blinked. 'You mean Giles as in

Powell?'

'Hmmm. He's here.'

'Here in the hotel?' Vania squeaked.

Harriet nodded. 'Registered under the name of Browning. You've probably seen him around.'

Vania did a quick mental run-down of their current guests, and gave a long slow whistle. 'Not that guy with the black hair and dark eyes? Harriet, he's gorgeous. All the maids are talking about him. Evelyn had to break up a near-riot yesterday morning, over who got to clean his room.'

Harriet laughed. 'It surprises me not,' she drawled. Vania frowned. 'Harriet, is that wise?'

This time it was Harriet's turn to laugh. 'Wise? What's wisdom got to do with it? Is it wise to love your Brett?'

Vania's lips twisted. *'Touché.'*

For a while the two women sat in a companionable silence.

'Let's face it girl,' Vania said at last, 'you and I are well and truly up the creek.'

'With paddles in short supply.'

Vania laughed. 'You know, I thought that you and James Larner . . .?' she probed delicately.

Harriet shrugged. 'No. He was just a handy piece of camouflage. I'm going to have to tell him . . . well I think he's getting the wrong idea . . .' she tailed off helplessly. 'Oh damn!' she snapped with a sudden show of

185

uncharacteristic temper. 'Everything's messed up.'

Vania gave a short bark of laughter. She knew just how her friend felt. 'Still, I'm glad you're not serious about James. I wouldn't trust him, Harriet, if I were you.'

Harriet frowned. 'Isn't there some history between him and your Brett?' she asked.

Vania shrugged. 'Yes, but that's not what I meant. I'm not sure that James is quite what he seems.'

Harriet sighed. 'Are men ever?'

Vania groaned in agreement.

Harriet chose a seat near the back of the charabanc, and with all the windows open and a pleasant cooling breeze fluttering in, the bus left Windrush Shallows dead on time for once.

Because he'd got on last and sat at the front, she didn't realise Giles Powell was on board until they arrived at Moreton-in-Marsh. Harriet waited until everyone else was off before walking to the front, and as she came down the steps was surprised when Vania came up behind her and hissed warningly, 'He's here'.

And out of the corner of her eye she saw a familiar figure step from under the shade of the big oak tree. Harriet quickly looked away, but not before the dark, mocking eyes had damaged her ability to breathe properly.

'Oh no,' Harriet groaned.

Varia turned and found Brett Carver

leaning against the front of the bus, watching her.

'Yes,' Vania said. 'I know.'

It didn't take long for the group to separate. The avid gardeners—of which there were many—headed straight for the plants, whilst the others headed towards the aviaries.

Vania cast a glance behind her. Brett's level grey eyes looked back. Since that incredible night when he'd finally become her lover, he was more than ever determined never to let her out of his sight. Not until he was sure she knew what she meant to him. Knew that she was life itself to him.

'What are we going to do?' Harriet's soft, despairing voice jerked Vania's eyes away from Brett's and back to her friend.

She took in the dangerous, dark presence of Giles Powell under the tree. He really was gorgeous. In a vastly different way from Brett, of course. Together, Vania mused, Harriet and Giles Powell would be perfect. What a contrast! He so dark, she so fair. Both so breathtakingly physically attractive. Vania found herself wondering what sort of children they'd have. She shook her head.

'Mine won't leave me,' she said flatly. And wondered what she'd do if he ever did. She cast Brett a look that was both longing and fulminating. She knew it was only a matter of time before they made love again—and again, and again. Now that she'd opened the floodgates, there was no turning back.

It was time to face up to facts. She loved Brett Carver more than anything else in the world. He meant even more to her than life itself . . . But where did that leave them? Where did it leave her?

Harriet shot her friend a puzzled look. 'Is it that bad?' Vania ran an harassed hand through her hair. 'It's—complicated,' she said at last. Harriet looked at Giles. Did she hate him or love him? 'Yes,' she said softly. Then sighed. 'Well, we can't stay here forever,' she continued, trying to at least get some kind of grasp on normality.

Vania turned and glanced around. 'No. I'll take mine to the arboretum. It's quiet in there and we need to talk. I want to ask him about that fight, for a start,' she said ominously. Harriet nodded. 'OK. I suppose I'll wander around the Falconry. What time do we leave?'

'Three o'clock. See you back at the bus.' She glanced at Giles Powell. 'And good luck.'

Harriet reached out and took her friend's hand as she passed. 'You too,' she said.

Brett followed Vania the instant she headed off. He looked with curiosity at the man still standing under the oak as he did so, noticing that he only had eyes for the beautiful Harriet. A strange look of comradeship passed between them as their eyes met. As if they sensed that they were both trapped in the same snare. But whereas Brett was where he

188

wanted to be, the Englishman looked deeply unhappy.

Harriet watched her friend go out of sight then her eyes flickered and moved back to the man under the tree. He was dressed in black trousers and a dark green shirt open to mid-chest. A summer breeze lifted the black wings of hair off his forehead. He reminded her of a black panther, which would growl or purr, depending on whether it was confronted by mate or prey. But, which was she?

And which did she want to be?

She turned suddenly, heading diagonally across the field, very much aware that he followed. Stalking her, just like the big cat he reminded her of.

Inside the wooden building she paid her fee, then was faced with open-fronted booths, each holding a tethered bird of prey. Small wooden perches a few inches off the ground supported kestrels, buzzards, hawks and dozing owls.

The birds watched her with disinterested, unblinking avian eyes as she walked slowly around. A huge eagle-owl, with lovely bright eyes and feathers for ears, watched her and winked one eyelid. Harriet smiled.

Watching the natural delight on her lovely, oh so perfect face, Giles felt himself finally surrender to the inevitable. He loved, and was in love.

Looking up, Harriet's eyes once again met those of her enemy. And found in them a look

189

that was at once both utterly unfamiliar and yet totally expected. She knew, if she had a mirror, that she'd see exactly the same look in her own eyes. Love.

But what happened now?

CHAPTER THIRTEEN

Vania glanced across at Brett as she pulled her car to a halt in one of Oxford's many small side-streets. Streetlights illuminated the famous 'dreaming spires' and domes.

'It's a lovely city,' Brett said.

'Yes, it is,' Vania agreed. 'The Ball is being held in a hotel just a few minutes from here. You always could get tickets for the best show in town,' she added wryly, and got out of the car.

Brett stood watching her lock up. Vania looked stunning. She wore a scarlet dress that left her shoulders and most of her legs completely bare. Her hair was a mass of ringlets and a garnet and pearl choker encircled her slim white throat.

'My life without you has been hell,' he said abruptly, his voice thick with emotion.

Vania turned abruptly away. 'Don't,' she said sharply. 'You know I hate when you talk like that.'

'You never used to have any problems with

the truth,' he said flatly, as he quickly began to walk away.

'The truth is, Brett,' Vania responded shakily as she felt him move up beside her, 'that my dad wanted us to marry just to secure his empire.'

'Your father knew I loved you,' Brett corrected her. 'He must have known about his heart condition, and wanted to make sure you were looked after if anything happened to him.'

Vania bit her lip. 'Looked after by you, you mean?' she asked.

The scent of night-flowering stock and lavender filled the air as Brett took her arm and tucked it gently under his.

'Don't you want to be looked after by me, Vania?' he asked softly. 'Would it really be so bad?'

'I can look after myself,' she snapped.

'Yes. I can see that. I'm not denying that you're a brave, independent, clever woman. But then, I always knew you were something special. Even as a teenager.'

Vania sighed heavily. 'Brett, let's not go over old ground, hmm? Not tonight? Let's just dance and enjoy ourselves.'

Brett smiled. 'So long as you save the last dance for me.'

Vania stopped as a college clock somewhere chimed the quarter hour. She looked up at him, his craggy face shadowed in the fading light, the overhead gleam of a streetlight turning his dark red hair into a halo of ruby around his head. 'I will,' she promised huskily.

Brett's head slowly lowered to hers, and their lips met, clung, parted, met and clung again.

Some half-drunk locals whooped as they moved around them on the pavement. Neither of them heard the raucous, good-natured cat-calls.

*　　　*　　　*

In the hotel foyer, James Larner reached up to take the black wrap from Harriet's shoulders. She was dressed in deep purple satin so dark it was almost black. The halter necked bodice criss-crossed her breasts, the skirt hung in straight lines to her ankles, with a long slit up one side which revealed the smooth, creamy-white skin of calf, knee and lower thigh. Her hair was loose, her jewellery a pair of long silver earrings, with a matching chain around her neck.

'It sounds like all the fun is coming from over there,' he murmured, glancing past open double-glass doors to the ballroom straight ahead. 'Drink? Or dance?' he asked softly.

'Oh . . . A drink please,' she answered, and they followed the arrows that led them past the warm, crowded ballroom and out onto a terrace. They'd arrived late, and it was already dark, but a full moon and pretty multi-coloured Chinese lanterns illuminated the gardens just beyond the terrace.

Roses, lilies, lavender and big white daisies danced in the evening breeze. Along the stone-flagged terrace were little tables, each with its own champagne bucket and flutes. James led her to a quiet, ivy-covered nook, before handing her a glass. 'To us,' he answered softly, clinking the glasses together.

Harriet's eyes flickered. 'James,' she began softly. 'I need to tell you something . . .'

Long white billowing curtains blew outwards from the ballroom, and amongst the dark shadows inside, Harriet didn't see the black, tuxedo-clad figure that lounged against one wall. Giles Powell had arrived with Laura Dixon, an actress. Laura was the kind of woman who needed a bevy of admirers around her, and had long since left him free to prowl the halls looking for Harriet. Once he'd noted her arrival, with her tame millionaire in tow, he'd shamelessly followed them. Now he watched them out on the terrace, experiencing a brand of masochism he'd never expected to find within himself.

It should be him sipping champagne with her out in the moonlight. Every atom that comprised his being—his heart, body and soul—was telling him so. She looked so glorious—a combination of light and darkness. With the orchestra playing only a very soft waltz, he could hear every word they were saying.

'You know, I never thought women like you existed in real life,' James said. 'Harriet,' he said softly, leaning closer, 'I've never been in love before. I wan . . .'

Harriet gave a soft cry of regret. 'Oh James, no. We hardly know one another.'

Giles, whose heart had given a lurch at the American's words, found himself almost wilting in relief at her lack-luster response.

James frowned. 'Harriet,' he said, his voice cracking a little now. 'Surely you must know how I feel?'

Harriet stared up at him dismayed. 'James. all we've done is have a few drinks together! Look, I'm sorry if you've . . . if I've . . . if things seemed . . .' Harriet shook her head.

'Stop!' James muttered. 'Stop right there.' This couldn't be happening. No way. No way was she turning him down.

Inside, Giles stiffened, sensing the mood turning ugly.

'Look, James,' Harriet tried again, 'you're a very nice man, and I'm very flattered you should be . . . well . . . attracted to me, but James, there can never be anything between us.'

James flushed. 'No, you look, Harriet,' he snarled, his voice colder and nastier than Harriet had ever heard it. He reached out to grasp her wrist as Harriet took a surprised step

194

backwards. 'I'm not used to women turning me down, and I . . .'

'Then I suggest you *get* used to it,' an Arctic male voice suddenly cut across the balmy night air, making both Harriet and James jump in surprise and glance around.

Giles Powell strolled lazily on to the terrace. Harriet's heart lifted. He was dressed in a tuxedo, the suit lending his already lean and handsome dark good looks an almost unbelievable air of power.

James stared at him, recognizing him briefly as a fellow guest at Windrush Shallows. 'Butt out,' James snarled. 'This is a private conversation.'

Giles smiled. It wasn't much of a smile; a mere twist of the lips, but James paled slightly. 'I think you should let go of the lady,' Giles said pleasantly, glancing pointedly at Harriet's wrist, 'before I make you.' Once again there was nothing in the voice but pleasant advice, but it sent chills down James's spine. James slowly released Harriet's hand, and she rubbed her aching wrist absently. Giles noticed it, however, and his lips tightened ominously.

'Harriet,' James said, turning to her, 'I want you to tell this . . . friend of yours to leave. We have to talk.'

'I'm not her friend,' Giles said softly, speaking no more than the simple truth. 'I'm the man she's going to marry.' Harriet gasped.

James's head swivelled around, taking in the

way the tall Englishman was watching him, his hands hanging loosely by his side, still with that same faint smile on his face. Nothing about him looked obviously threatening. But James felt infinitely threatened. 'Oh,' he said, instantly seizing on a way to save face. 'Oh. I . . . I didn't realise,' he said at last. He took a step back. 'In that case, of course . . .'

He glanced at Harriet, who was gaping at Giles in stunned silence, and then back again to the Englishman. 'Look, I still have some business in England, but I should be leaving the hotel soon,' he said, annoyed to find a pleading quality had crept into his voice. But something told him he shouldn't mess with this man. Not even to salve his wounded pride.

'Fine,' Giles said. It was a dismissal if ever James had heard one, and an ugly, embarrassed flush stained his skin as he turned and hurried away.

Giles turned back to Harriet, noting her stunned expression.

'Well, I can't say I think much of your taste in men,' he drawled, nodding at the hastily departing figure.

Harriet, realising her mouth was still hanging open, promptly shut it. 'I think . . .' she said, her voice emerging as nothing more than a whisper, 'I . . .'

'Want to dance?' Giles asked. 'Come on then.'

And before she could even think of

something to say, she found herself swept along into the ballroom. A big ball chandelier cast diamonds of light across the swaying bodies already inside. Harriet had a brief glimpse of Vania and Brett, locked in each other's arms, before the crowd swallowed them up again. The orchestra was playing another waltz, as smooth and slow and sweet as pouring syrup and suddenly Harriet was in his arms. And found that they fit.

Her head rested neatly against his shoulder. His hand rested perfectly in the middle of her back, the warmth of his palm sending ripples of awareness right the way through her. Her breasts, tight against his chest, tingled happily. Her legs, nudging his as they moved to the music, felt pleasantly unsteady.

For his part, Giles was very much aware of the smooth touch of her hair under his chin as he leaned his head down towards her, and the scent of her perfume—a combination of flowers and citrus, wafted over him. The sweet sound of violin, cello and flute, moved with them across the floor, a cocoon of sound that beat in time to their hearts and the sound of their breathing. Harriet closed her eyes. It felt so good here. In the dark with the music, the man, and the moment. Much too good to fight.

And when it was over, and they went back to the terrace, the moment went with them. Giles led her down the steps and onto the grassy paths between azalea and rhododendron bushes, where they had only the light of the full moon to guide them.

The sound of music and partying guests drifted further and further away behind them. In the distance, Giles saw the gleam of silver that was moonlight on water. The river.

Harriet, her hand in his, moved with him to a curve in the bank, where bushes screened them from the hotel, and the overhanging tender green screen of a weeping willow hid them from any eyes that might glance across the river from the other side. Without a word, Giles took off his jacket and laid it on the dry, still warm grass. He sank down, his hand tugging on hers and bringing her down with him.

With a sigh, Harriet lay back, her long white hair splaying around her on the grass as she looked up into the night sky.

She could see through the hanging green of the willows the velvet, dark night sky, the diamond pinpoints of distant stars and, away to her left, the shining clear white light that was the moon. And then his face. Dark wings of hair falling down, casting deep shadows over his midnight eyes and the sharp angles of his cheekbones and jaw.

Harriet sighed and reached up to brush the hair away, but the moment she dropped her hands, it swung down again, like black silk. She felt him tense at her touch, then sigh softly.

He was half-leaning over her, his hands

either side of her head, his straightened elbows bending as he slowly lowered his head towards her. 'This is insane,' Harriet said.

'I know.' His lips were only a hair's-breadth from hers.

'I love you,' she said, her words a mere whisper of regret and need.

'I know.'

'You love me too,' she added fiercely. 'Don't try and deny it.'

'I wasn't going to.' As he spoke, so close were they, she could feel the movement of his lips against hers.

'Giles,' she sighed. And then he was kissing her.

Shockwaves, like the silent underground ripples of earthquake tremors, spread through her, making her melt inside. She felt her whole body change—no longer hers to command, no longer even listening to the signals from her own brain, but to the signals from his body.

His hand, resting against her waist, had her shivering. Her lips were aware of every tiny movement in his—the pressure changes, the tiny sounds of their mouths as they moved, opened further, tongues delving, finding each other, touching, dancing . . .

Harriet moaned. It came from somewhere deep down inside her, and was at once primitive and seductive, making Giles quickly lift his head. He was breathing hard—like he'd just run a marathon. His eyes glittered above hers.

'Make that sound again,' he demanded harshly. It was the most wonderful sound he'd ever heard.

Harriet shook her head. 'I don't know if I can.'

Giles's hand moved from her waist, across her flat, quivering stomach and up, his fingers slipping beneath one criss-cross swathe of material to cup her breast.

Her nipple pressed hard into his palm and she moaned again.

Giles dragged in a harsh breath of delight. If he lived to be a hundred, he'd never get tired of that sound.

His hands pushed aside the rest of the dark silk and the summer breeze briefly whispered across her bare skin before his mouth gently closed around the rose-pink bud of her nipple.

Harriet gasped, head thrown back against the grass, her spine arching off the ground as her whole body responded to the mastery of his touch. She hardly felt him push the straps down her arms, and slide the dress from her hips. Underneath, she was only wearing brief silk white panties, which somehow magically melted away. When she opened her eyes he was taking off his shirt, the moonlight turning his shoulders silver, and darkening the smooth planes of his chest. His dark eyes were glinting like jet, and he shrugged the shirt aside, tossing it carelessly away to lie on the grass beside him. Then he was moving over her again, claiming her. This time bare skin moved against bare skin and Harriet moaned again. She loved the way the sound made him look— as if she'd just given him the world.

His belt buckle felt hard against her thigh, but then his hands were there, undoing it, shrugging gracefully out of even that garment until they lay together completely naked beneath the weeping willow and the Oxford moonlight. 'Harriet,' he said hoarsely, his lips on her throat, her neck, her ears, his tongue playing around the shaft of the earring, tasting metal and flesh. Harriet gasped as his hands moved down her, tracing the contours of ribs and sternum, hip-bone and thigh. Her own hands explored his back, the ridge of his spine, the smooth, silken feel of him. Lovers' lessons in Braille.

When his leg nudged hers apart, she opened her eyes quickly. 'Giles . . .' She needed to warn him.

But then his lips were on hers, and he was moving across her, using his weight to both cushion her, and press her down, in an age-old mating ritual. Harriet's body leapt, as if it had always known this man, and how his lovemaking would feel.

She felt him enter her, the hot, hard, pulsating length of him filling her. When he met the slight resistance of her virginity, his eyes shot open, but then her hand was against his buttocks, greedy to pull him ever harder into her, and this time it was his turn to moan as her body, so tightly clamped around him, drew him down into the very depths of ecstasy. He threw his head back, his face a taut picture of near-agony, as Harriet rose to meet his thrusts, her fit young body following wherever he led.

She felt the spiralling heat of climax claim her for the first time, and didn't moan but cried out, the passionate sound echoing across the river and drifting up towards the stars. Giles felt his own body and mind collapse, and then he was gasping against her, his cheek cushioned against her breast, her hand tenderly stroking the damp black hair from his face.

For a long time they simply lay there, helplessly and hopelessly entwined, body and soul.

*   *   *

Inside, they began to play the last waltz. It was nearly two a.m., and Brett Carver pulled Vania close. 'I want you,' he said softly. 'I want to make love to you again.'

In his arms, Vania shuddered. 'Yes,' she agreed simply. And leading him from the ballroom, she took him back to her car, and then back to her room at Windrush Shallows.

The time for running was finally over.

By the river, Giles lay looking down into Harriet's face. 'Harriet,' he said softly. 'I meant what I said. About marrying you.'

Harriet froze and turned her face away. 'I don't think that's such a good idea.'

She was so utterly different from what he'd expected her to be, that he was only now beginning to learn who the true Harriet Jensen was. Slowly, inexorably, Giles made her turn around and look at him. 'Will you marry me?'

Harriet shook her head. 'No.'

Giles laughed. He couldn't help it. Everything had been turned on its head, and he was feeling giddy. 'Why not?'

'Your grandmother . . .'

He sighed wearily. 'I'll talk to her. I'm not giving you up, Harriet.' His voice sounded as hard as granite. 'Come over tomorrow. We'll tackle her together.'

Suddenly, like an evil genie, into Harriet's mind flashed a picture of her grandfather's letter. Hadn't she wanted to find an excuse to visit Powell House and search the library? Well, here it was, being offered to her on a plate. And she didn't even want to think about it.

Betrayal and counter-betrayal! This was getting so incredibly complicated! She shook her head, feeling like someone being torn in half.

Oh Giles.' she wailed softly. 'No. No, no, no.'

But by the time they'd dressed, kissed and kissed again, she'd said yes.

He was to pick her up tomorrow at three o'clock. Grace, Lady Powell was to have a visitor.

CHAPTER FOURTEEN

James Larner dialled a number, and waited as it began to ring. And, across the Atlantic, in a residence located in Nob Hill in San Francisco, a maid answered.

'Mrs Glennister please,' James said affably. It was nearly two o'clock, and he couldn't wait to quit this place for good. Why the hell hadn't Harriet said she had a six-foot, menacing fiancé hovering in the wings?

'Yes?' A wary voice, full of fake Southern charm, suddenly filled his ears, and James gratefully turned his thoughts from his loss of Harriet Jensen to something much more satisfying.

'Rita-Sue Glennister? Hi there. My name's Larner. James Larner. You don't know me, Rita-Sue, but we have something in common.'

'Oh?'

'We both want something. In your case,

money and revenge. In my case, power. I've been thinking, and I've come up with a way that we can both get what we want. Now, don't you think that's clever of me?'

'Verah clevah,' Rita-Sue purred. 'What d'y'all have in mind?'

James grinned. 'I understand your divorce is running into a sticky patch?' Even over the impersonal wire, James could feel the temperature drop radically. 'I've never met your husband,' he went on quickly, 'but I'm "interested" shall we say, in what he and his company are up to.'

'Business. That's all yew gentlemen evah think about.'

James smiled. 'True, alas. That's why Robert had you sign that pesky little old prenup. I understand it's causing your lawyer all sorts of problems,' he added sympathetically.

Rita-Sue let rip with some very unladylike epithets.

'So, I'd be right in thinking that you wouldn't mind giving good of Robert a taste of his own medicine, and hitting him where it hurts then?' James said, when she'd finished. 'Not to mention earning yourself a nice little bonus into the bargain?'

'What do I have to do?'

James laughed. 'Oh, Rita-Sue, honey, hardly anything at all.'

'How do I know you're not just leading me on?'

James sighed. 'Look, phone up Jennifer Van Courten in Boston and ask her what she knows about James Larner. She'll tell you all you need to know—including the fact that I'm half-owner of McAllen's.'

'The car dealership people?' Rita-Sue squeaked. 'Robert's company deals in limousines,' she said thoughtfully.

'Yes,' James said grimly. 'I know.' Brett Carver was currently negotiating to take it over and set up his own empire. And if Vania McAllen ever learned that Carver didn't need her shares, the wedding would be tomorrow. The only thing James had going for him was the fact that no contracts with Glennister's company were yet signed—and the takeover might yet become a hostile one. He already had his men working on those shareholders who were against the bid, but he didn't have enough votes yet. Which meant he had to attack on another front. Which was where the dubious charms of Rita-Sue Glennister came into it.

'I'll tell you what. You ask around about me, satisfy yourself as to my credentials, and I'll call you back later. How does that sound?' he asked pleasantly. 'And think about what you could do with a hundred thousand in cash.'

'Yeah, but what d'yah want me to do for it, Mr Larner?'

James smiled. 'Why, nothing more arduous than to fly over to England and tell a certain lady a few home truths.'

'Home truths?' she echoed, puzzled. 'Oh, you mean lies.'

James grinned. 'Yeah, Rita-Sue, I mean lies. You know how to act like a wronged woman, don't you?'

'Mister, for a hundred thousand I can tell lies and act any part you want, good enough to win me an Oscar.'

*   *   *

Harriet slowly and reluctantly slipped out of the big Rover, as Giles stood holding the door open for her. She looked around at the impressive Powell mansion and Giles saw tension flicker at the back of her lovely eyes.

He held her hand, giving her fingers a quick, reassuring squeeze. 'Don't worry. She won't bite, you know.'

Harriet smiled, but wasn't so sure. 'I remember the last time I came here,' she said, biting her lip worriedly. 'I was half expecting you to throw me out by the scruff of the neck. And for your grandmother to cheer you on.'

Giles's smile vanished. 'Yes. Well, we didn't have the true picture about you then.' He paused. 'I've been wary of beautiful women since I was badly let down by one.' At Harriet's puzzled look he elaborated, 'I was married, very briefly, in my early twenties. Julie was stunning to look at, sweet, innocent and madly

207

in love with me—or so I believed. I was young and naïve and thought I loved her, too. Now I know it was simple sexual infatuation on my part. On Julie's part, well, it wasn't me she loved at all—it was the Powell name and our position in society. The moment we married my eyes were opened—I discovered she had a string of lovers she intended to keep, while she used my money to live in a style she hoped to become accustomed to.' He lifted Harriet's hand and brushed a kiss across her knuckles. 'Luckily, I had Grandmother, Aunt Frankie and a good lawyer looking out for me and now Julie is no more than a bad memory from a foolish summer. But it just shows how mistaken initial judgements can be. I made one about you and it was totally wrong.'

Harriet shot him a strange look, and Giles felt distinctly uneasy. 'Oh,' Harriet said. 'So you think you know me now?'

Once again, Giles had that weird feeling that there was something going on here that he didn't yet understand. 'You tell me, Harriet,' he said softly. 'Do I have the whole picture?'

Harriet flushed and looked away. She didn't like keeping so many secrets, but common sense told her that it was still far too early to trust him completely. As far as the Powells were concerned, Harriet had spent a lifetime mistrusting them, and that couldn't change overnight. Not even for the man she loved. 'Come on, let's not put it off,' she said, determinedly smiling and lifting her chin.

Giles grinned and led her inside. 'I've spoken to Grandmother,' he told her, dropping his voice as they crossed the hall and approached the open door of a pretty pink lounge. 'And told her how things are with us.'

'I'll bet that thrilled her,' Harriet whispered back dryly.

'She'll come around,' Giles said, which didn't exactly fill Harriet with confidence. 'Come on, bite the bullet.'

Harriet followed him into the lounge where Grace Powell sat, ramrod straight, on a dainty Louis XIV chair, her cane clasped firmly in one hand. She actually smiled at Harriet.

'Good afternoon, Miss Jensen,' she said, her voice diplomatically neutral.

When Giles had told her this morning that she was coming to tea, Grace thought at first that the boy had had some plan in mind. But when he'd gone on to tell her how wrong they'd been in their assessment of Harriet Jensen, that the hotel was a tasteful and well-run establishment and that the blonde up-start was really a hard-working and fair-minded woman, and that he'd fallen in love with her, it had taken every ounce of self-control she'd had not to hit out at him with her cane.

She'd never thought that Giles, of all men, could be so stupid. She'd believed that he'd learned his lesson after that ex-wife of his had taught him a thing or two. For him to fall for another gold-digger was so maddening! Still, she wasn't about to let his temporary insanity put her off her stroke.

Giles, pleased, if surprised, by his grandmother's civil tone, decided that his fears about advancing senility were just that—fears without basis.

A maid brought in a laden tea-tray, as Harriet was answering the old lady's gentle questions about how her garden was doing, and what she thought of the latest fashions. But Harriet couldn't bring herself to trust the old woman's change of heart. And as the afternoon wore on, she became more and more jittery.

She was right to be worried.

Grace was thinking about Thursday. And what the health inspector was going to say when he found rats on the premises of Windrush Shallows Hotel.

*   *   *

Harriet washed her hands under the cold water tap and looked up at herself in the mirror. Half an hour of her grandmother being spuriously pleasant was enough to make anyone feel haggard. She left the bathroom, and glanced at her watch. She'd been gone less than a minute. Curiously, she glanced around, wondering . . .

She opened the door opposite her, and

found herself in yet another drawing room. With the door opposite that one, however, she struck gold. The library. Before giving herself time to think, Harriet quickly nipped inside and shut the door behind her, closing it softly and feeling like a thief in the night. Looking around, Harriet was dismayed at the vast array of books.

Nevertheless she quickly located the fiction section, and found the H's in a matter of seconds. Hemingway's 'For Whom the Bell Tolls' was quickly levered out. And as Frankie had found before her, there was nothing there.

With another frantic glance at her watch (how long before Giles came looking for her?) she climbed the iron spiral staircase to the top floor. As expected, she encountered rows of volumes of poetry—from the romantic verse of Byron, Keats, Shelley, Wordsworth and Leigh Hunt, to the metaphysical John Donne, the war poets and the modems. These she ignored, all but racing to the locked cabinets at the far end. Here, sure enough, were the first editions. Harriet leaned down, cupping her hands against the glass and trying to read the titles.

These, too, were in alphabetical order. And . . . yes. There was another copy of the Hemingway novel. Gingerly, not really expecting the glass partition to be unlocked, she walked to the end and pulled the little metal handle. Unbelievably, it slid back with the merest sigh. *'Yes!'* she whispered.

And didn't hear the library door open behind her.

As she'd feared, Giles had begun to worry about her absence and had come looking for her He'd opened the library door merely to check that she wasn't there, not because he'd expected to find her inside. So when he saw her sliding back the glass panel on the rare and valuable book section upstairs, he froze in utter surprise.

Harriet, unaware of being watched, very gently and reverently reached for the Hemingway novel. The original dust-jacket was a little grubby, but still in excellent condition, and she was careful to handle it so that the natural oils on her hand came into as little contact with the paper as possible.

Behind her, Giles Powell noiselessly began to climb the spiral stairs. No doubt his grandmother would instantly jump to the conclusion that she was robbing the place, but Giles dismissed that thought even as it came to him. But what the hell was she doing up there?

Harriet very, very carefully held the book up to the light from the window, and peered through the gap between the jacket cover and the hardback binding of the book itself. Nothing. No folded piece of yellowing paper, no Last Will and Testament, or hidden treasure. She felt faintly ridiculous. Still feeling foolish, she carefully turned the book upside down and gave it a very careful gentle shake, just in case her grandfather had hidden the will inside its pages. But no tell-tale paper tumbled out to land on the carpet at her feet.

'What on earth are you doing?'

The voice was soft, but came from right behind her, and Harriet, giving a little squeak, nearly dropped the book, hastily rescued it, and spun around. Her face was flushed, her eyes wide with shock. 'What?' she whispered blankly. 'Giles . . .'

Giles glanced at the book in her hand, frowned, then turned back to her, one eyebrow raised. Harriet, caught red-handed, stared down at the book in her hand. 'Er . . . I er . . . I'm a Hemingway fan,' she stuttered.

'You're supposed to be in the loo,' Giles said, and couldn't help but grin. Harriet half-laughed, and hastily put the book back in its place. 'OK, you've caught me,' she confessed, thinking rapidly and hoping she didn't sound as guilty as she felt. 'I was just looking for an excuse not to go back.'

Giles sighed. 'Hmm. I think perhaps you're right. We shouldn't try Grandmother's patience too far. I'll just go and tell her we're leaving.'

Harriet nodded, and slid the glass door back in place. When she turned back, he was still there.

'I know Grace is a bit . . . hard to take sometimes,' he began softly, and taking one of her hands in his and drawing her closer, he

213

kissed her lips softly. His brown eyes met her violet gaze. 'But she's old. Give her a little time, hmm?'

At that moment, Harriet would have given him anything he'd asked for. Her hands tingled from the touch of his, her skin danced under his lips. She drew in a shaky breath. 'OK.'

Giles thanked her with a smile, dropped her hand reluctantly, then backed away a few steps as if he couldn't bear to let her out of his sight even for a moment, and then turned and headed down the twisting steps.

It wasn't until he was gone that Harriet had time to wonder about the will. So it was long gone. Lost. No doubt Lady Grace had found it years ago and burnt it. Or Giles had.

No. Not Giles, Harriet suddenly realised. If Giles had known of the will, or if his grandmother had told him where her husband had hidden it, he would have been as suspicious as hell to find her in here—and inspecting that book, of all books. Suddenly, any lingering sense of disappointment and anti-climax she might have felt melted away.

Because Giles hadn't cheated her. Giles, it was beginning to seem, might actually really love her. Might be the one Powell, apart from Frankie, that she could actually trust . . .

And that was worth far more to her than her grandfather's millions.

CHAPTER FIFTEEN

The afternoon river cruise, that started at Henley-on-Thames where the famous regatta was held, was always a popular tour with the guests. Vania watched the bus emptying, and turned to find Brett waiting right behind her.

'Aren't you getting sick and tired of following me around the Cotswolds by now?' she challenged, putting her hands on her hips and tapping her foot impatiently.

One or two of the guests, still milling about, overheard, and turned to look at them, smiling. 'Nope,' Brett Carver said. 'I'd follow you to the ends of the earth.' Several of the onlookers laughed openly at that, and Vania shook her head. By now, it was no secret at all that 'something' was going on with their pretty tour guide and the millionaire from Boston.

'The cruise starts promptly at a quarter-to-two!' she yelled in final warning to her group. There were general murmurs of 'don't worry' and 'yeah, sure' as they drifted away.

'Oh what it is to have such power over people,' Brett drawled. Vania thumped him on the upper arm. It didn't seem to have any noticeable effect on Brett.

It was amazing how things could change so fast. One minute she was just Vania Lane, tour guide, living a quietly contented life at

Windrush Shallows Hotel. The next moment, she'd looked up, and there was Brett Carver. Stormy weather had promptly followed—gales of protest, and downpours of defiance. Then the hurricane of their first lovemaking. Now, the storm seemed to be over, in some honest part of herself, and she knew that her life here in England, with Harriet and the hotel, was drawing to a close. She still wasn't sure yet where her life went from here though. But almost certainly back to the States. And, even more certainly, Brett Carver was going to play a huge role in it.

But as what? Husband? Friend? Lover?

'Want a cup of coffee?' he asked, as if sensing the weight of her thoughts.

The riverfront at Henley was one of the most popular places in town, and Vania quickly led him to her favourite riverside cafe, with tables on a flag-stoned terrace right at the edge of the Thames. She ordered tea and scones. A flotilla of mallards, and two snowy-white swans sailed towards them, sensing food. Vania smiled, cut one scone in half, and began tossing pieces to the hungry birds.

'Hey!' Brett said. Then grinned, and began to do the same.

'River pirates, Harriet calls them,' Vania grinned. 'Every summer we have an invasion at the hotel. Maisie starts to bake extra breakfast rolls from mid-May on, just because the guests always sneak out to feed them all.'

Brett leaned back in his chair and watched her. He was, at that moment, the happiest man on earth. Just because he was *there,* with her. And was her lover. And knew he'd see her again tomorrow.

'You and Harriet are close, huh?' he asked softly.

'Yes. We sort of . . . grew up together somehow.' Vania grinned but there was something about the way he shifted uneasily in his chair that made her look up. 'What?' she asked.

'Nothing.' Brett shrugged, 'It's just that . . . I'm beginning to get the feeling that you don't want to leave. England, or Harriet, or the hotel.'

'I don't,' she agreed, with a sigh. Then, seeing a dark, shuttered look cross his face, said slowly, 'But that doesn't mean I'm going to stay, either.'

Brett looked at her so hopefully, that Vania felt her heart contract with tenderness. 'I was thinking of going back to Boston,' she said casually. 'Starting up a business of my own.'

'Oh? Do you know what kind?' He couldn't help the surge of elation which rushed through him.

'I'm not sure. I was wondering . . .'

Brett lifted an eyebrow. 'Yes?'

'I was wondering if McAllen's was in need of another McAllen on the board?' she asked, oh-so-casually, running a fingertip across the top of her cup, and intently watching the motion of her hand. Then she looked up suddenly, and saw surprise, then speculation enter his expressive grey eyes. But not withdrawal or rejection. So, he was not feeling territorial. Or was he just a better actor than she'd supposed?

'You never showed much interest in the auto business before.' Brett scratched his chin, feeling his way carefully. He had the sudden but overwhelming feeling that the next few minutes were going to be important—vitally important.

Vania smiled. 'Brett, I was a teenage brat before. What did I know about anything?'

'What do you know about the business now?' he asked reasonably.

'Not a lot. But you can teach me.' She was endearing in her honesty and eagerness.

'True.' He couldn't tell her, but if he succeeded in taking over the limo company, he could bring her in on the ground floor. It would be their own business, without the spectre of Chuck McAllen hovering over them.

'You fancy yourself as an executive then?'

Vania grinned right back, but then suddenly, like a light going out, her smile went. She looked pensive again.

'What's wrong?' he demanded quickly.

Vania wouldn't look at him, instead her eyes followed a sleek riverboat as it headed south along the Thames, towards London.

'Honey?'

She stirred. Then took a deep breath, and looked across at him. 'I've been thinking about those shares that Dad left me in his will,' she said at last. If you had to handle dynamite, she supposed, it was best not to think too long and hard about it before you did.

Brett's eyes flickered. Those damned shares again! How much more trouble were they going to cause him?

'Yes. I thought that might . . . change things,' she said acidly and frowned as she saw the anger flicker into life in his eyes.

Brett slowly leaned back in his chair, feeling like a boxer who'd finally made it through to the final round. Punch-drunk and incredibly weary. 'All right, Vania. Let's talk about those shares. I admit I don't want them to go on to the open market—I know that James Larner has a coup all set up to take advantage of them if they do. But, even more than that,' Brett continued quickly, 'I don't want those damned shares to come between us any more. I'd rather hand McAllen's over to Larner on a silver platter than lose you.'

Vania took a deep breath, the pain of his words not half as strong as she'd thought it might be. She swallowed hard. Fine words. But did he mean them?

'You know, Brett,' she said softly, 'I've been thinking. In fact, that pre-nuptial agreement James set you up with gave me an idea . . .'

She broke off as his face lit up. 'Darling!' he exclaimed so jubilantly, that a few heads turned curiously their way. 'You believe me then—about that pre-nup being a fake?'

Vania blinked. Then she said slowly, 'Yes. Yes, I suppose I must do.' She'd spoken without thinking. Surely that indicated the way her subconscious was leading her. But was that so surprising? She loved the guy. What woman in love didn't believe the best of her man?

'You have no idea how many sleepless nights that damned stunt of his has given me.' Brett ran an harassed hand through his hair and said savagely, 'I tell you, having him around makes me want to . . . flatten him.'

The swans and ducks had found another sucker and were busy hoovering up cucumber sandwiches from the young couple a few tables down. Vania watched them and said nothing.

'Vania?' Brett prompted again.

'It's about the shares,' she replied reluctantly. If she'd got this wrong . . . Not unnaturally she'd been giving this subject a lot of thought recently. And, only a few days ago, an idea had begun to form in her brain.

At first she'd rejected it as foolish, insanely risky and fraught with hidden pitfalls. But she could see no other way out. Now she turned and looked at him, her face as expressionless as she could possibly make it.

'Suppose we were to marry,' she said, ignoring the way his eyes leapt with grey heat and the way his breath caught deep in his throat. His face became flushed, and, for the first time that she could remember, his expression was openly vulnerable. He looked like a man who'd just been offered the moon and the stars, but was afraid they would be snatched away again. Then she sobered. Now it was time to find out whether *she* was both— or her shares were the stars.

'And suppose we were to have a lawyer draw up our own pre-nuptial agreement?' she continued, choosing her words with care.

Brett was already nodding. 'Yes. Yes, whatever you want . . .' It was like a dream come true. After all those barren years without her, years of worry and mere existence. To suddenly have everything he'd ever wanted within his grasp.

'Not so fast,' Vania said crisply. 'Wait until you hear the terms.'

Brett waved a hand. What did terms matter? He'd agree to any terms she wanted. 'Fine. Fine.'

Vania took a deep breath. Well. It was now or never.

'The pre-nup should agree to both of us taking out of the marriage exactly what we brought into it. So any money you have, real estate, shares, whatever, you get to keep. And anything I bring into the marriage, my Dad's money . . . his shares in McAllen's . . . the Long Island mansion, everything reverts back to me in the event of a divorce.'

'Fine,' Brett said, already leaning over the table, his heart in his eyes. 'Do you want to be married over here, or in Boston?'

'Brett,' Vania said shakily, 'did you hear what I said? I get to keep control of my father's shares.'

'Sure, sure, I heard and I agree,' Brett responded impatiently. 'When do you want to get married? Next month? Or the fall? I suppose an autumn wedding in New England is kinda romantic.' He paused for breath. 'What kind of ring would you like? With your eyes, it should be emeralds.'

Vania shook her head. 'Brett, I meant what I said about joining the board of McAllen's.'

Brett nodded. 'If we have the wedding over here, we'd have the reception at the hotel of course. Harriet would insist. And . . .'

'And so,' Vania cut across desperately, 'when we're married, those shares will stay in my name. And I'll have the voting rights. And I'll sit on the Board and be active in all the decision making and, eventually, I'll want to take on the same role as my Dad did.'

'Yeah, yeah, whatever you want, sweetheart. Do you want to have kids right away, or wait till your career's established? Since I'm planning on us being together for a lifetime, I guess we've got all the time in the world.'

Vania stared at him. Then she began to laugh. She couldn't help it.

222

Either he was mad, or she was mad, or the world was mad, because, suddenly, everything seemed wonderful.

*   *   *

The big river cruiser lazily blew a few haunting notes on its whistle as another boat approached around the wide bend in the river.

Most people were gathered at the bar or sipping cocktails in the lounge. Near the front, Brett and Vania stared down into the dark waters below. Then he turned to her, and moved a step closer. 'When we dock, how long do we have before that ridiculous bus of yours leaves?'

'An hour. Why?'

'There has to be a jeweller's shop in that rinky-dink little town, right?'

Vania's eyes glowed. 'Right.'

'Then we'll have time to pick out a ring.'

He reached out and dragged her even closer to him; she laughed out loud as her shoes slid over the highly polished deck and she was pulled inexorably into his arms.

'You're in a mighty big hurry, aren't you?' she purred.

'You bet. I want you wearing my ring at the first possible moment. I want the whole world to see it.'

Vania laughed again. 'Do you know, feminism would have it that engagement rings

223

are just another form of shackle, a symbol of slavery, designed to show people that a woman is a man's property?'

'So, you buy me one, and we'll be evenly-matched,' he murmured. 'Now come here and kiss me.' Vania obliged with enthusiasm. A heron watched the kissing couple solemnly from the riverbank.

When he lifted his head at last, Brett gave her a devastating smile. 'You know,' he said, his voice impossibly thick and husky with emotion, 'there were moments, during the long winters back in Boston, when I despaired that this day would ever come.'

Vania's face puckered with pain. 'Brett don't. I'm sorry . . . more sorry than I can ever say, for putting you through that.'

'It doesn't matter.' Brett shook his head.

'But it does,' Vania said quickly. 'I didn't trust you, or myself. Worse, I didn't trust what we had together . . .'

Brett put a finger against her lips. 'Shush. It doesn't matter now. We're together, and that's all that matters.'

Vania nodded and sighed blissfully. 'You're a very forgiving man, Brett Carver.'

'I could forgive you anything.' His expression was whimsical, but he meant every word.

'I won't ever doubt you again,' Vania promised with a smile.

But as she kissed him, holding him tightly to

her, unable to believe her destiny could be so bright, she had no idea how soon that promise of hers was going to be tested. Or how hard it would be not to break it.

CHAPTER SIXTEEN

It was six-thirty in the morning when Arnold Faraday parked near Windrush Shallows Hotel.

He glanced cautiously up the drive that led to the hotel. He'd been warned that the kitchen staff were early risers, but he already had his route worked out. He only hoped the side door he remembered from his boyhood days, sixty years before hadn't been boarded up.

He opened up the back of the Land Rover and removed a cat basket. There was a slithering kind of scuffling as Arnold lifted it free from the back seat. Just feeling the shifting weights of the creatures it held was enough to give him the heebie-jeebies. As head gardener at Powell Mansion, he'd had to poison a few rats in his time, but he'd never had to handle live ones, and he hoped he'd never have to again.

Setting off quickly, he crouched down to waddle beneath the open kitchen windows. He wished he was back home in bed. If it hadn't been made clear to him by Lady Grace herself that his job depended on him doing her this 'little favour', he would be.

Once clear of the kitchen he found the side door unlocked, and he took a deep breath and stepped inside, where he found himself in a long, cool passage. Lady Grace had drawn him a map showing him where the cellars were, and so he moved confidently just a few yards down the corridor.

A single bulb lit up the square, musty-smelling room. He was shocked to see it was completely empty. A small door led off to his right, but when he tried it, it was locked. He upposed that was the wine cellar, and wasn't surprised it was kept under lock and key.

There were no windows at all in the cellar, and he knelt down nervously in the middle of the clean floor, gritted his teeth and opened the cage. Instantly, six large black rats swarmed out. One ran across his shoe in its hurry to get away, and the man leapt back with a barely suppressed curse.

Arnold backed away, hurrying up the stairs. At the top he cautiously opened the door, exited and closed the door behind him. He all but raced for the side door, fresh air and freedom. Once outside, he leaned back against the wall to get his breath, his heart racing.

*   *   *

'Let me see it again,' Harriet said, grinning at Vania across her desk. Vania smiled and held out her hand obediently. Harriet stared down at the emerald and diamond ring and sighed. 'It's beautiful.'

And it was. The huge rectangular emerald in the centre was encircled by alternate diamonds and emeralds. 'You must have been really thrilled when he chose it.'

Vania perched on the edge of Harriet's desk and smiled dreamily. 'I was. It was the one I wanted myself, and he just went unerringly for it.'

Harriet laughed. When her friend had come back from the river cruise sporting a ring and a sheepish look, it hadn't taken Harriet long to wangle the whole story from her. Even now she was amazed at the sheer romance of her friend's past. Vania running away from home and the man she loved, because she thought he only wanted her for her money. And Brett had been searching for Vania all these years, and now he had had found her at last and come to claim her. And to think, she'd been harbouring a fugitive using an assumed name all this time! She was still trying to get used to thinking of Vania Lane as the heiress, Vania McAllen.

'Harriet, are you really sure you don't mind?' her friend asked her now, for about the thousandth time. 'I can stay on until next summer if you like . . .'

'Don't be daft,' Harriet said promptly. 'You

227

can't stay working here forever. Much as I might want you to.'

Vania sighed, still feeling guilty. 'Once you've found a replacement, I'll be sure to train her well. I'll drill her like a sergeant-major would!'

Harriet groaned. She was due to start interviewing applicants for the post of a live-in tour guide next week, and she wasn't looking forward to it.

'So, have you decided on a date yet?' Harriet leaned back in her swivel chair and brushed some loose strands of hair back from her face.

'Yes. September eighteenth. What do you think?'

'Early autumn. What could be better? The late roses will be out by then. We can have a marquee on the lawn.'

She broke off as Vania began to shake her head. 'I still can't believe it's happening. I've got my first fitting for the dress tomorrow. Can you imagine?'

Harriet couldn't. 'Are you sure you want to be married in the village church here?' She asked delicately. 'After all, your home town is Boston . . .'

But Vania was already shaking her head. 'No. The Press would get hold of it and hijack it, and it wouldn't be our day anymore, you know? Not Brett's and mine. And, anyhow you and Brett are all the family I have now.'

Touched, Harriet nodded. Just then, Lydia Brack popped her head around the door. 'Oh, Harriet, there you are.'

'Has he arrived yet?' Harriet yelped, alarmed, sitting upright with a vengeance. The health inspector wasn't supposed to be due for another hour.

'What? Who? Oh no, don't panic! It's the couple in number fifteen. They wanted to know if we have a bottle of vintage champagne. They're celebrating their twenty-fifth wedding anniversary.'

'Of course,' Harriet agreed. 'We'll send something up.' She reached into her desk for the big old-fashioned key that unlocked the wine cellar.

'And Chef says those swordfish haven't arrived yet,' Lydia added. Harriet rolled her eyes.

Vania grinned and held out her hand. 'I'll see to the wine. You go see off the fishmonger.'

She made her way to the cellar door, humming softly to herself as she went. She found the light switch without difficulty, closed the door behind her and skipped down the steps. As she put her foot onto the bottom tread of the stairs, she heard it. An unmistakable squeal.

Vania froze. That was not the timid 'squeak' of an inoffensive mouse. Her dark head snapped up, her eyes swinging around the bare room. And then she saw it. A rat. Then another. Then another.

'Hell's bells,' Vania whispered, backing up the stairs. Suppressing a desire to scream the place down, Vania shot through the door, shutting it hard behind her.

For several seconds she just stood there, gulping for air. Ugh! Ugh, Ugh, UGH! Then she turned and raced down the corridor and into the kitchen. 'Harriet! Harriet!' she yelled, causing everyone in the room to turn and stare at her. And Harriet, who was still on the phone to the fishmonger, saw that her friend looked as white as a sheet.

'Vania! What is it?' Harriet asked, alarmed, hanging up. 'Are you OK?'

She pulled herself together. Realising it would hardly be prudent to advertise to one and all that they had rats on the premises, she took a deep breath and stiffened her spine. 'Er . . . Harriet, can I have a word with you outside?'

Taking Harriet's arm, Vania led her firmly down the corridor to the cellar. 'Vania!' Harriet hissed, thoroughly alarmed now. 'Tell me what's wrong?'

Vania looked at her with stricken eyes. 'The worst! Oh, Harriet. There're rats in the cellar.'

'What?' Harriet blinked, unable to believe what her friend was telling her.

'Rats,' Vania repeated. 'In the cellar.'

Harriet instinctively reached out for the

230

door-handle, intent on having a look for herself.

'Don't!' Vania gripped her friend's arm again, shaking her head. 'I'm not imagining things Harriet. There are rats down there. Big black ones.'

Harriet stared at her numbly. And then she went utterly white. 'Oh Vania,' she gulped. 'The health inspector!'

Vania, who'd forgotten all about him, suddenly clamped a hand over her mouth. For a few seconds the two women stood there, appalled, looking at one another helplessly. 'What are we going to do?' Harriet murmured at last, horrified.

Vania spun around and began to dash down the corridor. 'Where are you going?' Harriet yelled.

'To get Brett!' Vania shot back over her shoulder. She had no idea what Brett could do about it, but it was her first instinct. As she crossed the hall into the dining room, she didn't notice the beautiful woman watching her through the open door of the lounge.

Rita-Sue had been at the hotel for a day now, and she was confident that she knew her quarry well. And Brett Carver . . . what a hunk. Pity he was her target. Soon James Larner would want her to make her move.

Vania, unaware of Rita-Sue's speculations, skidded to a stop in the doorway to the dining room, unaware of how alarmed she looked.

The instant he saw her, Brett was on his feet and hurrying to her side. From his seat by an open window, Giles Powell too, sensed some kind of crisis, got up and followed Brett across the room.

The moment Brett joined her, Vania began to pull him into the hall. 'Brett, something awful's happened,' she whispered, but her voice carried clearly across the few yards to Giles, who was following their progress across the hall.

'Calm down sweetheart,' Brett said, holding her hand tightly. 'What's the matter?'

'You've got to come and help Harriet,' Vania hissed, and behind them, Giles went cold. A few steps brought him level with them. 'What's going on?' he demanded grimly, his voice making Vania jump a mile. 'Is Harriet all right?' he asked impatiently.

'Oh, come on!' Vania hissed, all but running towards the cellar, the two men hastily following.

Harriet was still hovering outside the cellar door, unwilling to open it. The moment he saw her, Giles felt himself relaxing. For a few seconds back there he'd thought . . .

'What's the problem?' Giles asked.

Harriet licked lips gone suddenly dry. 'There're . . . rats in the cellar,' she said feebly.

Brett, who'd been expecting something hideous, found himself laughing. He couldn't help it. 'Honey, is that all?' he asked, grinning at the beautiful, pale-faced blonde. 'There's always rats in cellars. It's a law of nature, I reckon.'

'Not in my cellars!' Harriet shot back. With that, she opened the door, and ran down the steps boldly. It was only when she reached the bottom, the two men following close on her heels, that she heard the scuttling, and stopped dead. She spotted one of the creatures immediately. Rising up on its two back legs, it sniffed the air, sensing danger with the sudden influx of humans. Beside her, Brett drew in his breath in a whistle. 'They're some fine-looking rats,' he drawled, impressed. Fat and sleek and black.

Giles shook his head, looking around. 'I count six,' he said, quickly thinking ahead and being practical.

Brett nodded. 'Yep. Me too. Look, honey, don't worry. We'll set some traps for 'em, and they'll be gone before you know it,' he said soothingly.

Giles, narrow-eyed and thoughtful, said nothing.

'You don't get it. The health inspector's due in . . .' Harriet shook her head in frustration, glanced at her watch and groaned. 'Oh hell. In three-quarters of an hour!'

Brett paled and swore softly under his breath. Then he glanced around, his brow furrowing. Something here wasn't quite right. 'You been storing food in here recently?' he asked.

Harriet shook her head. 'No, no. nothing's stored down here. Frankie and I had these cellars emptied out a while ago. We were planning to turn them into a leisure area for the guests. You know, table tennis, maybe an indoor swimming pool, sauna, that kind of thing . . .' Her voice tailed off. Her companions realised that those plans had probably died along with Frances Powell.

'Right. So the place has been empty since who knows when,' Brett drawled. 'That's what I don't understand.'

'So how did these rats get in?' Giles added. The two men looked at one another, and nodded.

Harriet looked from one to the other, sensing that they were a step ahead of her. 'What's going on?' she demanded.

'Harriet,' Giles spoke softly, 'rats only gather where there's food. But there's nothing here for them. So why are they here in the first place?'

'And rats usually gnaw their way into rickety outbuildings, or get down sewers and drains,' Brett added. 'But there's no way into this building. Look.'

Harriet did look, and saw only well-maintained dry walls, no windows and a single door which fitted into the frame too well to allow a rat access. 'But then . . .' Harriet suddenly stopped. She swayed a little, then slowly turned and looked at Giles. Her eyes were huge and stricken. 'Giles,' Harriet said, her voice seeming to come from a long way off. 'Did you have these rats released down here?'

Brett lifted his head from his contemplation of the scurrying vermin and gave her a quick, astonished look.

Giles was already shaking his head. In a flash, he knew that there could only be one explanation for all this.

'Oh hell!' he said. 'Grace.' He turned and quickly began to mount the steps.

'Hey, where are you going?' Brett called.

'To see a man about some terriers,' Giles yelled back over his shoulder. And pushing open the door, he was gone.

Vania moved a step closer to Brett. 'What did he mean?' she asked, nervously looking around at the rats.

'Dogs,' Brett stated prosaically. 'We can't shoot these damned rats 'cos the guests would hear us. And poisoning 'em would take too long. Nope, if we're to get this place free and clear before that inspector comes by, there's only one chance. Let loose some dogs in here. And terriers are the dogs for the job,' he added, nodding. 'You've got to admire the quick thinking of that man of yours, Harriet,' he added softly.

Although he didn't know what the story was between Harriet Jensen and the man who'd just left, he sensed they had a history as convoluted and complicated as his and Vania's.

Harriet said nothing, as Vania laid a comforting hand on her arm. 'You think it was your grandmother?'

'Yes. Yes, I think so.'

Brett shook his head. The girl's own grandma! He glanced at Vania who looked at him and again shook her head. 'It's a long story,' she said tiredly. 'I'll tell you about it later.'

Just then a rat hissed. 'Come on, let's get out of here,' Vania shuddered. And nobody needed telling twice.

*   *   *

The health inspector arrived dead on time. But by then, Harriet, Vania and Brett were ready for him.

Vania met him wearing a low-cut blouse, gypsy-style skirt and a winning smile, and asked him if he wanted to check out the ducks first. Harriet, she said, was a bit worried about the amount of ducks on the river this year, and wondered if their droppings could cause a health hazard? The inspector (not used to either women as beautiful as Vania, or someone being so open and honest as to actively draw his attention to a potential violation) was more than happy to go wherever she led. Which would be as far away from the

236

cellars for as long as humanly possible.

Brett was on lookout duty at the back door, and the moment he saw Giles's car, he checked that the coast was clear and beckoned them inside. Harriet had ordered all the staff to remain in the kitchens, so no one was there to see the peculiar sight of Brett, Giles, Thomas Carter and his team of yapping dogs descend into the cellars.

Inside, they winced as the snarling of the dogs and the squealing of the rats rose to a crescendo. But it was over amazingly quickly. Then Thomas gathered up his unharmed dogs and inspected them as, with grim expressions, Giles and Brett began to collect the furry bodies and bundle them into a plastic sack that Brett had procured.

'You get rid of them,' Giles said to the American, handing the bag over, 'and I'll get a bucket of water and some disinfectant from the kitchens and clear this mess up.'

'Right,' Brett nodded briskly.

*   *   *

Harriet looked up as Vania opened the door. 'And here's Miss Jensen. You needn't worry about the ducks, Harriet,' Vania said brightly, ignoring Harriet's blank look. 'Mr Warburton says they're too far from the hotel buildings to be a problem.'

Harriet blinked. 'Oh good. I'm really . . .

glad.' She rose and held out her hand. 'I'm sure you want to inspect all the paperwork?' she asked firmly, and almost wilted in relief as the innocuous-looking man nodded eagerly. The two women's eyes met. Was it all over?

*   *   *

The hole Brett dug in the woods was deep and large, and after disposing of the rats he quickly made his way back to the Hotel. He was just in time to see Giles help the old guy get the excited, yapping terriers into the car.

'All set?' he asked, and Giles nodded. 'Yes. Tell Harriet everything's all clear. I'm just going to take Thomas back.'

And have a word with his grandmother. 'Tell her I'll see her later,' he added grimly.

Brett nodded and moved on into the hotel. There he found Vania hovering nervously outside the cellar door.

'It's all right,' he said, taking her into his arms, where she shuddered and heaved a sigh of relief. He kissed the top of her head. 'Damn, girl, that was a close one,' Brett drawled.

'You can say that again.' Vania laughed. 'Where's Giles?'

Brett told her, then gave her a little push. 'You'd better go and give Harriet the all clear.'

As she tapped on the office door, and gave a small nod and a reassuring smile as Harriet

238

looked up, Vania wondered just how many more 'close calls' they were going to be in for.

It was obvious, now, that Lady Powell was in the throes of a real vendetta.

More than ever, she felt guilty about leaving Harriet in the lurch at a time like this.

CHAPTER SEVENTEEN

'He's gone,' Vania said feelingly as she watched the health inspector's pale blue Rover disappear. The two women looked at one another in silence for a moment, then Vania reached for her tea-cup and said softly, 'Harriet, you don't really think Giles had anything to do with this, do you?'

Harriet rubbed her left temple, a sure sign of stress and shrugged. 'I don't know. No. Oh hell, Vania, don't ask me,' she wailed.

'The old roller-coaster of suspicion and trust is one doozy of a ride, ain't it?' Vania smiled grimly. 'It gets you feeling sea-sick after a time. Believe me, I know,' she drawled sympathetically.

'Vania, how do you get off that particular ride?' Harriet asked, her forehead wrinkling with concern.

Vania met her friend's gaze levelly. 'You just have to decide once and for all which one you're going for—suspicion or trust—and stick with it,' she said fatalistically.

'Yes, but for you it was easy.' Harriet smiled. 'You set Brett a test and he passed it. And for what it's worth, I trust him. It's a sort of instinct.'

'But, Harriet, don't you think Giles's already passed his test? And you didn't even set it for him. Who thought of the dogs, and cleaned up the mess afterwards?'

'Yes. Yes, I suppose you're right,' Harriet admitted slowly.

'You know, if it's any consolation to you, I trust Giles, too, the same way you trust Brett.'

'You do?' Harriet's eyes sharpened. 'Or are you just trying to make me feel better?'

Vania shook her head quickly. 'No way. I wouldn't do that,' she answered earnestly. 'I think you and Giles are made for each other. Honestly, honey.'

Harriet's beautiful eyes flickered. If only she could be so sure. But how could they possibly be happy whilst Grace Powell was determined to cause trouble between them?

'Do you realise how close we came today to a real disaster?' Harriet changed the subject slightly. 'Do you know what it would do to a hotel's bookings if it got the reputation of being unhygienic?' Vania shook her head. 'We might even have been closed down. I wouldn't have been able to afford to pay off the final instalment to the bank. I'd have had to sell up. Lose Frankie's house . . .' She broke off as she

240

heard her voice begin to wobble alarmingly.

'Hey, no way. I'm rich, remember? In fact, if you need a loan . . .' Vania sat up sharply and patted her friend's hand reassuringly.

Harriet quickly sobered up. The last thing she wanted was for Vania to start feeling responsible for her problems. 'Thanks, but that's OK. I was just indulging in a bit of pessimism, that's all.'

'But what about next time?' a little voice piped up in the back of Harriet's mind. And suddenly, she was furious. If only that will hadn't been destroyed, it would've solved the problem of Lady Grace once and for all.

She picked up a pen and began to doodle.

Vania felt guilty. All this time she'd been sitting on her money when Harriet could really have done with a helping hand. But Vania had assumed that Frankie was fairly wealthy in her own right. Well, now that she was no longer in hiding, she could get some funds transferred to England straight away. What was the point in having all that McAllen money if she couldn't help out a friend? Whether she wanted it or not, Harriet was going to have some money other than the bank's to rely on.

Her thoughtful eyes fell to Harriet's pad and followed the progress of Harriet's doodling. Reading upside down, she murmured aloud the words Harriet had written. 'For whom the bell tolls . . .' Vania repeated. 'I didn't know you were a John

Donne fan.'

'Hemingway, you mean,' Harriet corrected absently.

Vania grinned. 'Hemingway got that title from the line of a poem by John Donne, one of your best metaphysical poets. Fancy you, a Brit, not knowing that.'

Harriet had become very still. Only her eyes, suddenly glittering with a bright light, showed any signs of animation.

'John Donne?' she echoed faintly. Hadn't she seen a big tome of Donne in the Powell family library? 'Vania, will you excuse me for a while?' Harriet said faintly. 'I've got to get on with something.'

'Sure thing.' Vania moved quickly towards the door, then turned and ordered, 'But don't work too hard. You've had a hectic morning.'

Harriet nodded vaguely as Vania let herself out. She had to find a way back into that library at the Powell mansion. Somehow.

*   *   *

The afternoon trip to Sudeley Castle and Gardens went quickly, but by the time the red and cream charabanc returned to Windrush Shallows, Vania was feeling beat.

She followed the wilting troop of contented sightseers across the hall and straight into the bar. Brett, who for once hadn't come on the trip with her 'just in case something else came up, rat-wise', rose from the barstool and watched her approach with a hungry, 'I've missed you' expression in his eyes.

'Hi, darlin'. You look like you could do with a good shot of Bourbon, girl,' Brett grinned.

Vania groaned. 'Make it a weak one. And make it a Scotch.'

'Scotchophile,' Brett teased, but lifted a finger to order the drink.

'So, everything's been all quiet?'

'Yeah. Giles came back a couple of hours ago.' Vania tensed. 'Did he see Harriet'?'

'Yep. Went straight into her office,' Brett reported, understanding that she was not so much curious as concerned.

'Did they start fighting?' Vania asked worriedly.

'I don't think so.' Brett shrugged. 'When he came out, about half an hour later, he looked happy enough.'

Vania slouched against the bar. 'Well, that's a good sign.'

'You wanna tell me about those two?' Brett invited.

And so, over an excellent single-malt whisky, Vania told Brett as much as she knew of the Powell family saga. When she'd finished, Brett shook his head in wonder. 'So neither the old lady nor Giles know Harriet's really their family?'

'Nope,' Vania said, draining her glass. 'And since it's up to her when she decides to tell

243

them, we're not going to stick our oars in either, right?'

Brett grinned, but was already shaking his head. 'Hell no. Besides,' he added slyly, 'we're the last ones qualified to go giving advice to the lovelorn and wary.'

Vania yelped in laughter, and gathered her bag off the bar. 'Too true. I need a shower before I change for dinner. Wanna come with me?'

Brett drew in a quick ragged breath. 'Do cows eat grass?' he drawled. The thought of Vania in the shower, of his hands, covered in soap suds, running over her smooth breasts was all the incentive he needed.

He followed her quickly from the room.

She was running with eagerness by the time she reached her room, and was laughing when she pushed open the door. 'Quick, get your things and meet me in the bathroom nearest to you.'

On the staircase leading to the third floor, Rita-Sue Glennister quickly shot back up the stairs as Brett Carver's shadow moved along the landing. She had only moments . . .

Vania put down her bag, slipped off her shoes, and walked to the dresser to extract a long, fluffy towel. Brett, just coming from his room, his own feet bare and a similar towel draped over one arm, swallowed hard as she walked towards him. Her eyes were glowing like emeralds.

'Let's hope the shower is big enough for two,' she said huskily, reaching up on tiptoe to kiss him.

Brett's big body trembled under her touch. 'It will be,' he promised thickly, when she drew away. At the bathroom, Brett reached for the handle. Laughing, Vania gave a shove and they both tumbled inside. A beautiful blonde woman, wearing only a towel twisted into a knot at her breasts, spun around.

'Oh . . . sorry ma'am,' Brett stuttered, as, behind him, Vania gave a gasp, then stifled an embarrassed giggle.

Rita-Sue looked at Brett, her face a mixture of surprise, then growing pleasure. 'Brett, hon-eee,' she cooed, her Southern drawl as ripe as molasses. Vania blinked. Brett stared at her. 'I'm sorry?' he responded, puzzled. He'd never seen this woman before in his life.

Rita-Sue let her brows knit together in a small, puzzled, frown, and half-laughed. It came out just right—a touch defensive, a touch unhappy. 'Brett, hon-eee, what's going on heyah?' Her eyes flickered to Vania nervously, then back to Brett. 'I thought we were gonna meet back in my room?' she drawled suggestively. Rita-Sue turned a little more towards them, the better to let them both feel the impact of her deep cleavage, the sun-tanned shoulders, the luxurious cloud of blonde hair.

An icy finger ran up Brett's spine. Set-up!

This situation had the smell of a set-up all over it. He began to turn back towards Vania. As he did so, Rita-Sue let her eyes travel over his shoulders again and alight firmly on Vania.

Vania distinctly saw on the older woman's face that peculiar, shame-faced look of aggressive obsession that a woman got when faced with a rival. 'Hon-ee, who *is* thiy-yis?' Her Southern accent elongated the last word into two syllables—both of them packed with angst and worry.

Brett looked back at Rita-Sue. 'Look,' he said flatly, 'I don't know who you are, or what you're up to, but . . .'

'Bre—tt,' she squealed his name in a rising tone of convincing panic. 'What are you talking about? You asked me to come over.'

Vania shuddered as a vicious, stabbing, jealous pain shot through her. Brett and this woman. Right here at the hotel . . .

'How much is Larner paying you?' Brett demanded flatly, and Vania felt her breath feather out of her in a relieved woosh. Of course, it was all Larner's doing. It had to be. And, anyhow, what kind of a man would invite his mistress to stay at the same hotel as his fiancée? He'd have to be a fool the size of Everest, and Brett was nobody's fool.

'Larner?' Rita-Sue echoed, her voice as puzzled as could be. 'Who's he? Look, dah-ling,' she said, taking a step closer to him, for all the world like a wronged woman who'd

246

been mortally wounded. Two enormous tears appeared in her eyes and rolled down her cheeks. Both Brett and Vania watched them with appalled fascination. 'Hon-eee, ple-eeeeese,' Rita-Sue wailed, sniffing. 'Babee, I did what you asked me,' she cajoled, losing (or appearing to lose) all sense of personal dignity. 'I've got all that information you wanted on Robert.'

Brett stared at her blankly. Vania did the same. Only now, something cold and ugly was replacing the pain. 'What are you talking about?' Vania asked, her voice surprisingly calm.

Rita-Sue shot her a quick, worried look. Hell, this little cookie was taking this calmly. 'Why, I'm talking about mah husband,' Rita-Sue sniffed. 'Robert Glennister.'

At the sound of that name, Brett stiffened suddenly, reacting before he could stop himself. Neither woman missed it, and Rita-Sue gave a quick mental sigh of relief.

'This man heyah,' she cooed, looking at Brett lovingly, 'is doing some business with him. Isn't that right lovah?' she asked, reaching out to run her hand up his arm.

Brett flinched at her touch. But what could he do?

Negotiations to take over Glennister's West-Coast limousine company were nearly complete, but it would only take one shockwave to rock the boat and ruin it all. All

Robert Glennister needed to do was to get one last share-holder in the bag, and he'd be a very rich man, and Brett Carver would own his own empire.

But . . . if this woman really was Glennister's wife, how might he react? Would it blow the whole deal? If Larner really had got something going on . . .

'Brett?' It was Vania's voice. He turned to her, trying to grapple with his thoughts.

'Vania, sweetheart, I don't know this woman,' he began softly, ignoring Rita-Sue's cry of anguish. 'I didn't ask her to come here. I'm not her lover. Never have been.' And he looked so sincere, Vania thought. He sounded so sincere. She believed him—her heart did anyway. But . . .

'Do you know this Robert Glennister?' Vania asked. And saw his expression change. His eyes darken. There was something going on there, Vania thought, agonized. She looked back at the blonde. 'What business is your husband in?' she asked flatly.

Rita-Sue sighed. 'He owns a huge limousine company,' she said grimly. 'Not that it's any business of yours. Brett heyah wants to take it over, and needed a spy in the camp, so to speak. He . . . wee-ell, I suppose you could say he seduced me,' Rita-Sue said, holding her breath to make guilty-looking colour rise to her cheeks. 'Oh, I know what you're thinking, but Ah love him,' she cried passionately,

248

staring at Brett, who merely looked disgusted and turned away.

Rita-Sue turned to face Vania proudly. 'If mah man wants to be a big shot in the auto industry, and Ah can help him get what he wants, then Ah don't care what Ah have to do to help him. Ah love him!'

And she watched, with smug satisfaction, as that last declaration caused the colour to drain from the beautiful brunette's face.

Vania felt agony lance through her. This woman had just voiced every fear she'd ever had—that all Brett wanted was to be an auto king, just like Chuck McAllen.

Rita-Sue bit back a triumphant smile.

Leaning against the door, Vania looked at Brett, who was staring blankly at the wall. In fact, he was thinking furiously.

He couldn't do anything to jeopardise the deal now. Then he looked at Vania, and took in her stricken face. But there was no way he could lose her either. If it was a choice between the company, money, and losing to James Larner, or having Vania, then Vania won every . . .

'Brett,' Vania said flatly. 'Is becoming some big-shot power in the auto industry all you care about?'

And suddenly, shockingly, he wondered if he hadn't lost her already. Perhaps he'd been living in a fool's paradise these last few weeks. For if Vania still didn't trust him now, when would she ever? Suddenly, he had a bleak vision of the future—with Vania his wife, but still wondering if he loved her, or if he loved what she could give him more. What kind of a future was that—for either of them?

Vania swallowed hard, wondering why he didn't answer her. Why he stared at her like that. 'Brett?' she whispered.

Behind them, Rita-Sue fidgeted restlessly. Now that she'd spread her poison, she wanted out of there. Once she'd collected the cheque from James Larner, she was on the first flight back home.

Brett shook his head. He wasn't aware of making a conscious decision, but suddenly he just knew that he was about to take the biggest gamble of his life. One that he'd never even have dreamed could exist a mere month ago. Brett took a deep breath.

Vania's heart pounded, as if she already knew that something . . . momentous was about to happen.

Brett looked at her, his grey eyes utterly expressionless. 'Vania, do you remember what you promised me on the boat? What you promised me on the day I gave you that ring you're wearing now?' he asked softly.

Vania glanced down automatically at her engagement ring. And remembered her words. 'I'll always trust you,' she whispered. And felt her promise to him throb within her, like a living thing. She looked up at him, her heart in

250

her eyes. 'And I will. I'll always trust you,' she said again, her voice stronger this time. Then she glanced at Rita-Sue, her look contemptuous. Then back to Brett. 'When can you tell me what this is all about?' she asked, her voice almost matter-of-fact now.

Brett let out a deep, shaken breath. 'In a few days. By the beginning of next week, at the very latest.' By then he'd know whether the deal was on or off.

But he'd already won everything he could ever want. Vania loved him, and trusted him. Anything else was just the frosting on the cake.

Vania nodded. 'All right,' she said. And turning to Rita-Sue, she smiled savagely. 'Get dressed, hon-eee,' she drawled in a perfect imitation of the fake Southern Belle accent. 'Nobody heyah's buyin' what y'all are sellin'!'

And she threw open the door with a triumphant flourish. 'Out!'

CHAPTER EIGHTEEN

As she walked towards her room, Harriet checked her watch. It was nearly seven o'clock, and Giles was meeting her downstairs in half an hour. She made straight for the bath, filling it with gardenia-scented foam, her hair, piled up on the back of her head, making a natural cushion as she leaned back.

251

Harriet contemplated her talk with Giles that afternoon. He'd begun by telling her that for some time now he'd been worried about his grandmother's health, and had fears about the onset of senile dementia. This made Harriet feel a little better towards the old woman. But when Giles had confronted Grace, she at first denied all knowledge of the rats. It was only when Giles threatened to question every servant in the house that she'd admitted she had given the orders, but had refused to name the employee who'd carried them out.

It was then that Harriet felt even more of her resentment towards the old lady fade away. Whatever else she might be, Grace Powell was still a woman of principle.

After that, Giles said, things had become a bit rough. Especially when he'd insisted that Lady Grace be booked into a private hospital to undergo some tests. She'd accused him of only wanting her to be declared incompetent so he could squander the estate's money on his new ladylove.

Harriet had felt her heart melt for him as he'd told her this. It must have been really hard for him to see his grandmother in such a state. In fact, he'd been so alarmed by the wildness of her reactions, fearing that she might do herself harm, that he'd called in their local doctor, who'd promptly agreed with him that a visit to a discreet private hospital was the best thing for Grace Powell in her current condition.

Harriet had sat in her office feeling alternately relieved, guilty and glad. But at least, as Giles had said wearily at the end, if his grandmother was suffering from the onset of senile dementia, she was now in the best place. Until, he'd added, looking her straight in the eye, he employed some nursing staff and brought her back home again. Grace needed, he'd continued, to be surrounded by familiar objects and people who loved her, and he wasn't prepared to let her spend her remaining days in some impersonal home being cared for by strangers.

But Harriet hadn't said a word against those arrangements. In fact, she'd agreed with him. It would be cruel to keep an old lady away from the home that meant everything to her. And, as she'd said softly to Giles just a few short hours ago, his grandmother couldn't be held responsible for her actions.

At that, Giles's face had lit up with relief as he'd swept her up in his arms, and they hadn't done much talking for a quite a long while afterwards. All in all, Harriet thought now, reaching for the loofah and half-heartedly running it along one arm, it had been a cathartic meeting.

She'd learned so much about him that afternoon, and most of all that he was the kind of man you could always rely on. And that was something Harriet, who'd had so much tragedy and uncertainty in her life, found extremely attractive.

And he'd learned about her too—namely that she didn't have a vindictive bone in her body. It had made them both feel so much better. The only thing that had spoiled it was when Giles had invited her to go over to his place tomorrow morning. He wanted to show her around the house and estate, properly, he'd said. And she'd had no other choice but to agree. But, even as she accepted his offer she knew that, if she had the opportunity, she would search the library again. Because, once and for all, she had to know.

But then what? Harriet sighed and sat up in the bath, feeling as tired and oddly dispirited as when she'd got in.

How would Giles take the news that she was a Powell, too? And if she found the will, she'd have to confess where, and under what circumstances. He was bound to think she'd only been using him to get her hands on her share of their grandfather's estate . . .

Harriet groaned. Was there no end to this nightmare?

*　　　*　　　*

Rita-Sue Glennister was packing the last of her clothes when James Larner knocked on her door. 'Come in,' she called.

James strolled in, hands in pockets, the epitome of the all-American playboy. 'Well?' he drawled, expecting only a good report. 'How did it go?' He had the eager expression of a foxhunter, at the moment of the kill.

And Rita-Sue was not about to disappoint him. Hell, if she told him the truth, he might not agree to pay her! 'It went just like you said it would, sugah,' she laughed, tossing the blouse in her hand into the case and undulating over to him.

'I was undressed and in the bathroom when they walked in. You should have seen the looks on their faces when I threw myself on Brett Carver and gave him a real Southern welcome.'

James laughed. 'Go on. What did he do?'

She gave him a highly fictionalised account, and snapped her case shut. 'Now, hon-eee, you haven't forgotten my little ol' cheque, have you?' she asked, looping her arms around his neck and narrowing her hazel eyes at him.

James reached into his pocket. 'I thought you might be wanting this in a hurry,' he acknowledged, and handed it over.

Rita-Sue snatched the slip of paper and looked it over carefully, before stowing it away. 'I hope it won't bounce, lov-uh,' she said. And hoped even more fervently that he didn't realise how she'd duped him before it had time to clear. 'Well, I'm outta here,' she said breezily, and blowing the triumphant James

255

Larner a kiss, she sauntered out.

*   *   *

In his room, Brett put a call through to Glennister's West Coast office. Because of the time difference he thought he might just be lucky and find him in. He was.

'Brett! I'm glad you called. We finally got Lucien Harper to sell. I'm transferring his voting rights even as we speak. Between us, that gives us overall control.'

Brett let out a long, slow sigh of relief. 'That's great, Bob. When will you have the papers ready?'

Over the line, Robert Glennister laughed. 'Hell boy, they'll be ready for you to sign by the time you can hop on a plane and get over here. Say, what you doing in England anyway, or shouldn't I ask?'

'Getting married,' Brett grinned.

There was a startled silence for a second, and then a deep chuckle. 'Well, congratulations.'

'Listen, Bob,' Brett said, launching into what he needed to know right away. 'There's something I need to ask you. And it might sound . . . nosy. But, is your wife there with you?'

There was definitely a surprised silence then, and Bob Glennister said cautiously, 'Rita-Sue? Heck, no. We're in the middle of a very messy divorce, son. I don't want her anywhere near me, if I can help it.'

That fit. 'Tell me, Bob, is she about five-six, blonde, hazel-eyes, and speaks like Scarlett O'Hara?'

This time the silence was a touch chilly. 'Yeah, that sounds like Rita-Sue. What's going on, Brett?'

A fair question. And it deserved a fair answer. So, taking yet another risk he gave the other man a brief summary of events so far. 'Look, Bob, I'll swear on a stack of bibles that there's been nothing going on between your wife and me,' Brett finished grimly, but suddenly there was a bark of laughter over the phone lines.

'Heck son, I know that. I've had a team of PI's on Rita-Sue's case since last January. You think this Larner fellah hired her to drop you in the brown stuff, huh?' Bob mused, his voice a touch thoughtful now.

'It looks like it to me. But if I'm square with you . . .'

'Heck, yes son.'

'Then the deal's still on?'

Over the line Robert Glennister laughed again. 'Still on? Son, I'm gonna get those papers drawn up and fly with them to England myself.'

This time, Brett didn't try to stop the laughter. 'Thanks Bob. See you soon.'

Brett put down the phone and then leapt

up, a fist raised triumphantly into the air. 'Yes!' He hurried to the door. He had to find Vania. She wouldn't have to wait for her explanation after all.

*   *   *

As Vania and Brett slumbered on, exhausted after a night of passionate lovemaking and tearful avowals of everlasting love and trust, Harriet Jensen arose and dressed, feeling nothing much at all. She was back in a state of limbo, and she wasn't sure that that wasn't as good as it was going to get.

As she headed for the dining room to face Giles and whatever fate might hold in store, she felt that at least she was looking her best.

'Morning,' Giles said softly, his dark eyes caressing her face as she sat down to join him. It was amazing how she could take his breath away just by walking into a room. Her beautiful hair was like a loose silver curtain flowing around her slim shoulders, she was wearing a light summer dress, which floated around her ankles as she glided towards him, and she looked . . . lovely.

'You're going to enjoy seeing the real Powell Manor,' he promised. He'd grown up in that house and loved it. He loved the farms, the land, the house, and the people who lived and worked there. 'Have you ever played a computer game?' he asked, and Harriet, who was doing her best to look cheerful, found herself staring at him blankly.

Giles laughed. 'I'll take that as a no. I've got an office at the manor—I'll have to show you the sword-and-sorcery game I'm in the middle of designing.'

Harriet smiled. 'I'd forgotten about your computer company. Don't you get confused—being both gentleman farmer, and whiz-kid?'

Giles shrugged. 'Not really. I've got one foot in the past, and one foot in the future, but instead of feeling torn apart, they tend to balance me out.'

Harriet, fascinated by the complexities of this man she loved so much, shook her head. 'Now you've made me curious,' she said. And she was. And so, as he drove her back down the now familiar route to his home, she found herself looking around, but not as an outsider. The deer park, gardens, ancient yews and cedars, all made her feel as if she was coming home. But she was honest enough with herself to know that the absence of her grandmother had something to do with this new feeling of peace.

'So, what do you want to see first?' Giles asked, opening the car door and helping her out. It was getting towards the end of the month now, and she found her eyes drawn to a splash of colour against one wall. 'The gardens?' she suggested softly, and felt like crying when his hand reached out to take hers.

Because she knew where this was all leading. When a man you loved, and who'd said he loved you, took you on a tour of his home like this, it could only mean one thing. He was going to ask her to marry him again. And she felt the tears well up again, because she still didn't know what her answer could be. But she took his hand and smiled, and didn't cry.

*   *   *

The morning had passed in a blur of information, sensation and satisfaction. The size and beauty of the formal gardens had stunned Harriet. News of her presence had spread like wildfire throughout the estate, and speculation was rife. Nor did it take long for the word to spread that Giles's companion was none other than the infamous Harriet Jensen.

Luckily, both Harriet and Giles were unaware of the gossip as they made their way back to the house itself. There, on the cool, shadowed, east terrace, they lunched on smoked salmon and prawns, delicious salad, freshly baked rolls, and peaches just that minute picked and still warm from the greenhouse. Harriet, drowsy and replete, felt herself falling asleep in the chair, and jerked upright.

'Tired?' Giles murmured, reaching across the wrought-iron table to take her fingers in his. He kissed the tips of them gently. Harriet

260

hastily averted her eyes from the way the cool breeze pressed the rippling white shirt against his ribs, revealing expanses of tanned, dark skin. Her body ached for him, remembering every last detail of that night on the riverbank.

'Yes,' she admitted. 'I haven't been sleeping well.'

'Same goes for me. Why don't I have Jenkins set up some hammocks under the apple trees?'

Harriet laughed. 'I'll fall out.'

'No you won't! Come on, I'll show you how it's done.'

And within ten minutes (after a hilarious and, for Harriet, nervous few minutes) they were swaying gently under the apple trees, the drone of bees buzzing in the lavender that lined the orchard, and the twittering of swallows and sparrows as they went about their bird business, filtering through the warm air.

To Harriet, it was yet another reminder of far they'd come. Giles Powell, once her arch-enemy, now slept by her side. Loved and loving. She could look across and trace the pattern of his dark lashes against his cheeks, and touch him if she wanted to. That was more, much, much more, than she'd ever thought would be hers.

But when she awoke a few hours later, it was suddenly time for action. One quick glance told her that Giles was still asleep.

'Grandma' Grace was out of the way, at least for a time. And the library would be empty. She didn't want to do it . . . She got up, careful not to make a sound, and picked her canvas bag off the ground, where she'd left it.

She had to make her way to the front door, not knowing her way around the house enough to go through the east wing. Luckily, she passed no servants. Wasting no time, she went straight up the first set of spiral stairs in the library to the large poetry section.

There she found no less then ten volumes of John Donne.

Fate, it seemed, was still not about to make things easy for her.

It was in the sixth book that she finally found it, slipped beneath the leather binding. Her heart suddenly thumping with a mixture of dread, excitement and disbelief, she hooked her nail carefully into the concealed document and pulled out two pieces of paper. Her hand was shaking as she put the book carefully back in its place. Her heart thumped as she walked, on legs she couldn't quite feel, down the stairs and to one of the round cherry-wood tables. She carefully opened the folded, faded sheets, wincing for fear they would crumble to dust beneath her fingers. Of course they did no such thing.

Harriet, with a sense of fatalistic calm, read the first few words.

I, Francis George Henry Powell, being of

sound mind, do hereby add this codicil to my Last Will and Testament . . .

Harriet stopped reading for a moment and looked up, breathing deeply. It was here. It was real. She bent her head again, still hardly able to take it in, and read the document through to the end. It was relatively simple, and even she could understand her grandfather's intention. The house and estate, title and deeds, all went to Arthur, his oldest son and heir.

But, the codicil stated, Francis George Powell now wanted all the private Powell money, not entailed, to be divided into three equal parts, to be given to his daughter, and two sons—including Mark. Harriet swallowed hard. He'd done it then. At the end, he'd realised how unfair he had been to her father. It was, in many ways, a vindication of Elizabeth too. Harriet felt the tears roll down her face, hastily re-folded the document, put it into the zipped side pocket of her big handbag and breathed a sigh of relief that the will was now in her keeping.

She walked back to the front of the house, then out into the grounds, and back to the orchard, where Giles was still sleeping.

For long, long moments, she simply stood looking down on him, balancing what she could see, and feel, with what she knew. He was the most handsome man alive. That black hair that always tumbled over his brow. The

263

strong line of jaw, nose and cheekbone. Those melting chocolate eyes that would smile into hers when he awoke. His pride in his heritage. His modern streak—as embodied in his computer company. His loyalty to those he loved. His strength. His intelligence. She knew she loved him. She believed he loved her.

And Lady Grace was an old, sick woman.

Everything she knew told her that things would be all right. Must be all right. And yet . . . Her handbag seemed to weigh a ton. As if her grandfather's will was heavy enough to drag her down . . .

Giles's eyes snapped open. For a second, in that moment between sleeping and waking, he was the fierce alert animal scenting danger. Then he saw her. She saw the recognition flash across his face.

And his melting eyes smiled into hers, just as she'd known they would. 'Hello you,' he said softly.

'Hello you,' Harriet said back.

He got up, with a fluid ease that told her he'd slept in a hammock many times before. 'What time is it?' he asked, rubbing his face sheepishly. 'I was really out of it.'

Yes, you were. And while you were asleep, I was rummaging around your library, and robbing you of half your inheritance . . .'I don't know,' Harriet said.

Giles grinned. 'Wanna go play Kings and Castles and Lost Maidens?'

'Why not?' Harriet laughed. 'I take it I'm the lost maiden?' And if her voice faltered, Giles didn't seem to notice.

'Come on, I'll let you win,' he promised, and Harriet very nearly burst into tears on the spot.

It was as they were walking towards the terrace, surrounded by blooming roses, that he stopped, turned to her, took her in his arms and said softly, and with just a touch of uncertainty in his voice, 'Harriet, you will marry me, won't you?'

CHAPTER NINETEEN

Harriet walked nervously into the Cheltenham solicitor's office, and approached the desk.

'Miss Jensen?'

Harriet nodded and the young man held out a long, knobbly hand. 'Sam Phillipson. Please, won't you sit down?'

Harriet sat. Now that she was here, she wasn't sure where to begin, and she took several deep breaths. Then she looked across the table at him.

'Your father, or perhaps your grandfather,' Harriet began quietly, 'drew up a Last Will and Testament for one Francis George Powell. I don't know exactly the year or the date, but I think, before I go on, that it might be best if

265

you could have someone fetch a copy of that for you.'

For some seconds, Sam Phillipson said nothing, his eyes assessing her. Then he reached forward, pressed the intercom and gave his secretary the details, asking her to bring Francis Powell's file. He played with a pencil idly, a habit of his when he was thinking hard.

'You knew Lord Powell?' he probed casually.

Harriet smiled. 'Yes and no. I never met him. But he was my grandfather.'

'Ah.' For a while there was silence, neither one willing to go further. It was broken when the secretary returned with the file and left as quietly as she'd arrived.

'May I?' Sam indicated the file, and Harriet nodded. For long minutes, the room continued to be deathly silent as Sam acquainted himself with the contents of the file. Finally he leaned back. 'Seems straightforward enough. And it was my father who drew up the will, by the way. It was duly signed and, after Lord Powell's death, legally probated.'

'Yes,' Harriet said. And opened her bag. 'Please, it's a long story, and rather complicated, so be patient and let me start at the beginning,' she asked, and began to pile onto his desk certain papers. 'My name is Harriet Jensen, but I was born Harriet Powell. Here's my Birth Certificate.' She handed it over.

She'd done a lot of thinking about this meeting, and was determined to keep everything business-like and unemotional. 'After my mother re-married, I took my step-father's name.' She handed over the documents detailing her mother's marriage. 'My father died . . .' She stopped, but only to add Mark Powell's Death Certificate to the sheaf of documents on Sam's desk. 'This, you understand, is just to prove that I am who I say I am. Mark Powell's daughter.'

Sam, who'd studied each of the papers carefully, nodded his head. 'These are all satisfactory. And if necessary, can be corroborated, I'm sure.'

Harriet nodded. 'All right. A few years ago, my mother died,' once again she handed over the relevant documents, 'and I came to live with my Aunt Frankie. Frances Powell, daughter of Lord Powell. As you may have heard, she also died recently. I don't have any paperwork for that. I assume it went to my grandmother, Grace, Lady Powell?'

'Go on,' he said slowly, leaning back in his swivel chair, and twiddling his pencil furiously.

'About a week or two ago. I began sorting through my aunt's things, and found this letter from Lord Powell.' Here Harriet handed over the letter from her grandfather. She watched Sam Phillipson read it. Saw the frown appear on his forehead. Saw him scramble through the file for a letter in Lord Powell's handwriting, which was a distinctive, old-fashioned copper-plate. He quickly found one, and holding the two documents in his hands, carefully checked the handwriting, which looked, even to his layman's eyes, almost identical.

Harriet watched his frown deepen as he took in the implications of a missing will. When he looked up, with one eyebrow raised, Harriet smiled faintly. 'Turn it over,' she said softly.

Sam did so, and found Frankie's notes. 'That's my aunt Frankie's writing,' Harriet supplied helpfully.

Sam too, had little trouble deciphering it, especially when Harriet briefly described Lord Powell's heart trouble. She then went on to tell him how she and Frankie had come to the same conclusion—namely that Lord Powell had hidden the new will, or codicil, in a copy of Hemingway's book. Again Sam looked at her levelly, his pencil all but doing a ballet in his hands now. 'You searched for this alleged document in the Powell family library?' he asked outright.

Harriet smiled. 'I did. But didn't find anything in the book "For Whom the Bell Tolls".'

'Ah.' Sam relaxed slightly.

'Then my friend told me that the original line for the title of that novel was taken from a poem by John Donne,' Harriet said, reaching into her handbag for the final document and placing the faded two-page script carefully on the desk. Sam's eyes fixed on it like glue. Without a word, Harriet pushed it across to him. Sam read it through, word for word, twice. Then he checked the signatures. 'Have you verified that these names correspond with the names of gardeners on the Powell Estate at the time?' he asked quickly.

Harriet shook her head. 'No.'

The pencil finally stilled, as Sam nodded thoughtfully. 'What I want to know,' Harriet said finally, 'is whether that codicil is valid?'

Sam glanced down, re-checking the dates on both this new document, and the old will, which had already been probated. The codicil post-dated it. Making it possibly valid and enforceable. If it was genuine.

'You understand we'll need to authenticate this document with a handwriting expert?' Sam said cautiously. Harriet nodded. 'Yes.'

'Just to be sure there's been no . . .' He hesitated tactfully.

'Fraud?' Harriet offered, managing to smile, in spite of everything.

'Mistake,' Sam corrected her.

But he already knew there'd be no mistake. The evidence was too great. 'Of course, this corroborating evidence,' he tapped the letter to Frankie from Lord Powell, 'is very strong, and, quite frankly, may prove invaluable.'

269

Harriet sighed. 'So you think . . .'

'Hold on. Not so fast. It's complicated.' Sam held up his hand. 'The original will has been probated and the terms been carried out for some . . . what . . . twenty-two years now? It's possible, in law, to get the original probate revoked. Another possibility we may have to consider, is to make the original executors liable, if it can be proved they were negligent. However, you'd be opening up a whole can of very messy worms . . .' His voice trailed off as his quick and agile mind went over the legal ramifications of all this.

He shook his head. His first instincts were to keep this whole affair out of court, if at all possible. Slowly, he leaned back in his chair. 'The estate is clearly Giles Powell's, and there's no argument about that. But the rest of the private money . . .? This document rescinds the previous bequests, and leaves a straightforward third of the money to each of the children—which, in this case, has now been handed down to their descendants. Tell me, your Aunt Frances . . . did she leave any heirs?'

Harriet blinked. 'I . . . I don't know.'

'She had children?'

'No.'

'But she'd made a will?'

'Yes,' Harriet said faintly. And a kind of sick dread began to rise up in her.

'Who did she leave her money to?' Sam

270

continued to dig ruthlessly.

Harriet swallowed hard. 'Me,' she said faintly. 'Or at least, she left the Hotel to me.' Briefly, she told Sam about Windrush Shallows and as much as she could remember about the phraseology of Frankie's will.

'Well, I can always get a copy and make sure,' Sam said, sighing heavily. 'But if you're the main beneficiary of both your father's estate and your aunt's, you're going to be a very rich woman. Provided, of course, we succeed in getting the original grant of probate revoked.

'Tell me, what does your grandmother say about this?' Sam asked bluntly. Harriet stared at him with appalled eyes.

'I take it,' he said heavily, 'that you don't believe your grandmother would be willing to settle this matter . . . amicably?' Harriet continued to stare at him blankly.

'Because,' Sam continued, a little desperately now, 'in cases like this, it's best by far to settle the matter out of court. I can find out how much money you should have inherited, and ask the family to reimburse you. Surely you can see the advantages in having a family conclave and discussing this matter and coming to some mutually agreeable settlement?'

Harriet was shaking her head. 'They don't know,' she said at last. Sam blinked. Harriet shook her head, as if trying to clear it. 'Giles,

271

and my grandmother—they don't know.'

'You didn't tell them about finding the codicil?' Sam gaped.

'No. And they don't know that I'm Mark's daughter, either.'

This time it was Sam's turn to stare at her blankly.

*   *   *

Bob Glennister strode into the Windrush Shallows Hotel lobby and looked around with curiosity. Small, countrified and cosy. Evelyn quickly directed him to the lounge where Brett and Vania were drinking morning coffee and reading the papers.

Saturday mornings were tour-free days, and Vania had never been more thankful. So when someone else walked into the empty room, Vania felt a brief stab of disappointment. It was the only disadvantage she'd found to living at the hotel—the lack of privacy in all but your own bedroom.

But the moment Brett saw him, he reacted with pleasure.

'Bob!' he yelled, getting up to pump the stranger's hand enthusiastically. Vania, too, got slowly to her feet. Eyes gleaming, Brett turned to her. 'Sweetheart, I want you to meet Bob Glennister.'

Vania's smile was instantly sweet and welcoming too. Last night, Brett had finally been able to tell her all about this deal he had going to take over Glennister's limousine company. It had certainly explained why Larner was so desperate to set up that ridiculous scenario with Rita-Sue. But this deal, she quickly realised, also finally put the last vestiges of her fears to rest. Brett was now, without any help from the McAllen millions, a millionaire auto king in his own right.

He didn't need her shares. Didn't want her shares.

They were now able to marry in the sure and certain knowledge that they were doing so only for love.

'Mr Glennister,' Vania said, holding out her hand. 'You have no idea how glad I am to see you,' she said, with feeling.

Robert Glennister beamed. 'Miss McAllen. I knew your father slightly. A real auto man.'

Vania smiled, suddenly sensing that, wherever he was, Chuck McAllen was looking down on them all and smiling. 'Yes,' she said softly. 'He was quite some man.'

'Well, son,' Bob said, brandishing his leather briefcase, 'I dare say you wanna get down to some signin'?'

Brett grinned and hastily pulled out a chair set next to a small occasional table. 'You bet.'

Vania came around to stand behind her lover, her hand resting on his shoulders as she watched him sign the papers that would make him the controlling owner of a fleet of luxury limousines.

She couldn't have felt prouder if she was signing the deal herself. She guessed she was Chuck McAllen's daughter after all.

*   *   *

James Larner ordered himself a stiff bourbon, but hadn't taken his first sip before Vania and Brett walked in, their eyes zeroing in on him like twin missiles.

Brett began to smile as he approached. 'James!' he said jovially, for all the world like meeting a long-lost friend. 'You're just the fellah I wanted to see,' Brett beamed. 'You can help Vania and myself celebrate. Bartender, champagne all round. On the house.'

The other people in the bar, not surprisingly, suddenly perked up at that. 'I'm in the mood for a toast,' Brett continued loudly, grinning broadly into James's sickly looking face. 'This young lady here has just agreed to marry me,' he added, and received the usual congratulations from the other guests, and the beaming good wishes of the bar-tender, who, like all the employees at Windrush Shallows, had a soft spot for Vania.

James swallowed hard. His felt the colour leave his face. What the hell was going on here? According to Rita-Sue, their relationship should be in tatters. His eyes darted nervously between the two of them,

274

sensing disaster.

'And don't forget our other reasons to celebrate, baby,' Vania prompted softly.

'Too true!' Brett said, and gave James's shoulder a 'friendly' squeeze which caused the blond American to actually wince. 'I've just this second signed a deal that makes me the proud owner of the Phoenix Luxury Limousine Company.' Once again the others in the bar, all businessmen of various kinds, gave a good-natured cheer, and Brett ordered more champagne.

James winced.

'Oh yes,' Brett added, as Vania again nudged him playfully, 'Vania, here is going to join the Board of her father's company—and become the next in a long line of McAllens to provide America with cars. And with her business and mine combined, we'll have an outfit fit to beat the band. Isn't that great James?'

James stared at them and licked lips gone suddenly dry. Unable to bear to meet Brett's mocking grey eyes he looked at Vania instead. And what he saw in Vania's eyes was Chuck McAllen, looking back at him. The same drive and determination backed up by the same immutable power. Instead of being under Chuck McAllen's thumb and long, long shadow, his daughter would now be in the driving seat.

And with Brett by her side, already running

the company, that was a duo which couldn't and wouldn't fail.

James felt sick. All that time, all his planning . . . And, at the end, to have to kowtow to yet another McAllen—life was not fair!

'Champagne, James?' Vania asked sweetly, handing him a glass.

'Yes, I insist,' Brett said, as James reared instinctively back. Eyes glinting, Brett pressed the fluted glass of champagne into James's hand instead. 'You'll toast the continued success of McAllen's. won't you James?' Brett said. 'And to Vania's eventual chairmanship? And, of course, to our forthcoming partnership—both in and out of the Boardroom.'

And something in his voice forced James Larner to lift the glass and drink to all this.

* * *

It was later, much later, when Brett and Vania stood on the small bridge over the river Windrush and watched the sun slowly set. The orange glow touched the water, and rippled across their reflections as they stood together, pressed close, with Brett's arm around her. Vania lifted her head to the warm summer English breeze and sighed.

'I love you, Brett Carver,' she said softly. 'You have no idea how good it is to be able to say that at last.'

Brett turned and looked down at her, and slowly, slowly, kissed her.

'I love you too, sweetheart,' he said, his voice full of emotion. 'I always have, and I always will.'

CHAPTER TWENTY

Harriet glanced across at Sam Phillipson, who was busy driving, and wondered if her own face looked as grimly set as his. He was obviously expecting trouble, and Harriet couldn't blame him. She'd really dropped a live grenade in his lap, and he must, by now, be regretting ever setting eyes on her.

'I wish things were . . . different,' she said at last, and saw the solicitor smile.

'So do I,' Sam said, not taking his eyes off the road.

It was nearly two weeks since she'd first contacted him. Two weeks in which so much had happened. For a start, Vania and her fiancé had told her all about the intrigues that had been going on in *her* hotel right under her nose, and in return, Harriet had told them the incredible story of the missing codicil. So when Sam Phillipson had called her that very morning, and told her the results of his investigations and consultations with the top legal brains in the field of Wills and Probate.

277

they'd been over the moon for her.

But then Phillipson had asked her to arrange a meeting at Powell Manor for Giles, her grandmother, Harriet and himself, and that was something that had filled her with a kind of sick dread. Nevertheless, the moment the solicitor had rung off, Harriet had telephoned Giles. And when she'd asked if she could come over that afternoon, he'd sounded delighted. His grandmother was back from the hospital, and he agreed it would be a good idea for them all to sit down and have a 'talk'. She simply hadn't had the heart to tell him about Sam and their bombshell.

Now, as Sam's Mercedes ate up the miles to Powell Manor, she could feel the cold chill of apprehension scudding up and down her spine.

The solicitor turned into the driveway, his mind on the upcoming interview and all the research he'd done. He found himself whistling quietly between his teeth at his first sight of the big house. No wonder Harriet Jensen had wanted to get her fair share of all this.

He parked and turned to her. 'You're not looking forward to this, are you?' he murmured. Now that he knew her family history, he wasn't surprised she'd never spoken of it to her estranged grandmother. But all that had to change, now. 'You know, it might not be as bad as you think,' he tried to reassure her. 'I'm sure your family will see sense, when they realise what's involved here,' he added, wishing he believed it himself. He'd done some checking on Grace Powell, and she didn't seem to him to be the live-and-let-live type.

Harriet sighed. Of course, Sam was only thinking in terms of law and money. How was he to know that more, much more than that, was riding on what happened next? If Giles rejected her . . . She slowly got out of the car, pulling down her jacket as she did so. She was dressed in a plain black jacket and skirt, with a white blouse.

'I've told you that Giles thinks Lady Grace may be ill, haven't I?'

'Yes, you did.' Sam agreed nervously. 'But we'll be dealing mainly with Giles Powell, right? And from what I've learned about him these last few days, I'm confident we're going to leave here with a fair settlement.

Harriet said nothing as at that moment the door opened, and the impressive butler stood in the doorway. His eyes flickered to Harriet, and . . . wonder of wonders . . . a smile touched his lips. Unbeknownst to her, the staff at Powell House had come to suspect that she was soon to be the new 'Lady of the Manor'. And as such, she deserved respect.

Sam stood aside to let Harriet precede him. As she stepped into the hall she heard a firm, familiar step, and her head shot up. Coming through from the west wing, Giles had heard her arrival. He was dressed casually in a pair of grey slacks and a black and white designer shirt. It was a startling complement to his raven-black hair and dark eyes. As always, at the first sight of him, Harriet's pulse skipped a beat. He was smiling at her, his mouth wide and welcoming. Then she saw a slight shadow cross his face, and realised that he'd just spotted Sam, who had come in behind her. Harriet licked her lips nervously. 'Giles. This is Sam Phillipson. My . . . solicitor.'

She saw him dart her a quick questioning look, but then Sam was holding out his hand and Giles was taking it. A querulous voice, sounding much older than the last time Harriet had heard it, wafted through the open door at that moment.

'Giles? Arthur? Who is it?'

At the name of her dead uncle, Harriet shot Giles a quick look. Giles shook his head in warning, glanced, still obviously puzzled at the solicitor, and then indicated the open doorway.

'Please, come on through. Sally's bringing some tea. But perhaps you'd like something stronger, Mr Phillipson?'

How polite we all are, Harriet thought miserably and once again the old familiar enemy—pessimism—raised its head. Was she going to leave here a rich but broken-hearted woman? Or stay a poor but happy one? Because, although she hadn't told Sam this yet, if things looked like getting too unbearable—namely, if she thought she was going to lose Giles—she was going to waive all her rights to the Powell inheritance.

And yet . . . she knew, in some deep dark, utterly female part of her, that she had to test him. She had to see what his reaction was. She had to know, once and for all, if he loved her enough to both forgive her for her deception, and share every part of his life with her. Because if he couldn't, then he didn't love her as she needed to be loved by him. Together, they would have it all, or alone they would have nothing.

Harriet found her eyes going straight to those of her grandmother. And was surprised to see Lady Grace looking so much older. She looked . . . diminished in some way.

Harriet winced and looked away.

Lady Grace allowed herself a small smile. So, the little upstart thought she'd scored a big victory did she, convincing Giles that his poor old grandmother needed to see the quacks. Hah! There was nothing wrong with her brain. She knew the Jensen girl thought she was going to be Lady of the Manor but she wouldn't get her foot in the door as long as the present Lady of the Manor drew breath!

Sam Phillipson blinked at the look of evil venom on the old woman's face as she stared at Harriet Jensen and realised that Harriet hadn't underestimated one jot the likely reaction to her news.

Finally the old lady noticed the stranger, and as she looked at Sam, a puzzled expression came into her old eyes. 'I know you,' she said at last. 'You're that string-bean of a solicitor of George's.' Her husband had always been known as George, even though that was, officially, his second name.

'I think you must mean my father,' Sam smiled and said, in the gentle tone of voice a man might use around a very old, very sick lady. 'He was your late husband's solicitor.'

Lady Grace still looked puzzled.

Giles managed to catch Harriet's eye, and nodded to the door. 'Would you excuse us for just one moment?' he said to Sam, casting the solicitor an apologetic look as Harriet followed him out into the hall.

Giles turned to her, looking none too pleased. 'Who's he? And why's he here?' he asked her abruptly. 'You must have known that I wanted to talk to you about Grace.'

Harriet wearily brushed a strand of hair off her face. 'She's worse, isn't she?'

Giles nodded. 'Yes. I didn't want to tell you over the phone, but the doctor's confirmed it. Senile Dementia.'

'Oh Giles, I'm so sorry. I think . . . I think Sam and I should talk to you alone.'

Giles's eyes narrowed slightly. 'Harriet, what's going on?' He wasn't used to being kept in the dark. He didn't like not being in control.

'Giles, we have something to discuss that . . .

282

I think will upset your grandmother . . .' Harriet's voice faltered.

Suddenly Giles knew that the time had come, and she was going to lay all her cards on the table. The reason for all those times when he'd felt that she was holding something back was about to be revealed. But when she looked at him out of those amazing violet eyes, he found it hard to think about anything but picking her up and carrying her upstairs to the master bedroom, and the big, Queen Anne four-poster in his room. 'Why?' he asked softly. 'Harriet, why have you brought a solicitor? Why on earth should you and I need one?' He reached out and gently stroked a hand through her hair. 'Can't you just tell me simply and straightforwardly what's happening?'

Seeing the way Harriet's eyes flickered with pain, Giles added hastily, 'Harriet, darling, don't worry. I hate to see you looking this way. If it's to do with Frankie leaving you the money that's worrying you . . .'

Harriet shook her head. 'No. It's not that. It's something else entirely.'

Giles tried not to let the way she couldn't meet his eyes scare him, but it did. If she was going to tell him that she didn't love him after all . . .

'Well, let's get on with it then,' he said bleakly. 'Just a minute.' He walked to the wall and pressed a bell. A few moments later, a tall, robust nurse appeared. She was in her forties, and exuded warmth and efficiency. 'Nurse Fenton. Would you please take my grandmother upstairs for her nap?'

The nurse nodded. 'Of course. The wheelchair has arrived, but Lady Grace is refusing to use it.' She smiled. 'She's quite a character isn't she?' she added cheerfully.

Harriet stood aside as Lady Grace emerged after a few minutes, leaning on her cane and the nurse in equal proportions. As she passed them, she paused to give Harriet a puzzled look. 'You remind me of Mark,' she said devastatingly, then demanded, 'Who are you?' She reached out a hand and patted Harriet's cheek. 'You're a very pretty girl.'

Harriet opened her mouth to speak, but by then Lady Grace had turned back to the nurse. 'I want some brandy in my milk, mind,' she said querulously. 'If I'm to sleep during the afternoon, you've got to give me something to help me nod off. And none of those horrible pills of yours. I won't take 'em,' she warned.

The nurse laughed. 'I think a drop of brandy is just the ticket.'

'You've picked a really good nurse, haven't you?' Harriet watched them go, her eyes brimming and said. 'I feel so sorry for your grandmother,' she added simply.

Giles's smile was tinged with sadness. 'Yes. I wish you'd known her before . . . well, before she became so difficult.' Then he turned abruptly back to her. His grandmother, he knew, would have the best of care, and all the love she needed. Right now, he wanted to know how secure his own future was. And once again, the moment he looked at her, Harriet's lashes veiled her eyes. Then she made a visible effort to pull herself together. 'Come on,' she said flatly. 'Let's get this over with.'

She led the way back into the lounge, where Sam Phillipson waited. He looked relieved to see them and cast Harriet a speculative look as she took a chair opposite him. Giles, after the briefest of hesitations, took the chair that was at right angles to both Harriet and the solicitor. He felt like someone attending his own trial. But what was he accused of? And what would his sentence be if he were found guilty?

If he was going to lose Harriet to this other man, this solicitor, he knew it would break his heart. Giles Powell, quite simply, had never felt so scared in all his life.

But not a flicker of his feelings showed on his face as Sam opened up his briefcase and began to bring out the documents. When he had them all arranged to his satisfaction, he glanced at Harriet.

'Do you want to start?' Harriet bit her lip. Now that the time was here, she just wanted to get it over with. As quickly as possible. She forced herself to look at Giles. Seeing the repressed fear in his eyes, that she'd put there, made her want to put her arms around him.

'Giles, there's something I haven't told you,' she said, her voice weak with fear and tension. Here it comes, he thought bleakly, not knowing what to expect. Was she already married? Did she have a fatal disease? Had she fallen in love at first sight with Sam Phillipson? What?

'I'm Mark Powell's daughter,' she whispered at last.

Giles, prepared for anything, wasn't prepared for that! He simply stared at her. 'What?' he finally managed.

And slowly, fumbling a little, Harriet told him her story. Everything, from her mother's funeral, Frankie finding her there, the reason Frankie had left her Windrush Shallows, and the fact that she was Lady Grace's long-lost granddaughter, and Giles's adoptive cousin.

From there, as he still continued to simply sit and stare at her, she went on to tell him about finding her grandfather's letter amongst Frankie's things, and the search for the codicil. It was at this point Sam took over, and repeated to Giles what he'd told Harriet that morning. Namely, that they'd tracked down one of the witnesses, who was now retired but distinctly remembered signing Lord Powell's 'new will'.

Sam then went on to tell him that the top legal experts believed that Harriet had a case for revoking probate, but that, ideally, the matter would be best settled out of court. Sam assured Giles that Harriet would agree to a mutually acceptable settlement of her share of the Powell money, without the need for courts, lawyers and litigation. All through this recital, Harriet had watched Giles fearfully. But, try as she might, she couldn't tell how he was taking the news at all. Apart from surprise, he looked more . . . relieved . . . than anything else. And that couldn't be right.

It was only when Sam finally finished his spiel that Giles spoke. He turned and looked at her—this, the only man she'd ever love.

Her breath caught. Here it was—the moment she learned whether her future was to be played out here, in this house, with the man she loved, or whether it lay in the cold, cold comfort of career and solitude.

'Is that it?' Giles asked, his voice so surprised she didn't know how to respond.

Slowly Giles leaned forward. 'Is that what's been coming between us all this time?' he demanded, dimly aware that he was both angry and so utterly, utterly happy. 'The fact that you're my cousin?' he demanded, his voice rising a little. 'And not even *real* cousins. Is that all, Harriet?'

And when Harriet stared at him, wide-eyed and too surprised to even think, Giles began to shake his head. 'Bloody hell!' He gave an explosive bark of laughter. 'Harriet, I thought it was something . . . serious.' Now that he'd stepped back from the brink of the abyss, he felt the same euphoria that followed a near-tragedy. He wanted to kiss her . . . and kiss her.

'Mr Powell,' Sam Phillipson, sensing that something private and intimate was about to disrupt this meeting, coughed discreetly. 'Do I take it you have no objection to er . . . coming to some fair and equitable monetary arrangement with my client?'

Giles dragged his eyes away from Harriet and gave the lawyer an impatient look. 'What? Yes, of course,' he said dismissively. He ran a harassed hand through his thick, black hair. 'Hell, she can have all the Powell money if she wants it. I've got the house and estate and my own computer company. I don't need it.'

Sam blinked. The victory was so sudden and complete that he felt wrong-footed. 'Er, I'm sure Miss Jensen doesn't want it all . . .' he began, flustered, but Harriet was suddenly on her feet. 'I don't want *any* of it,' she said, her eyes sparkling, fixed on Giles. 'I never did. I only wanted . . . justice. For my mother. For my father. Because of what Lady Grace did to them . . .' But now, it hardly seemed to matter.

'Giles,' she said, her voice cracking. 'You're saying you don't mind? About the way I sneaked into the library trying to find the codicil? You don't care about me lying to you all this time, about keeping my identity a secret? You really don't care?' she breathed,

288

still unable to believe her good fortune.

Giles too got to his feet. 'Harriet,' he whispered emotionally, 'of course I don't care. And when you think of the way grandmother and I treated you to begin with, I'm not surprised you kept quiet about your parentage. It serves us right! In fact, I hope that you had a damned good laugh at our expense.'

And Harriet had *never* loved him more than at that moment.

'And about what happened afterwards . . . hell Harriet,' he laughed, 'I did wonder why the library held such a fascination for you.' He was laughing helplessly now, and shook his head. 'But I thought you must have some kind of book fetish!'

Harriet was laughing too. She couldn't help it.

Sam Phillipson stared at the two individuals shaking with laughter and shook his head. This really was the damnedest case . . . Still, at least he could report to his partners that there'd be no ugly lawsuits. Discreetly, he bundled his papers together, said something about seeing himself out, and headed for the door.

Slowly, Harriet's and Giles's laughter, along with the tension that had produced it, drained away. And they found themselves alone. Looking at one another with wonderment in their eyes.

'So, will you marry me, Harriet Jensen? Or Harriet Powell. Or whoever you are?' he asked softly.

Harriet swallowed hard. 'If you'll still have me,' she whispered. 'Yes. Yes. A thousand times, *yes!*'

And before she'd finished speaking, Giles swept her up into his arms.

The butler watched, amazed but outwardly granite-faced, as Lord Powell crossed the hall, carrying his beautiful blonde 'Lady' triumphantly in his arms, and all but ran up the stairs to where his four-poster bed patiently awaited them . . .